I SEE RED

By Amy Piers

For Daniel, forever.

CHAPTERS

I am Dallas.

I am six and a half.

[I see red.]

\#

Zoe Fletcher, 26

Behavior Specialist

[I see you.] I see who you really are, Dallas.

(And I love you anyway.)

CHAPTER ONE

Hot Dog

[I see red.]

"You're making me die! Let me go!" I scream and shout, with all my breath.

The *Evil She* is holding my arms across my body, with my hands rolled up in a ball. I try to get free by sticking a fingernail out of my fist to scratch *She*'s skin. It's working, but her is holding me so much more tighter than before. I'm going to die; I know it. I am so angry, everything I see is red. I smash my head back it into hers, and I hear it crack on the wall. *She*'s arms get looser so her can grab that walkie talkie that's usually clipped onto *She's* belt.

The *Evil She* presses the button and yells, "Hot dog!"

Now is my chance. The stupid idiot can't hold me with one arm, and this thing is for sure: I am very much faster than her has ever been.

So, I run.

[I see you.]

"Shit," I say under my breath, as I grab the walkie talkie again. "He ran," I admit, while five teachers come to my aid.

The principal shrieks, "You have to use the code, for God's sake, do you want parents hearing this?"

It wasn't my fault that this asshole of a child ran away again. Six adults are out looking for him now, and you're worried that I didn't say, "Hot Dog." Three more teachers join the search, with one running outside to cover all bases.

My head is pounding.

[I see red.]

Don't tell anyone, but I'm hiding in the bathroom. I'm sitting on top of a toilet with my knees tucked under my chin. I heared how they're looking for me, and I wonder if they think a homeless person stole me? I wonder if they were thinking a car flatted me like a pancake? I like how they are so worried, like chickens with the heads cut off. Them are running around all panicky and scared thinking I might be dead. This is the funniest thing because I was almost dead when *She* was holding me, and I am really very alive now that I'm freed from The *Evil She*'s grip.

I am the boss of this place, and this time, they'll all learn their lesson; then nobody will mess with me ever again.

[I see you.]

"Has anyone checked the bathrooms?" I yell.

"Yeah. Nobody was in there," a frenzied voice replies.

I know the intricacies of Dallas's brain pretty well by now—an achievement carved out of spending seven hours a day with him for the past two weeks. I know when he's up to something, particularly when he's up to no good. I have a hard time trusting other people to understand him like I do, especially considering it's only our third day at this new school. Jeez, Dallas, we can't even get through three days without wreaking havoc. You know what they say about second chances at first impressions? Yeah, we blew it. I can't say I'm surprised, though, because as far as kids go Dallas is definitely the worst.

I walk into the boys' bathroom. The stall is closed and locked, curiously with no feet showing under the door. A small body breathes almost silently, and I watch his shadow shift carefully on the floor. Lifting the walkie-talkie to my mouth, I press the button and say, "Hot dog found."

I'm going to sit here and wait this one out.

[I see red.]

7

No! Hot Dog is still missing. Hot Dog ran away to Mexico for all you know. I could be any kid crouched up on a toilet; I could just be a regular guy taking a poop. Why are you so sure you found the Hot Dog? I think The *Evil She* wants to wait for me. Oh, I can wait too. I can sit here like this all day until the night, and she will not win.

She will not win.

[I see you.]

"Dallas," I whisper, "I know you're in there."

There's no reply, which is another thing that doesn't surprise me in the least. God knows how long I'm going to need to wait for him to come out of the stall. What I do know is that he hates being ignored. So I wait.

"I know you're in there and just so you know, I don't care. I've got plenty of other things I can do right now, so I'm going to go eat lunch—you can have fun sitting here on a boring, stinky toilet," I say, walking out the door. Sitting on the cold, hard floor outside the bathroom, I know it's only a matter of time before Dallas runs again. There's only one exit point from this bathroom, so I plan to catch him as he goes to make a run for it.

I sit, I watch, I wait. I'm ready to pounce at any second.

[I see red.]

Nobody ever knowed that I can fit through the window in here. I tested it a different day in case I ever needed an escape route. Today seems to be the day I needed it most. The trick is about taking out the middle glass bit, which actually slides out easy. You have to be careful, or you'll get blood coming out your hands.

I slide it out and set it down gently. Now there's a kid-sized hole for me to climb through. Lucky I only ate half my bagel for breakfast because if I ate the full thing I probably wouldn't fit through this tiny window.

[I see you.]

It's been a while. Dammit, I thought the little shit would come out by now—I'm starving, and I need some ibuprofen. My head throbs in pain, and there's a bruise forming on my cheek.

Suddenly, a familiar face smiles and waves at me through the window to the play yard. No—it couldn't be? How the hell did he get outside? He laughs at my apparent bewilderment.

"Hot Dog," I say through the walkie talkie.

"What? Again?" a voice replies.

I sigh, "Again."

He raises his eyebrow and smiles before running out of view. Here we go again.

[I see red.]

I used to know what was the F-word, but I have forgotten. I would like to yell it, but I am running so fast, and I haven't got time to remember. Here's something I know: The *Evil She* will not catch me. The biggest reason why her will never, ever catch me is because I am always the best. I know how to make people yell, I know how to make people cry, I know how to get the biggest piece of cake every time. People are like big fat toys, with all kinds of buttons to press. The buttons make lights and sounds like sirens— people buttons are the funniest things. Press a button, and just like that—I maked someone angry.

"F-word! F-word!" I yell as I run, checking to see where The *Evil She* is behind me. The look on her face is too good! Her is all red—puffing and panting again. Her can't run much longer. Like I said, I always always win.

"Catch me if you can!" I say as The *Evil She* steps pretty close to me this time. I am an artful dodger, and of course, her didn't catch me.

[I see you.]

I'm so mad that I might explode; I swear Dallas will be the death of me. I have to admit that I am also trying not to bust out laughing, since ironically, there's so much comedy in the ridiculousness. Apparently, he's forgotten the actual F-word but knows it gets a huge reaction. About a week ago we were listening to music on my computer, and he chose a song with explicit language. I tried to change it straight away, but I wasn't fast enough. Dallas looked at me and said,

"Oh, so it's fuck?"

"What did you just say?" I died.

"Fuck means the F-word," he mused.

He yelled the F-word so many times that day; I thought it would never leave his vernacular. Right now he's the one appreciating the comedy, laughing at me as I chase him through the school. The mood changes as he heads for the gate.

"This isn't a game, Dallas," I say with false confidence. "I won't chase you."

"You already chasing me," he replies in a sing-song tone.

The truth is I have to chase him, because this is San Francisco and he's nearing on Geary Street. I walk a fine line between pretending not to care and being ready to catch him at any moment. I turn and repeat, "Hot dog. Hot dog at the Geary gate."

Three grown ass adults run towards us like grade schoolers responding to the recess bell. I have to admit if I were a child I would find hilarity in this scene. A round middle aged lady (I think she works in the library), a nerdy tech dude with a beard (I don't even know if he works here, seriously never seen him before) and a pretty young thing in heels all attempt to close in on us. None of them can run for shit—it's like one of those movies where they rally a motley crew of misfits to achieve the impossible. Dallas is in hysterics, and at this point I'm starting to become legitimately scared. There are only a couple of feet between his body and cars speeding down the road. Like most San Franciscan children, I can assume he's got pretty good street smarts when he's present, but right now his common sense is completely out to lunch. He seems to leave his body when he's in this state. His eyes narrow and lose focus, and it's clear that someone (or something) else is at the wheel.

Now I'm caught between a rock and a hard place—if I go too close, he'll run onto the street to spite me. If I don't go close enough, he might still run on the road. The vacant version of this kid doesn't give a shit about the value of his life because his core belief is that he's worthless. He won't let anyone put him in danger, but he is completely unafraid to die, so he has no qualms about putting himself in the line of fire. His arms twitch in atypical movements, and he jumps up, laughing.

[I see red.]

I am winning! I win every time and every thing. Cars are zooming down the street, and I step a little closer to feel the breeze on my face. A car almost flats me, and it's the funniest thing because the driver beeps the horn so loud after. I like how there's this wind that messes my hair when a car goes by; it's the most exciting thing. I wonder what it might feel like to step out in front of them and be squished? I'm the boss of my own self, so if I wanted to, I could. I own my life, and I can die any day. Anyone can, you know? You never know the day that you will become dead.

If I was dead I would become an angel; maybe I would grow wings and spend lunch time with God and Jesus. I think dead means you're quiet and still, and people will love you more. People are always nice about dead people, putting up their photos in their house and giving them a grave. And they cry and say what a beautiful soul they were, and how they wish they could give their legs to be together again.

The car breeze smells like jet fuel, and I like it. Smack! I'm on the ground now, and The *Evil She* is on top of me with my arms behind my back.

[I see you.]

"Fuck," it slips out as I pin him to the ground. My blood pressure is at an all-time high.

"Oh yeah, fuck means the F-word," I hear, muffled under his giant jacket. While I'm using all of my might to hold back tears, his affect is entirely flat. In fact, his mouth kind of curls at the side in a strangely grimaced grin. He freaks me out, and I look away. The motley crew of misfits joins the scene.

"Are you OK?" one asks.

"I'm fine," I lie, still avoiding the gaze of the creeptastic child in my grip.

"Hot Dog found," the round lady reports on the walkie talkie, with the enthusiasm of someone winning a cruise on a gameshow. She's way too into this.

"I'm going to need help getting him up the stairs," I explain.

The random guy with a beard grabs Dallas's feet, the lady in heels does her best to support his middle—but honestly, I have no idea why this girl is wearing such an inappropriate outfit to work at an elementary school. Kids this age will cover you in snot, pee, tears, and yogurt. Frankly, I've got no time for heels. The round lady tries to act like she's being useful but obviously doesn't know what the hell needs to be done, so I just grab his head, and we start walking.

I expect Dallas to thrash around and try to get away, but he's oddly calm to the point where I'm afraid to look at him. He locks eyes with me and rekindles that maniacal smile. I hate to think it, but Dallas looks like the kind of person who might just turn up to school one day with a gun and kill us all. His eyes sparkle murderously, and I quickly avert my gaze. The hairs on the back of my neck stand on end, as I try not to let a brief shiver weaken my grip.

"Ahh...This is the life," he jeers, laying his head back like he's enjoying champagne at a day spa.

"Goodness. He needs a swift kick in the pants," the round lady remarks. "It's the parents' fault though—they need more boundaries."

I can't even right now. So I hold my tongue, as well as my kid. This lady is about as useful as an ashtray on a motorbike. Next minute, he thrashes as I'd expected, and kicks the beardy guy in the face. He drops the legs for a second, and I'm terrified Dallas will run again. Beardy Man whispers the elusive F-word and manages to grab the boy's feet before he can escape. The look on his face says, "How did I get roped into this?" and I feel genuinely sorry my client became his problem.

Finally, we're back inside the school building, and I sit on a couch with Dallas in my lap—crossing his hands in front of his body. Dallas has an underdeveloped Moro Reflex, which he should have outgrown by four months of age. You know how newborns throw their arms out when they're startled? It makes them feel like they're falling, and that's why parents swaddle babies. Since he still has this reflex, Dallas shows dysregulation by the movement of his arms jerking and flapping all around his body. I hold them close so he can get a hold of himself.

For someone with the reflexes of an infant, my God he's strong when he's upset. The motley crew goes back to whatever the heck they were doing in the first place—the round woman a little reluctantly. I tell her I have it covered, and she looks back twice on her way out. The bearded guy grabs his bag and leaves the premises immediately, confirming my suspicions that he was, in fact, a visitor. The principal calls Dallas's parents straight away, while I'm just waiting for the storm to pass.

Dallas kicks me in the shins once more, and I am convinced this will be the meltdown that never ends.

[I see red.]

The *Evil She* is trying to kill me again. Her arms are around me squeezing all my breaths out, and I am choking.

"You not allowed to do this!" I scream. Her ignores me another time, and I know her is getting tired of me kicking and hitting all the time. I will win, you just wait and see. I know that *She*'s muscles can't keep up all day. Pretty soon, her will get tired, and I'll run.

"I am the boss of this place! I am going to kill you, and send the police to kill everyone at this school!" I growl.

[I see you.]

I want to tell him police are for helping, not for hurting, but with what's happening in the news lately I can't say that with full integrity.

"I will talk to you when you are calm," I remind him, yet again.

[I see red.]

The *Evil She* smells like shampoo and laundry soap. Her leans close to me, which is my biggest hate, and her says all the things I hate most.

"I like you every day, Dallas. It doesn't matter what you say or do; I will like you every single day."

No, no, no, no, no. Not. Gross, I will throw up on you, disgusting witch lady. I am not to be liked or loved—I am the baddest bad guy. I am smart, and bad. One time I even farted on a book my teacher loved, and I will easily do something like that to you. You don't like me; you never have, and nobody has ever liked me. There is nothing to like, so stop F-Word lying. I kick her about forty hundred times and I manage to bite her finger. *She* pushes her hand back into my mouth, and that makes my mouth open too wide to bite anymore. So, I let go.

"You're not going to win," her whispers quietly in my ear.

I am a winner and winning is what I do. I break free and snap her glasses in half. Her catches me and tries to kill me again.

[I see you.]

Dallas keeps telling me to take my arms off his tummy—but the arms around his waist are his own. He's disassociated so far this time he can't tell where his body ends and mine begins. He's gasping for air now, his own hand grabbing his throat. I take it away, as the principal approaches.

"That boy is out of control," she says with eyes wide.

No shit, Sherlock.

"This…" I struggle to hold him. Still, he tries to grab my hair, but I bring his arm back down, "This isn't him. He's not home right now."

"How do we get him back?" the principal asks, sarcastically.

"Honestly, it's not the best time for conversation," I say. "I wish we had a more private space to see this meltdown cycle through."

She looks somewhat offended, but sticks around to watch the train wreck, regardless. He's screaming bloody murder and scratching my arms. I remind myself this will pass, it always does. I need to focus; I need to be strong—and for God's sake, this kid needs some dignity at the moment. Yes, he is absolutely out of control, and it's not his choice: this is a child possessed. Somewhere deep inside this raging body is a soul that is eternally valuable, a little boy without a father, a six-year-old desperately afraid of who he might become. I see him, while he sees red.

I turn him around to face me.

"What's your name?" I ask. He spits in my face.

The principal interjects, "Dallas! Stop this right now. You're very naughty at the moment, and we just won't tolerate that kind of behavior at this school."

"Please, let me deal with him," I request, shooting a death stare at the principal, whose reprimand was as insulting as it was ineffective. You know what naughty means? *Naughty* comes from the root word *naught*. Do you know what that means? Nothing — it means *you are nothing*. The principal throws her hands in the air and walks away. I bare through five extra minutes of blatant rage, thanks to her input.

He calms, as I ask, "What's your name?"

"Dallas," he says, eyes flicking from left to right.

"We're alone now—look at me. What's your name?"

"Dallas," he says with locked eyes.

"Tell me three times, what's your name?"

"Dallas, Dallas...I am Dallas," he says.

Right then he goes limp. I hold him in my lap like a baby, all curled in the fetal position.

I run my fingers through his sweaty hair as he weeps, rocking him back and forth.

"I'm sorry… I'm bad," he sobs, voice muffled in my shoulder. "Do you still like me?"

"No matter what," I admit, holding him close. "I like you every day."

He violently weeps; tears are pooling on my shirt. His knuckles are white as he holds onto me for dear life. This moment reminds me that I'm his biggest cheerleader, his only safety net. Even though I struggle, I am alone in being able to see him for who he is, however, shrouded in the dust of his actions.

"It's OK Buddy. You're safe now," I whisper.

His breath slows, growing deeper before he falls asleep on my chest.

CHAPTER TWO

Ultimatum

[I see you.]

The principal shifts in her seat and leans forward, "He's just not a good fit for this school."

I'm not stupid; I knew this was coming. Dallas's Mom picked him up not five minutes ago, and the school didn't have the balls to kick him out then and there. I'm not their messenger—if this principal is going to have him expelled from yet another placement, she has to tell his mother herself. Meanwhile, where is he supposed to get an education? I want to tell her to shove her precious school up her ass, but I'm a professional. I've finally figured out how private schools work: tell parents that all kids are welcome, then exclude the weird ones three days later when they "don't work out."

"I know he's hard work," I sigh, not quite finished with my sentence when she interrupts.

"Hard work?" she scoffs, as I brace myself for a lecture.

"Zoe, I've worked in education for longer than you've been alive," the principal begins. "*Hard work* is teaching a kid how to share the red crayon. Hard work doesn't even scratch the surface of what we are dealing with here."

"He needs you to give him a chance," I respond.

The principal explodes, "Dallas Jensen is a psychopath!"

"Conduct disorder," I snap. "It's impossible for a child to be a psychopath."

She suddenly looks repentant, and unsuccessfully scrambles for a way to save face.

"Well, from where I'm standing, that kid is one episode away from becoming a murderer—or killing himself in the process," the principal replies, with no less unprofessionalism. I can see that Dallas has brought this lady to her knees.

I'm livid, but there's no refuting her argument; I just don't want it to be true. I know he has potential, but I can't let it overshadow his current reality. We have to take him for who he is, right now, at this moment. Is he capable of being in a mainstream school environment? Truthfully, I don't know. I'm walking a constant tightrope while trying to lead others to join me on the precarious cable. Unsurprisingly, I'm having a hard time getting people on board—especially staff at this school. I never thought it would happen, but somehow over the course of the last few months, I guess I've fallen in love with this ridiculous child. As a Behavior Specialist, it's my job to extend hope to families and schools by providing interventions that change circumstances like this. The sad part is, at this moment—holding my broken glasses with a pounding headache, with scratches all over my arms and bruises to match—I totally agree with her. Although he's never had a formal diagnosis, his future looks bleak. I'd be lying if I told you I thought he was sane and safe.

"Can you *please* give him another chance?" I try not to sound too desperate. "You know, these kinds of behaviors often get worse before they get better."

"We're already seeing major red flags, and it's only the third day of the school year," the principal responds.

"He's the new kid—weren't you ever a kid at a new school? It's hard to be an outcast," I plead. She looks at the ceiling. The silence is deafening.

"I don't know if I can risk that kind of liability," she says, exhaling.

"Dallas is going through a lot at the moment, with the new baby at home and a new father figure joining the family—he's got no stability," I remind her.

"We can't sit here and wait for his mother to get her act together," she says, seeming like she's already made up her mind.

"You knew about his situation when you accepted his enrollment!" I say, a little unprofessionally, but heck, I'm in good

17

company. "I thought you believed in giving every student the right to learn?"

She retorts, carefully, "We didn't understand the… magnitude… of the situation at the time."

"Can we just put off making any further decisions until the end of the week?"

"I don't know, Zoe."

"That's two more days," I negotiate, "He's already gone home today, so just Thursday and Friday. If the next two days go south, then I agree—it's time for the school to cut ties with this family."

Because I work for his family directly, I don't risk losing Dallas if this placement goes awry. He's never been at a school longer than two weeks, and that's why the family hired me. Well, at least his Mom hired me—his step-dad hates my guts. The principal sighs and puts her face in her hands. She's exhausted. I'm exhausted. From her facial expression, I'm preparing myself to be more persuasive. I need to think quickly... I'll say something about equality, and how every child deserves—

"Fine," she says.

Wait—what? I try not to look excited. Game face, Zoe.

"He's got two days to prove he can be a functioning part of the group. If he passes, we will only keep him here on continued good behavior," she says as she makes very intense eye contact.

"Thank you," I smile.

#

I walk to my car with a blank stare. I open the door, sit down, and turn the key in the ignition. Finally I'm alone, and I don't have to pretend it's OK anymore. It seems like 85% of my energy as an adult woman is used up by figuring out ways not to cry in public. My head falls to the steering wheel, and I'm weeping involuntarily. A great, big, ugly, snotty cry. The tears are heaving from the pit of my chest, and I wipe my nose on my sleeve. Looking down at my arms, I see tiny pieces of torn-off flesh and hints of the red blood beneath. I hate myself for having let that happen to me, and I hate myself for having to hold him.

What if I am the monster? What if I have this all wrong? What if I'm just choosing to believe I am helping this boy, when maybe I'm making it all worse? He thinks I'm trying to kill him, and while I know my intention is quite the opposite I believe he thinks I'm here to make him die. I pull my sleeve down and lift the emergency brake to drive away.

I guess so much of life is simply about forward motion.

[I see red.]

Home smells different since Jacob moved in. It's smokier, smellier, and there's more yelling. Yelling isn't a smell, but it's also something that fills the air and makes us feel weird. I don't know why Mommy choosed to live with him—they only like each other because they maked a baby. I thought he would move out quicker if I was more bad, but so far he's stayed around. Most people think it's good when adults stay together, but I only think it's good if it's your real Mom and real Dad. Even if I never see my real life Dad ever again, Jacob will never be my real Dad. He's mean, and Mom's mean for letting him be that way.

It's only lunch time, and I have to be at home because I got sent home from the new school. I can hear Jacob yelling at Mom; he's telling her something about how he doesn't like me. I found the game playing tablet and I crawled into the tent I maked under my desk table. I really want to play all of the gun games but actually… I'm so… tired. I'm trying to stay awake but, I'm falling… asleep.

[I see you.]

Walking into my house, I throw my backpack down on the ground and fall into bed. There are a thousand things I want to do, but I can't think straight. I close my eyes, just for a minute.

#

I hear my roommate, Julia, banging on my bedroom door.

"It's time to go!" she yells through the wood. "Are you coming or not? We needed to leave, like five minutes ago."

I look at my phone, and it's 6:05 pm. I swear I only blinked, but I must've fallen asleep for three and a half hours. Julia and I are supposed to go to a fitness class tonight, but after all that's happened today, I don't think I can 'people' right now.

"Sorry," I groan, "I'm not feeling well."

"You could have told me earlier," she sighs, as she grabs her keys and slams the front door behind her. Julia and I have been friends since we went to high school back in Santa Cruz, and we were lucky enough to find a rent controlled apartment here in this crazy city. We don't live in the coolest neighborhood, but it's nice only to have to live with one other person. Most of our friends are packed like sardines in houses of six or more (gross), and I don't think I could handle that.

At the end of a day of Dallas, I tend to want nothing and no one, which is a far cry from my formerly extroverted self. I find myself being able to handle less and less of what people my age are supposed to enjoy. Julia bears the brunt of most of my isolation. I should spend more time with her, but I can't seem to get my head above water. I want to tell her it's me, not her—but instead, I just make stupid excuses. I've sold her out to be there for kids like Dallas. Over the past three years, I've had around six other versions of Dallas—all boys under thirteen. All troubled in their own ways, all struggling to make life work, yet none of them so much as Dallas.

I try to get out of bed, but I feel like I've been hit by a bus. I flick the switch on my lamp, and it seems so much brighter than usual. Squinting reflexively, I catch my reflection in the mirror, looking like a haggard, crazy-haired cat lady. There's a bruise forming on my cheek from where Dallas headbutted me and I'm starting to worry that I slept so long because I might have a concussion. I reach for the ibuprofen again.

The recurring thought crosses my mind: what if Dallas can't do this? What if he has another episode this week, and all of my advocacy falls flat? What if there's something profoundly wrong with this boy, and I'm perpetuating the problem? Do I honestly believe people can change?

The pills hit the pit of my stomach and stay there.

[I see red.]

I wake up under my desk tent, and I hear Mommy singing to the baby. Babies cry all day and all night long, and they are bad friends. They actually do nothing but eat and poop, and also they sleep. I can't know why Jacob likes the baby more than he likes me because I can do all the things, like win games and play baseball and I also sing really good too. The stupid baby can't even walk. Her doesn't even say words.

"You're so pretty," Jacob says to the baby. I hear a kissy sound, and then he tells my Mom he loves her. Gross. I never heared my Dad ever say that to my Mom, and that's the way it should be. My Mom will win for her own self, and nobody needs to win things for her. My Dad wins things for himself, even though I don't know what kinds of things because I haven't been to his house in a hundred years. I heared he has like 2 or 4 stupid new babies at his house, too. Why everyone's gotta have more babies?

I walk out into the living room to break up their disgusting party. Jacob looks at me, and leaves the room, and that is because I always win things I want.

"We need to talk about today," says Mom.

"What about it?" I shrug.

"Why did you run away again?" she asks.

"Because I am sneaky and fast," I smile.

"What the hell is wrong with you?" yells Mom, and walking back and forth in front of me. She grabs her phone and types in some things. I hope she's getting me a game to play—I mostly hope it's one with laser guns.

"Jacob, I think we need to call that psychiatrist the school recommended," she says, and I start to think she's not about to let me play gun games.

"We've already had this conversation, Sarah. The fees are sky high," he responds, "We can't afford it."

"We also can't afford to raise—" Mom stops half way in the middle of her sentence, and Jacob interrupts. Interrupting is rude, everybody knows that.

"Call a spade a spade, why don't you?" Jacob says. (Duh, why would you call it anything else? Jacob isn't smart)

"Dallas, go to your room," she tells me, and I know there is about to be a lot of yelling. I am starving, because all I ate was half a bagel in the morning and I'm about to die of hungry. I know better than to ask for dinner right now, so I grab a box of crackers off the table and go to my bed (I sleep on the bottom bunk). The crackers start to taste like a cardboard box after a while, and I am thirstier than I have ever been. I have a juice box in my backpack, which is extremely lucky, and I drink it in three long gulp, gulp, gulps. When it's empty, I can suck the air and only small bits of juice come up the straw with a lot of air and it makes this loud sound like a fart. It's almost loud enough to block out what Jacob is saying about me in the kitchen.

"Wake up to yourself! He's not a normal kid. I don't need to know a shit ton about childhood development to know he's not normal," I hear him say when the juice runs out.

"Well, are we going to just throw our hands in the air and say he's a psychopath, or are we going to help him?" Mom yells back.

"We're paying a million dollars for that girl to follow him around all day at school. She should be able to fix him for the amount she's charging," he says.

"I know, and I appreciate how much we pay," Mom tells him.

"I don't think you do, Sarah," he says. "You just piss my money away on that kid. He's not even mine."

"I'm sorry," she says. "I shouldn't have brought it up."

I've had enough of this conversation, because I hate the girl that follows me around at school. And I think Jacob is actually more right than my Mom, but Jacob can't win, so I am stopping listening to what they are saying. I have headphones around here somewhere—here they are, they're tangled as F-word. Untangling them is the worst punishment, so I start singing as I try to get them undone. I am a really very good singer. They're still sort of tangly but enough undone for me to plug them into my extremely old music player, which is where all my good songs live.

CHAPTER THREE

The Extremely Important Day

[I see you.]

My 6am alarm goes off, and I'm about ready to snooze when I remember the vital importance of today. I shower, make my hair look nice, and spend an extra few minutes on my makeup because a woman should never underestimate the value of perfectly winged eyeliner. My breakfast is full of protein and whole grains, and my coffee is locally sourced. I even ate chia seeds for Pete's sake—I'm not about to let Dallas go down without a fight. I stuff my bag with a bunch of resources that will help him learn with the other kids. Today is going to be the day he shows everybody that he is smart, that he is amazing, and that he adds value to their school community. Just you wait and see.

On the way, my car playlist is on point: calming my nerves and building up my bravado. I find a parking space straight away, which is a miracle in and of itself. I walk up the stairs with my head held high—oh, I can't wait to see Dallas and tell him how he's going to win this one!

The minute I walk into the classroom, one of the morning teachers accosts me at the door.

"He's hiding under the couch," she says, rolling her eyes. Suddenly I'm feeling all Mama Bear. I can roll my eyes at Dallas, but she sure can't.

"He's not even supposed to get here until 8 am," I snap, considering it took less than three seconds for one of these morons to rain on my parade. Looking at my watch, I continue, "It's only 7:55 am right now! Who dropped him off?"

"I guess it was the Dad?" the teacher divulges. "A guy, anyway."

(Thanks Jacob, that was really helpful. Way to get on board with the intervention, douchebag.)

Before nine, all the kids are cared for by the extra staff who cover teacher breaks and after school care. They're all about eighteen if they're lucky - some looking barely older than the kids in the upper grades. The morning staff aren't the brightest sparks, and few of them have a clue about early childhood development. It pains me that they say, Good Boy/Good Girl to these kids—their lack of separation between child and behavior makes me cringe. They're too young to be looking after this many kids—I know, because I've been there. When I was their age I thought I knew it all, only to soon find out I knew nothing about the tiny humans before me. Being excellent at working with children doesn't come from books, it comes from building a relationship with each child as an individual person. To effectively change the course of a child's life is to stop viewing them as a child, and start respecting them as a person.

Maybe these teachers don't have a clue, in part, because they're not reading the room. I guess I've always been an emotional sponge, soaking up the feelings of everyone around me like some kind of superpower. It's the most wonderful blessing, and simultaneously a terrible curse. I only wish I were oblivious to the emotional temperature of the room; I'm jealous of ignorant bliss—if I want to bury my head in the sand, I have to make the conscious decision towards oblivion. Maybe there aren't enough people born this way, and that's why so few are able to see Dallas the way I see him. Like x-ray vision, I see through the wild exterior to the bare bones underneath that prove we're all human; we're all imperfect, we're all trying our best, even when we completely miss the mark.

I have decided to use my oblivion card and ignore the morning staff, doing my own thing instead. I walk over to the couch and take a seat, pretending I have no idea Dallas is on the rug below. I grab one of his favorite books from the shelf and begin reading:

"The Army Ant is a name that is applied to over 200 species of ants, known for their aggressive predatory raids."

I see his arm poke out from under the couch. I have no idea why he loves this book, I think it's about as entertaining as watching paint dry—but for some reason he's got a real attachment.

"There are workers, queens, and males. Workers are the lowest caste of Army Ants. Colonies of Army Ants only have one Queen, and her job is to reproduce new ants by laying eggs."

Dallas slides his torso out from under the couch, and I pretend not to care. I continue reading aloud this vapid exposé on the Army Ant.

"Army Ants forage for food, sometimes a colony can devour up to half a million prey animals per day. As you can imagine, this kind of raid has a tremendous impact on the surrounding ecosystem."

A warm body sits beside me, and finds a front row seat to the Army Ant show. Again, I'm playing it cool and intend to keep reading. His leg is careful not to touch mine; his body turned away, ever so slightly.

"The Queen is the winner," Dallas whispers.

"What does she win?" I whisper back.

"All of the power. Her is the boss of everything."

"What's better, love or power?"

His eyes widen. He whispers, "Power."

I get close to him and say, "I want to give you some power today."

"What kind of power?" he curiously inquires.

"Today, you're the boss of something really important."

"Yeah?"

"What kind of day do you want to make for yourself?"

"A good one."

"That's your power."

"I don't get it," Dallas admits.

I wonder if I've lost him, as he slides his body off the couch and onto the rug again. I might need the innocuous Army Ants book to continue. Like magic, he jumps up and looks at me.

"How do I make a good day?" he asks.

"One step at a time," I say.

He thinks first, then inquires, "What if I make a bad step?"

"As long as most of the steps are positive, you're using your powers for good."

He falls on the rug again, "What's the point of a good power?"

"All of the true winners have good powers," I explain.

"Nuh uh...the bad guys win," he retorts.

"I disagree. They might win for a moment or two, but not in the end," I say as he grimaces. Clearly, this was not the news for which he was hoping. "Let's just try it out for today."

"Okay," he shrugs.

I take him over to the table and show him today's schedule.

[I see red.]

The *Evil She* is showing me a schedule of things what are happening today. Her is kind of a nice girl some days when her isn't being super bad. You might be wondering why I think that *The She* is evil, and I can tell you a few of the reasons. First, The *Evil She* stops me from doing things that I want to do. When I have good ideas, her catches me and holds me until I can't breathe—like yesterday when I wanted to draw at writing time. The stupid lady wouldn't let me, so I ran away from her, but she sent a hundred grown-ups to kill me. They didn't win though because here I am—alive and ready to play with blocks. I won't write though because I don't know how to do writing.

This is the list of things she is making me do today:
- Check in with Zoe (That's The *Evil She*'s name, but I never call her it)
- Morning choice; blocks, drawing, reading (I'm absolutely doing building, I have a plan too)
- Morning meeting; 5 min with group, then body break (I don't like the first bit, but I love the second bit, so one minus and one plus is a nothing)
- Snack (For your big fat information, I only eat animal crackers and never ever disgusting yogurt)
- Writing; 3 sentences about your weekend (I would write if I knowed how to write, but I don't so I'm not doing it)

- Lunch (Mom packed chicken nuggets in a warm thing with a strong lid)
- Recess (Best, but I wish I had friends)
- Quiet time (I usually make this into loud time)
- Math (I never do this because mostly I am kicked out of class when I'm bad and that happens before lunch mostly)
- Closing circle (never been to this, I wonder if it's fun, but probably isn't)
- Pick up (I hope it's Mom today) by Jacob (ugghhhhhhh)

I grab a marker with my fist (they're hard to hold) and check the first item. The *Evil She* looks happy about this, so I check off the next thing, and her takes the marker from me. I wonder if she forgot how I can't read or write?

"Wait! You haven't done your morning choice yet," her explains, and what she said is really true. "What are you going to choose?"

"Building," I say, running to the blocks. Her grabs my body, which I hate.

"Dallas, plant your feet," she says. I keep my body still, but it doesn't mean I like doing nothing. I'm just doing it for extra time with the blocks, not because I am listening to the stupid instructions.

"Eyes," she reminds me. I look at her.

"I want the blocks," I say, looking at her. I'm bored of this already, but she looks happy. I wonder if her thinked I couldn't talk or stay still? I'm not stupid, I'm just bad. These things are two different things.

Her sticks a golden star on a paper with lines.

[I see you.]

I'm so excited. Today is going exceptionally well so far, especially considering the lemonade we made from this morning's citrus cocktail. He's making eye contact, he's speaking clearly, he's calming his body with prompts. He's getting it! Thank God.

"Buddy, you earned a sticker! Only nine more, and then what do you get?"

He doesn't reply. That's OK, I guess Dallas is done talking for the moment, and maybe I should stop pushing my agenda so hard. I sit beside him on the rug as he pulls out various blocks.

"In nine more stickers, you'll get ten minutes on the…" I'm leaving a gap for him to finish my sentence—this way I can check that he's tracking what I'm saying, and he has processed what he is working towards. No reply. I count in my head: five, four, three, two, one.

Still, no response.

[I see red.]

"On the game tablet," yes, I already knowed that. I wish her would stop talking to me and leave me alone. I have a good idea about not answering she when her speaks—if I stop answering, her will stop talking to me. I do this all the time, and mostly people get tired of talking when nobody talks back. They say it's like talking to a brick wall, which I never knowed if they did or not. I don't feel like trying to talk to walls because that sounds stupid and really not fun. Also, people who get prizes for being good are people who aren't me. I don't need a sticker for talking, and I like games, but I don't need a prize.

I didn't do work for a award.

[I see you.]

"You'll get ten minutes on the game tablet!" I say, in a voice more condescending than I'd care to admit. He doesn't acknowledge what I've said.

I know he likes having time on the game tablet, but I also know he's not big on rewards. Maybe he is, but he hates the educational game selection the school allows? Hmm. He's playing his cards close to his chest. I find myself getting worked up in the confusion of all these things. This is the part of the job that I hate the most—am I actually supposed to understand this kid? I'll tell you something for nothing—I don't get Dallas Jensen in the slightest. What if today turns to shit? I'm supposed to have it all together. What if I'm wrong and he runs away? What if we don't catch him this time? Forget catching Dallas, first I need to catch myself. I take a deep breath, relying on affirmations to keep myself afloat.

Zoe, we can do this.

I decide to choose my battles and back off while he plays with the blocks. The more I trust his behavior, the more space I put between the two of us. I feel like a weight has been lifted off my shoulders. I'm breathing easier. He looks so normal right now, like every other kid in the room. Every now and again we get these windows into who Dallas could be—who he might become with an early intervention. Why Dallas is the way he is is still a mystery, one I can only attribute to an omission in parental communication between home and school. He strikes me as a kid with attachment issues, but I'm not sure that's the whole picture. I think there's something neurological going on, but heck, I can't diagnose. But I do wonder.

I became a Behavior Specialist three years ago after completing an Education degree at college. Somewhere along the line, I realized I wasn't made for classroom teaching, and came to resent the idea of wiping snotty noses and tying shoelaces all day. I was knee deep in a four-year course, and subsequently in student debt. I decided I would see the degree through, thanks to the encouragement of my parents, then take a look at my options later on. During my last teaching internship, I was given the responsibility of handling the behaviors of an eight-year-old boy with Autism. I was thrown in the deep end just as I realized I had been born to swim. Quirky kids were my field and I found endless joy in building a relationship with this boy.

After finishing the degree, I landed a Behavior Specialist position where I could learn on the job. I rang in my first day with a four-year-old boy who had torn up his living room from floor to ceiling. He stood there holding a key, which he had used to carve expletives into the wall (I was equally horrified and impressed with his literacy skills). He scowled at me with a certain kind of look in his eye, one I now see in Dallas. I've known so many little guys with the same narrow eyes, the same flailing limbs, the same proclivity to succumb to power outside of themselves.

But right now, I'm here watching Dallas play like any other kid. His eyes are clear, his face innocent. No matter what happens today, we have this moment. This super friggin' normal throwaway moment. I snap a picture, both in my heart and on my camera.

Hope rises.

CHAPTER FOUR

The World's Most Normal Kid

[I see red.]
  I told you I had a plan for these blocks, and I really do. The long ones are the road, and I made a church out of the ones that are a bit like an arch, but they have a flat pointy on the top. Next to that, I builded a hospital which is mostly rectangles. I think we need a shop, too, where people can buy things they want and need. The teacher said I can't bring out the toy cars if I already have the blocks out, so I have to be smart and use blocks as cars. I don't mind because I can figure out what to do without any help, and now the smallest blocks are my cars.
  There are imaginary people in these little block cars, and they are all sick in different kinds of ways. Every person in the town is sick, but them aren't all sick on the same day. That way, the healthy ones can take good care of the ones who feel like they're all broken. Them can choose to go to the shops and buy things to feel better; them can go to church and say wishes that God will take all the sickness and throw it far far away, or them can let the doctors heal them at the hospital. I wonder where the people will choose to go today? I always listen to them, and let them choose for their own self.

[I see you.]
  I'm taking notes on Dallas as he plays:

Notes by Zoe Fletcher
Time: 8:55 am Situation: Block Play, Classroom

Before: D asks the teacher if he can use toy cars in his block play. The teacher explains that he can only play with one thing at a time.
What Happened: D makes eye contact with the teacher and says, "Why?" Teacher says, "We have to make sure everyone has something to play with." D shrugs and says, "OK." He then finds small blocks and uses them as cars.
After: D continues playing independently.

His regular classroom teacher, Mrs. Garcia, walks over towards me. She's professional, in the sense that she makes an effort to cover how uptight she's feeling rather than letting it all hang out. I see it in her eyes and her clenched fists. She's newly married, strikingly beautiful, with long black hair and a charismatic smile. She's carrying skeletons in her closet; it's all there in those almond-shaped eyes.

"He's being so normal right now," Mrs. Garcia says. "I'm sorry, I know it's more PC to say typically developing, but you know what I mean."

"Yeah," I cringe. Maybe I spoke too soon about her professionalism. "I don't really know what to do with myself when he's settled like this."

"Use the restroom. Grab a coffee—enjoy the down time!" Mrs. Garcia encourages me.

I'm not too jazzed about the idea of actually leaving the room, but the restroom is only a few feet away. I feel like I can make that one happen (Look at me! Living on the edge!) He's been playing so well for an hour and a half now, and here I am justifying a trip to the bathroom. Truth be told, I usually don't drink any liquid in the morning, so I won't need to go to the bathroom. Dallas is likely to punch someone in the face the minute I leave the room, as was the case two days ago. Mrs. Garcia didn't see, so I pretended it wasn't Dallas. Today, he can't do that or he'll be expelled, as he probably should have been on day one. I remind myself that he's doing great right now, and all we have is this moment. I can step out and go to the bathroom, right? For Pete's sake, I shouldn't be so conflicted about whether or not to go pee.

"I'm going to use the restroom," I say as I start walking away. "If anything changes with Dallas, can you just grab him like a bear hug and sit him on the bean bag? I'll only be a minute... maybe I should just hold..."

"Zoe," Mrs. Garcia says, in a condescending tone. "Look at him. He's fine!"

"OK, OK... I'm going," I say as I walk away smiling.

Honestly, I don't even need to use the bathroom anymore, but I could use a minute to check my email. I sit in the stall and take a deep breath, then I leave and (even though I didn't use the bathroom) I wash my hands, so I don't look like a gross weirdo. I didn't even check my email—this isn't the day for putting distance between me and the kid. Walking back into the classroom, I'm relieved to see Dallas is still playing safely.

"Thanks for watching him," I say to the teacher.

"It was less than a minute. What mischief could he get up to in that time?" she laughs.

I'm also laughing, but I sense it's for a different reason. Oh, lady, you have no idea what this little slice of heaven can get up to in less than a minute. This kid can shit on demand—no joke— he peed on his last teacher's favorite book. Just found a quiet corner, opened the book, peed on it, and closed the pages. Two days later, the teacher opened the book to read aloud to the class and the pages were all stuck together... and smelled disgusting. Don't be fooled by this angelic face—he'll change the time on all your clocks while you're putting a band-aid on someone else's scraped knee, and he'll steal your cell phone from your pocket if you're not making eye contact. Give him a minute and he'll run halfway to New York—a lot can happen in a minute. But thankfully, this time, it didn't.

Since our primary goal today is safety, I let the teacher know it's OK to leave Dallas in the block area rather than transitioning him to snack. As we speak, he's already missing out on the morning meeting and frankly, I don't care. When I look around the classroom, I see at least two other kids working on individual projects, so technically he's a functioning part of the group right now. He's still building that block city, and it's becoming more elaborate by the minute.

It's so refreshing to see him acting "normally." A little girl from the class approaches him to see if she could join the activity. My heart begins to race—this kind of situation doesn't usually end well. Surprisingly, he seems to welcome her into his space, and it looks like they're actually playing together.

[I see red.]

Carolina is a girl in my class. Her is still only five, which makes me better because I am a bigger number. I only knowed her for three days but I think I win more things than her does, but here is one thing to know: Carolina is so pretty. Her won at being pretty, but I didn't even enter that competition. Her wants to play with me and I think that is OK because last time we played her wasn't bossy. Carolina only likes me on some days and today might be one of them.

"What are you building?" her asks.

"A city," I say.

"What place?" Carolina says.

I don't want to tell her because they're my ideas from my own head and I can share this area with blocks but I can not share all my ideas. Some things are only for me.

"Hey, I said, what place?" her says another time.

"It's just a city, you can make up in your head which is what place," I a little bit yell at her with a tiny bit of an angry voice. Oops—that made The *Evil She* walk over to us.

"Hey guys," *Evil She* says. "Is everything OK?"

"He...he...he... isn't sharing him's ideas," Pretty Face tattles. Now she looks less pretty.

"I don't have to share my ideas!" I yell again.

"He's right, Carolina. It's really nice of you to be interested in what he's doing, but it looks like he might need some space right now. Is that what you want, Dallas?" The *Evil She* says.

I nod my head.

"Let's use words. Can you politely tell Carolina that you need space?"

I nod my head another time.

"I need space," I say all mumbly into my sleeve.

"Meany!" Carolina yells, "Dallas is a bad boy. That's why he has no friends."

Carolina stomps her foot before she leaves the block area in a huff, and I'm mad that she talked bad about me. I've only been at this school for a little bit of days, that's why I don't have friends yet. The *Evil She* is all happy and gets out the gold stars again. Why *She's* happy? I just told a kid to go away. That's not needing a sticker.

[I see you.]

Yes! He's getting it!

Mrs. Garcia checks in with me, and assure her everything is under control, but ask her to follow up with Carolina. Things are better than alright—Dallas is using words and complying with directions. Finally! I wish the Principal would randomly walk by right now so I could brag, but funnily enough, she only responds to 'Hot Dog.'

[I see red.]

Now I am back to work in the city I made for myself, by myself. I have added tons of things, like for example a pool for people to swim or take a bath. When people are sick, them shouldn't just swim for fun because they might catch their death, but at the church, I heared a story about a sick man who sat next to a pool all day, every day. Rachel told me. I used to know a grown up called Rachel, and her was my Sunday School teacher. Her liked me, even when everybody else didn't want to be my friend. Her held my hand, her hugged me, her told me about Grey in heaven. Rachel said all these prayers with me, and her said that no matter what happens in my whole wide life, God and Jesus will be my friend. Jacob won't let us go to church anymore, so I never see'd Rachel again.

Rachel told me about the sick man who was lying on a yoga mat by the pool because him's legs didn't work anymore and he just waited and waited for him's turn to get in the pool, which would heal whoever went in the water because an angel stirred it. The problem was, the guy couldn't do a magic swim when him couldn't move, and nobody helped him. Jesus didn't let someone help the guy, but he just made him's legs better and told him to walk away with the yoga mat. That's why we have a pool in this city—so Jesus can decide if he wants to help.

Jesus and God are the same, like how ice is made from water—that's what I got teached when I went to church those times. Jesus lived on the Earth, and him could heal whoever him wanted but also the people had to want to be healed. God is the Dad, and dads can choose to listen to kids or drink beer instead. I think God is a big dad, the kind of dad who lives at your house forever, not like my Dad who left. God could leave us all if he wanted to, but I don't think that's the way him wants to be. God has billions of kids, but him can be their dads all at one time.

About three or five minutes ago I pretended to get a tissue for my snot, but in real life, I took two toy cars from the box near the shelves. Them are in my pockets now, and they poking my leg, but I don't mind because I have a plan for later. Right now, I am making the doors to the shop real wide so that the sick people can easily go there and buy things. Them will be tricked into thinking they got healed when them buy cool clothes and phones, but guess what? The people forget to buy medicine! Them buy too many lattes, so their credit cards run out of money, and they don't pay their banks and then the men yell at the Moms, "Imma throw you and that kid out on your ass if you ever speak to me like that again, crazy bitch."

Uh oh! The mail carrier is delivering a letter to the Mommy. Her opens the letter and it says, "We are taking your car away because you's credit card is called Max." The Mom in this game is crying and her man tells her to shut up.

Him is angry and her needs to watch out before him blows up like a volcano.

[I see you.]

Notes by Zoe Fletcher
Time: 10:35am   Situation: Block Play, Classroom

<u>Before:</u> *D has been playing independently for 2.5hrs, building what appears to be a block city.*

What happened: *Noise level increased at 10:32 am, as he began to look angry. D speaking to the block (people?) I think I heard him say, "I'm going to throw you out on your ass, crazy bitch" or something to that effect. One of the (people?) blocks in his left hand crashed into the building made from the arch-shaped block. The left-hand block then said, "Don't listen to their bullshit, you can't go there anymore, it's closed forever." He then knocked down the whole block city.*

After: *I approached D to see if he needed to take a break. He did not respond, remained stable but mildly dysregulated. Proximity used to prevent escalation/elopement.*

[I see red.]

I hate this city. I never liked it in the first place, so I knocked it all down, and you know what? I'm not going to clean it up. There's a rule in this classroom, "You make it, you break it." I made this city, and it is my job to break it. I won the right to break it down, and I also won these cars in my pocket. I deserve these cars at every minute of the day because the stupid teacher doesn't know I am the boss.

I run away from the block area, straight to the bathroom. I slam the door because I like things LOUD LOUD LOUD. I told you I had a plan for these cars! Vrrrroooom, VROOOOM, I say. Plop! The blue car did a long fall down into the toilet, and he sinked to the bottom. He can't swim, so he's dead from drowning. Goodbye, car! Flush! And now, the red car… he has a long journey ahead. He's going somewhere other than the toilet. I need some tape, which is also in my pocket with my teacher's phone. Nobody knowed I took it, because she set it down on the table and I am the winner of the sneaky award. If you act normal, stealing things is easy.

Tape makes a loud sound when you wrap it around a phone and a blue car. I am trying to be quiet because everyone knows sneaky people do things quietly. The *Evil She* is calling out my name through the main door of the bathroom. She can't come in, because teachers aren't allowed in a kids bathroom unless someone is dying or dead. I tell her, "I'm OK!" and, "I'll be right back!" and her tells me she's giving me a gold star for using words. Now the tape is definitely sticked on the car, and it is back in my pocket. Time to breathe in and make my tummy little, because the glass is out of the skinny window and I am climbing out into the wide world.

[I see you.]

Third gold star in less than three hours! I had nothing to be nervous about today. He's been pretty solitary, but apart from that, he's acting like the most normal kid in the world. Seriously, thank goodness for these moments to breathe. He's been talking to himself in the bathroom lately, I think he was acting out car noises just before. When he gets out, I'll get him to pack up the blocks and I think we can just take a game tablet break. The schedule I made this morning was OK, but not exactly realistic. If we can just get through the day without anything major, we'll be fine, and he can stay at this school. I honestly don't care if he learns anything today, as long as he can hit some really basic social expectations. I'm setting the bar so low a mouse could do the limbo.

Jeez, he's been in the bathroom for a while. I'm trying not to be too much of a helicopter shadow (worst kind of support professionals—they don't give kids any space), but I guess it's time I checked in.

"Dallas? Are you OK?" I inquire.

I count to five in my head, because you know, he rarely answers the first time.

"Dallas? Are you OK?" I repeat verbatim because it's important I don't change the wording of questions the second time I ask. He generally processes changed wording as though it was a different question, so I don't want to confuse him. He doesn't answer again, which isn't unusual. Personally, I don't like to repeat a question more than three times, so the third time has to be more than pissing into the wind. I walk into the bathroom, and the cubicle closest to the wall is locked. I look under—lo and behold! No feet.

Dammit. I'm so embarrassed I let this happen again—so much for trust! The friggin' window is open, too, and I start to suspect this is how he Houdini'd his way out of here yesterday. The open part is less than a foot high, so if he got out of there he must've pulled some mouse level shit—mice can squeeze through holes as small as 1/4in. I guess we discovered the kid equivalent.

CHAPTER FIVE

Flight of the Blue Car

[I see red.]

The red car is in for a much bigger adventure than the blue guy could ever do. The red car is always better because it's a faster color like Fire Engines. You don't know how important the red car is until the blue is dead and gone. The red car will sometimes remember his friend Mr. Blue, but thinking about him will never bring him back. That is why the red car sometimes hates the blue car in his memories. Remembering is stupid and boring.

I found a ladder on the outside fire escape, which is way too high up for me to reach, but I have a plan. I always have plans, don't you know? Kind of close to the ladder is a tree, which is not the strongest but also not the unstrongest. I grab a hard box from the play yard and stand on it. Hmm—too small. I grab another box because that will make it two times big, and when I stand on it, I am tall enough to climb onto a branch. I jump up, and the boxes fall down, but lucky I am in the tree now.

I hit my knee on the bark, and it's got blood but I don't care. I hate band-aids, mostly I hate when people try to put them on for me. The blood falls down to my sock. I climb to the next higher branch stick, and I am close enough now to get onto the ladder. The branch is a bit skinny for climbing and bends when I stand on it. I think I have to do this lightning fast so the branch doesn't snap, so I get down low and BURST my energy like a rocket. I jump and grab onto the ladder like a cat. That was tricky, but I won.

I climb up the ladder fast, fast, fast. Now I am where I want to be—I'm on the roof. Did you know most of the roofs in San Francisco are flat? I did. Even if they look pointy at the front it's all fake—they're flat behind the front. I wanted to climb this roof the minute I came to this school, but I never got the chance. Well, today is my day. Red car and phoney are in my pocket, so I get them out. The phone lights up under all that tape, and I see a picture of a stupid man giving a kiss on Mrs. Garcia's cheek. I slide open the lock, and there isn't a passcode. Her doesn't have any games that I like, so I open her music. She has two songs the same as me but a hundred songs I hate.

The green square with the speech bubble is for texting. There's a red circle in the top corner, and it says the number two. I tap the green and it opens a page with texting from a guy who's name is Will, and there's a love heart picture beside the word. He wrote a text that I can't read, so I press some buttons, and it spells words automatically which makes me seem very smart. I press send. Oh! I know! I will add a photo to send to him. I open the albums and send a picture of Mrs. Garcia kissing a different man than the one when the phone was locked. OK, enough time wasting. Now it's time for red car and phoney phone to have the ride of their lives.

I walk to the edge of the roof.

[I see you.]

I lift the walkie-talkie to my mouth and press the button reluctantly.

"Hot dog," I confess (famous last words).

I sense the principal is shining her shoes, readying herself to kick us to the curb. It must feel good to be right all the time. I run outside, but I can't see him anywhere before help arrives. I ask one teacher to look in the bathroom and another to check all the staircases. The principal bursts from the building like mints in a cola bottle, and I can tell she's absolutely livid.

"He's gone! He's out!" she says with her beady eyes melting a hole in my already deflated soul. "I shouldn't have let you talk me into keeping him here a single moment longer, Zoe. I had faith in your ability to change him."

I interrupt her rant, "Can we talk about this later? Right now we have a child to find, which I am sure you'd agree is more important." Suddenly something falls from above and crashes into a thousand pieces on the cement.

"What the f...udge?" I alter my speech to remain professional. On the ground before me is a red toy car, wrapped in tape, connected to a device that once was a phone. The blood drains from my face, and I look to the roof of the building. F-Word. Dallas is laughing and yelling, "Blast off!"

I slowly grab the principal's arm and calmly whisper, "Don't make any sudden movements, don't talk, just stand here. I'm going to tell you something, and I am trusting you not to react. I need you to act as natural as possible—can you do that?"

"Yes," she whispers confusedly, "What is going on?"

"Dallas is on the roof," I murmur.

Her eyes grow wide, and I'm pretty sure she just shit her pants a little bit. "Are you serious?"

"Don't look up," I say, as she is frozen like a deer in headlights.

"What if he jumps?" she says, as though I hadn't already thought of that possibility.

"We will get him before he has the chance," I lie through my teeth.

"How?" she says, almost inaudibly.

How indeed. I need to think fast.

"We have to look as though we're still searching for him. Get some staff out here, and just direct them to look for him like we did yesterday. Make him think he's winning," I convince myself. "I am going to climb up on the roof."

"Don't be stupid. You can't get on the roof," she whispers bluntly. "Call the fire department for God's sake!"

"Not yet—trust me," I say, without fully believing what I am about to do. "Call them when I catch him, and not a moment before."

Why did I volunteer myself for this? This is the stupidest plan I have ever hatched, and with one wrong move both of us may need scraping off the sidewalk. This kid may literally be the death of me, and here I go like a lamb to the slaughter. The principal rallies the crew, and I hear them starting the fake search party. I run to the fire escape, extend the ladder as quietly as possible, and climb on and on not stopping to look below.

When I reach the top I see Dallas standing on the other side of the roof looking towards the city. He's singing with all of his heart, and I see the lengths to which he's gone in order to get a moment he can call his own. I don't want to scare him—I'm trying to be sneaky, not stupid. When I get within ten feet, I know it's time to say something.

"Buddy," I say quietly.

"I won!" he laughs, "You better watch out, or I'll fly like the car."

The moment passes in slow motion, as I realize the gravity of the situation. There is no time to be afraid, and by the look in Dallas's eyes, he's definitely not 'home' right now. I cease talking to the boy, and I begin conversing with his demons.

"Who are you?" I ask.

"I am the boss," he snarls.

"Dallas, listen to me," I assert confidently, "Dallas, take the wheel."

He jumps on the spot, arms flailing.

"What's your name?" I say.

"D... Damn you, asshole!" it screams.

"Dallas. I see you, Dallas. You're called Dallas," I say, trembling.

His eyes close and face winces.

"I'm Dallas," he says through clenched teeth, and he returns to me, so slightly. I need to seize the moment—and fast.

"Have you ever played this game? It's called Undead Pirate Ransom. They're zombies, and also pirates. I think you'd like it," I mention casually, my heart beating like a hummingbird's wings. I sit down in my place and put the phone's volume on full blast. Zombies moan words like, "Argh!" and, "Shiver me timbers!" The sound of swords brandishing fills the air, and Dallas follows it like catnip. He runs towards me.

"Let me see!" he says, trying to take the phone.

"No way, I'm playing right now!" I retort, grasping my phone tighter than ever before.

"Can I be next?" he begs.

"I guess. But you have to watch me now, so you know how to play," I reason.

Dallas sidles up beside me, and without a second's hesitation, I extend my arm and scoop him into my lap. My phone leaves my hand, and bounces twice on the roof. I have him, thank God, he's safe with me for now—but I need backup before he escapes. I can't risk the walkie talkie, so I scream more desperately than I ever have before.

"HOT DOG! I have him!"

The principal is mid-call to 911, and I wait, painstakingly on this roof with Dallas. He's kicking and screaming—I'm going to need superhuman strength to hold him until the fire truck arrives.

Finally, I hear sirens.

[I see red.]

I've been tricked! The *Evil She* is trying to kill me again, just when I thought her was nice. There's no such thing as a nice killer, so she is now the most evil person I have ever knowed. I have no breath left, and I'm trying to scream to tell everyone I'm dying, but no sound is coming out. I think this has to be the start of what dying feels like. I have to kick and scratch her so I don't die before they all find out who the bad guy really is. This lady whispers lies to me, she follows me everywhere, and she takes away my choices. I have to tell the police about her as soon as I can talk again.

I throw my head back to crack hers again, but it doesn't work. She seems stronger today, and she's holding me tighter than any other day. Her leg is over the top of mine, and she is not letting me win at all. I need some new ideas to make her stop killing me. Wait—is that a siren? The police heared my wishes, and they are taking her to jail. I hear sirens getting louder, and louder, then they stop. I just have to survive until they take her away.

[I see you.]

Dallas elbows me in the side, and he's kicking like crazy. He reaches his mouth down to my arm and plants his teeth, which hurts like nobody's business. Instinctively, I push my arm into his bite, which opens his jaw and he releases. His screams are husky, and he seems breathless. I hear him trying to scream, but it comes out all breathy.

"You're killing me!" he wheezes, "Why are you making me die?"

My arms are loose enough around his waist to know that I'm not actually taking his breath away, but the stress of the situation seems to be choking him. If I let him go, he'll jump off the roof, but if I hold him, he might hyperventilate. Luckily, I see the cherry picking extension rise up beside the roof. A firefighter climbs out and approaches us.

"Be careful," I ask, "He runs. If you're going to take him from me, you have to promise that you won't let him go."

"OK—I won't," the firefighter agrees.

"I mean, from the second you take him from my arms to the second you put him back in my arms you can't let him go," I reiterate hysterically. "He is hard to hold, so make your grip tight enough to contain him—but you have to make sure he can breathe. Also, don't talk to him. Just get him to the ground safely."

"I promise you, I won't let him go," the firefighter confirms and reaches over to take him. I've never let anyone take Dallas from me while he's raging—not even his own mother. What if this firefighter (albeit a 6'3" man) loses grip—just for a second? A second is all it takes for Dallas to run and jump.

"DON'T LET HIM GO!" I scream with empty arms, as I watch the fireman carry Dallas from the roof to the cherry picker. They climb inside, then I hear the hydraulics mark the cherry-picker's descent, watching strangers take him as they fade from view. I'm alone on the roof right now, and I cry from the pit of my stomach. By the grace of God, we both survived. I'm angry and thankful, relieved and terrified—all at once. I assume the firefighters will come back for me, so I make a decision to trust their ability to keep him safe. I can't do anything from up here, except take in the beauty of the San Francisco skyline, which will be forever associated with this unfortunate moment in time. Soon enough, the cherry picker returns and I'm ushered into the bucket with a different firefighter.

Once we're on the ground, the first firefighter hands Dallas back into my arms, and I walk him to the front entrance of the school. I corner him by the doors, blocking his ability to run.

"What's your name?" I ask.

"You're killing me!" he says, cowering.

I stand him up again on his feet.

"Dallas, I like you every single day. It doesn't matter what you do, I like who you are. You're safe, Buddy. You're safe with me," I tell him, "What's your name?"

"Dallas," he whispers, almost silently. "I'm Dallas."

He falls to the floor and weeps, so I scoop him up onto my lap. He's not at risk of running now, he's 'home' within himself. He melts like wax into my arms and cries, as I stroke his sweaty hair away from his eyes.

"You're OK, Buddy. You're safe now," I whisper, gently rocking him back and forth. He falls asleep in my arms, intermittently sniffling as he starts to calm in his sleep. The principal stands there with her mouth open, not sure whether to be enraged or impressed. She walks over and sits beside me on the ground.

"He's not welcome back here, I know," I say, trying to save her breath.

"Sorry," she replies. "His parents are on their way over."

I'm a little worried about what might happen next.

"Zoe," the principal says quietly, "Are you OK?"

"I'll be fine. This is part of the job," I brush off her concern.

"Maybe you need to rethink your involvement with this family," she says carefully, knowing that her suggestion is unwelcome. "For your own health and safety."

"Things always get worse before they get better," I insist. "We'll find him another educational placement, and we'll start again."

Nobody ever screws up so much that they're beyond help. I believe that with all of my heart.

CHAPTER SIX

Last Resort

[I see red.]

I waked up in my bed, and suddenly I miss the red and blue cars. I wish them were still here in my pocket because them were so cool. I wonder where the blue guy went after he drowned in the toilet? Same place the poops go I guess, but I never knowed where that was. I do know I can never go there. The loudest things are happening in my house right now. There's a grown-up who is crying and crying, and I think the cry belongs to my Mom. Moms can yell, moms can hug, moms can read books—but moms shouldn't be crying like babies. Them are too old for that. I wonder why her is so sad? Wait—can I hear The *Evil She*'s voice? Here? At my house? I hope that's not real. I walk to my bedroom door and press my ear to the wood. I listen closely:

"I'm sorry this happened, but I'm confident I did everything I could," *She* says.

"I believe you—it's Jacob that..." Mom says without finishing the words. "I'm just at a loss as to what to do with Dallas. I don't think we're making progress at all. I think he's getting worse."

"I see where you're coming from. To be honest with you, it's my belief that if we can manage his anxiety we're more likely to see progress. Any kid who has a behavioral intervention taking place is likely to get worse before they get better," *She* says.

Mom asks, "Zoe, can you seriously look me in the eye and tell me you think he's going to grow out of this?"

Her does a deep breath and then some seconds go by (they feel like a hundred years), and then The *Evil She* says, "I couldn't honestly come to work every day and do this job if I thought he couldn't change. It's not going to happen quickly, or without a lot of work, but I honestly believe it can happen."

"Have you seen these kinds of interventions actually change kids? I mean, have you been personally involved with a child who has made significant, lasting change?" Mommy says.

[I see you.]

I rack my brains for a case that will throw her a lifeline. I have seen plenty of kids improve, but I think she's looking for someone who is "completely normal" now. I haven't got many squeaky clean stories from which to draw inspiration. My first kid changed schools without notice, and his parents decided he didn't need help anymore. I waited all day at the school, but he never arrived. I heard through the grapevine that that child has since been kicked out of five schools, so obviously his folks made the right choice in ditching the intervention (not). My second kid stabbed me with some kind of stick fashioned into a shiv, and I was never allowed to be in the same room with him again. Third kid ended up going to a special education placement, which turned out fantastically—but that case isn't relevant to Dallas, because he's not eligible for that kind of thing. My fourth and fifth kids moved away, and I never heard from either of their families ever again. I often wonder what became of these guys, and mourn for the fact that some of their interventions were never properly realized.

Thinking over this list, I wonder why I'm so intent on continuing with this job, since the success rate appears to be so low. Big picture, it's hard to see change—especially when the parents aren't on board. But on a day-to-day level, each of these boys progressed by leaps and bounds. Little things like learning to greet people appropriately, making eye contact, considering others before themselves, learning their body's limits, and paying attention to the still small voice inside their hearts that some may call a conscience. I have seen glimpses of change, breakthroughs unimaginable… but somehow they struggle to translate to a full success story.

Sarah persists, "How? How did they change?"

"Time," I say. "And a lot of really consistent adult interaction. I'm talking about interactions so predictable that they're boring. Kids need to be able to expect something stable from their adults."

Now I'm the kid with the shiv, and Sarah is me. A guilty expression washes over her face and remains like stagnant water. My words are like knives to her heart, yet I don't regret my cruelty. For me to have integrity, these things need to be said.

[I see red.]

Mom starts talking quiet as a mouse and I have a harder time hearing through the door. I crack it open just a little, and you wouldn't believe how much more clearly I can hear now. Her is talking about Jacob being an angry butt head.

"Jacob doesn't understand the time aspect. He wants a magic wand—he's not interested in a long-term intervention," Mom cries. "He thinks it's bullshit. If I disagree, he gets angry."

"You are Dallas's mother," The *Evil She* says. "Start by changing your own interactions with him. You're ultimately in charge of your son."

"I am doing the best I can," Mom says, sounding a little angry. I think The *Evil She* maked her mad.

"I know that, Sarah. Just remember that every little interaction causes Dallas to weigh up whether or not you can be trusted. Make schedules, stick to limits, eat three square meals with him—pick him up on time," *She* tells my Mom, like a bossy kid.

Mom cries more, "It's hard to do it all on my own. Jacob only looks after Aurora."

The *Evil She* puts her arms around Mommy, and I wonder if her is going to hold on until Mom dies? I am about to run out and kick she's legs, when her lets my Mom go.

"If you don't mind me asking, what happened to Dallas's biological father?" *She* says, and I do mind her asking about that. I know that means my real Dad, and that is none of her beeswax. That's exactly something that's just for me to know. I want to interrupt her so bad, but I know I am already in trouble, and that means no screen time. I don't feel like also having no dessert, so I think I just have to let my stupid Mom tell The *Evil She* about my Dad.

"We divorced three years ago, after a death in the family," Mom tells her. I want her to stop telling that story, so I start humming. Now I can only hear parts of what Mom is telling the *She*. I hear her saying sorry to Mom and I shut the door, put my hands in my ears and hummmmm.

Hummmmmm…. "Dallas and Grey—" ….hummmm….. "He was six and Dallas was just three—"…hummm….. "You know, all kids love swimming in the summertime—" …..hummmmm.... "They were good swimmers, but—" …. hummmm… "It only takes a second, you see that's the part that people don't take seriously—" ...hummmm…. "By the time we realized, he was blue—" ...hummmm… "Dallas never truly understood what happened to his brother. He's never really recovered from that day. But we don't talk about it."

She's lying! I know what happened to him—he died. Him breathed in water, and his insides were supposed to have air. I was next to him, I was supposed to save him, and I didn't. Dad told me it was my fault, and I can never ever say sorry to Grey because he's gone. He went to heaven, and we never saw him again, and he lives with Jesus now, because I made him die. If I want to be near Jesus, I need to go to church with Rachel, but I can't because Jacob told my Mom that church was bullshit, and we aren't allowed to go. Rachel said it wasn't bullshit, Rachel was more right than Jacob, but now I have no Rachel. Also, there's no Grey, and there hasn't been one for a very long time. Sometimes I can remember him, and sometimes I can't. Sometimes I don't remember him on purpose because he'll never come back. Jacob said dead people just get eated by worms in the ground, but Rachel said there's heaven. I know there's a heaven, I just don't know if I'll ever get there because I'm bad.

I find my music player and untangle the earbuds again. How do they get so tangly every single day? I do my most happy playlist because I'm feeling the most sad. I put the earbuds in and close my eyes—it's the closest to invisible I can be.

I think I disappear when I do this, so I do it for hours and hours.

[I see you.]

So, after three hours of damage control at Dallas's house, we've come up with an educational solution for the immediate future: I'm going to homeschool him. It's really great timing because this week Jacob finishes his paternity leave, and the baby starts daycare next week so we'll have the house to ourselves. Despite the fact that today was the scariest day of my life, I'm feeling confident about the future. I've been face-to-face with death many times in the past three years, and I guess today was our closest shave. By the grace of God, Dallas and I are both alive and kicking. (Maybe he's kicking a little more than I am.)

Meanwhile, if we were looking for a reason why Dallas is the way he is, then today we hit the nail on the head. I can't stop thinking about Dallas's brother, Grey, who drowned three summers ago. His death ultimately fractured the family—Mom's alcoholism threw her towards rock bottom, while Dad had multiple affairs within a year, resulting in a new baby with a girl barely out of college. Dallas has been through so much, and that's why he disassociates.

There seems to be a cloud around the story of how Grey actually died, though. What Sarah told me doesn't exactly add up. I know it's an incredibly emotional story to relay, but there seem to be some significant gaps. All I know, and all I need to know, is that they've all been through significant trauma. Dallas's mind was frozen in time.

Just when I think I've had enough of this kid, I open my phone and flick through my photos. I keep a cute picture of Dallas in my album, so every time I'm at the end of my rope I look at his first kindergarten photograph. There's something about the way his nose is scrunched that makes it hard to hate him, his pointy chin and baby teeth add to the cuteness. He's just a little boy, isolated from the shitshow that is his life. I'm convinced children are adorable to ensure that we continue reproducing, despite the fact they can be the absolute worst. Having worked in this field, I'm not sure I'll ever have my own kids—they're far too unpredictable for my liking. My feelings for Dallas run the gamut from deep affection to pity, anger to indifference, and deep down inside of me is a feeling I am embarrassed to admit, but I guess I need to be honest with myself.

There is a part of me that truly hates Dallas.

#

[I see red.]

It's Friday today, and Mom said I'm not going to school. I asked if it was just today or forever and Mom said it was for always.

"But why I can never go back?" I ask.

"Do you remember what you did yesterday?" Mom says.

"The cars had adventures. Also I made this city out of blocks for hours and hours," I explain. Mom grabs my face, way too rough and her hand hurts my cheeks.

"Dallas, you're not welcome back at school. Do you know what that means?" Mom tells me in a yelly voice, then lets my face go.

"It means they don't want me there."

"Yeah! Sound familiar?" she growls like a bear. "This is your fourth school in a year!"

"Do they just need space? If they tell me with words, they'll get a gold star," I remind her. Mom doesn't look nearly as happy as The *Evil She* when I get stars.

"What the hell is wrong with you?" Mom yells, very meanly. "You don't get a damn gold star for risking your life and having no remorse for the effects of your behavior!"

"I didn't say I get a gold star!" I am yelling now, too.

"I don't fucking care," Mom swears.

"Listen to me! I said the teachers would get a gold star!" I yell with all my voice.

"GOLD STARS AREN'T REAL!" she yells back. "Grey never needed a single gold star in his life. A thousand gold stars won't make you a good kid. Gold stars won't get you a school that sticks, dammit."

"Well, how am I gonna learn to read if I'm not in school?" I say.

"Zoe is going to homeschool you."

"What's a homeschool?"

"School at home," she says, "As the name would suggest."

"So the teacher and all the kids will come here? That feels like too many people for the house," I tell her, because she mustn't have thought of that yet.

"No. You and Zoe—that's it. That's your school now," Mom says, and I hope she's lying.

"That's not fair! You know I hate her!" I scream.

"You did this to yourself—you chose to put yourself in this position," Mom says.

"I hate her!" I say the loudest—and I mean it.

"Well, that's too bad. She likes you, whether you like her or not," Mom says because she's a mean liar. "God knows why."

God probably does know why, because him knows everything. Here are some things I know:

- I know when the ketchup is the wrong brand, because it tastes weird.
- I know you can yell as loud as you want, but people in heaven can't hear you. Unless they do, and they don't feel like saying a reply.
- I know Army Ants can be used as stitches when someone cuts themself. You shouldn't do that if there's a doctor in your neighborhood because real stitches are cleaner.
- I know I will never like The *Evil She*. I will never let her teach me things at homeschool, which is home and not school.
- I know for a fact that this weekend will be so boring, and my stomach will hurt the whole time because that's how my body feels when I don't know how to expect home school to be like.

#

[I see you.]

It's easier to agree to homeschooling a child than it is to actually plan a program. I've been preparing content for the upcoming week while we wait for a legitimate curriculum to be delivered. I ordered one from a school of distance education, and I am hoping it will meet Dallas's needs. He's all over the map academically—unfortunately, his behavior has taken him out of the classroom too often for him to have any kind of consistency.

I know he's capable of being a smart kid, he just hasn't had the opportunity to prove it. From what I've been told, he formed a secure attachment with his parents from birth through three; then he experienced major trauma. I'm not sure I fully believe things were peachy before Grey died, but that's the story I've been fed. In the light of what I heard yesterday, I have a feeling the family were hanging by a thread at the point of Grey's death. Regardless, everything he should have learned and developed after the age of three is severely stunted. He's a three-year-old toddler in a big boy body.

I take a look at the last report card he was issued. It was written before the summer, so it might not be completely accurate to where he is now.

Ivy Elementary

Transitional Kindergarten Report Card
School Year 2015-2016

Student: Dallas Jensen   **D.O.B:** 2/28/2010
(6y 3m)
Teacher: Mrs. Adrienne Barber
Principal: Ms. Celinda Kwan
Date: 6/6/2016

Absences: 10/49 days   **Tardies:** 30/49 days   Part
Days: 40/49 days

COMMENTS:
Dallas has moments where he is able to engage with the curriculum, though unfortunately the majority of his time is spent off task. He requires enormous amounts of adult supervision and presents with some very concerning behaviors. As discussed, Dallas will not be joining us next year. We encourage your family to find a MFT, and highly recommend that Dallas has 1:1 support in class.

ACADEMICS:

A= All the time   M= Most of the time   S= Some of the time   R= Rarely   N= Never

MATH		LITERACY		FINE MOTOR	
Can count to -	12	Identities rhyming words	N	Correct pencil grip	N
1:1 Correspondence	S	Identifies Upper vs Lower case	N	Can trace lines	N
Able to classify objects	S	Identifies sounds of consonants	N	Correctly writes first name	N
Able to make patterns	R	Identifies sounds of short vowels	N	Can use scissors	S
Able to match like items	R	Listens for sounds at beginning of word	N	Uses pencil with control	N

SOCIAL LEARNING

Listens while others speak	R	Cleans up after work	N	Respects others	R
Follows directions	R	Follows directions	R	Shows empathy	R/N

Works well independently	M	Hands to self	R	Displays self control	R/N
Puts forth best effort	R/N	Quiet when necessary	R	Self regulate after upset	N
Attentive	R	Cares for materials	R/N	Accepts correction	N
Completes work on time	N	Shares	R	Shows honesty	R/N

I know he can sing the alphabet, because he loves music—but he'd be hard pressed to identify any of the letters by sight. He knows colors, which I assume he learned before the trauma occurred. He speaks with an inconsistent mix of pronouns and is yet to grasp an age-appropriate understanding of changing words to past tense (basically, he talks like a three-year-old). He doesn't enjoy picture books or animated characters, preferring information texts with photographs. He *can* make friends easily, but his motivations are very narcissistic—he chooses the socially weak children and manipulates them to do things for him. His friendships have a high turnover rate, very few returning for more—usually because whoever he spends time with ends up doing something that lands them in the principal's office.

Dallas's world has been turned upside down since his brother's death, and the biggest question for me right now is why his mother didn't tell me earlier. Amidst the intense grief, his brain development strayed from typical to atypical, and his parents haven't been able to address the profound effect this has had on Dallas. The reason his Dad moved out? Dallas and Grey share a striking resemblance, and it was too much for their father to bear. Also, he believes Dallas is responsible for Grey's death—and three years later, he avoids seeing Dallas. Result? Neglect, attachment trauma, dissociation.

I have no idea how I'm going to teach this kid, or if this hairbrain scheme of homeschooling is anywhere near what he needs. All I know is he's a human being who deserves a chance at life, and if I can give him a leg-up, I will.

CHAPTER SEVEN

A Brand New Day

[I see red.]

The doorbell ringed, so I am hiding under my bed. I know who will be at the door, and because of The *Evil She* my stomach hurts so bad. I hear Mom let her in, and I hear them talking about the day.

"He's nervous about all the change," Mom says. (Shut up, Mom)

"Yeah, I'm sure he is," She says in a stupid way. "How do you feel about everything?"

"Well… it is what it is," Mom tells her. "Anyway, he has chicken nuggets in the freezer if he gets hungry—he can just throw them in the microwave for a few minutes. If he doesn't eat that, there's also some corn dogs. Ketchup is in the pantry."

(I want chicken nuggets right now, but I'm too busy hiding.)

"No problem, I'll take him from here," She says, then wonders, "What time will you be home?"

"Jacob will bring the baby home about 3 pm," says Mom all rushing around. "I've gotta run—good luck!"

The *Evil She* says goodbye to Mom and then I hear the garage door go up. I hear the black car with four rings symbol start up and then drrrrrr, the garage door goes down, down, down again until the noise ends. Now I can only hear my breaths and my heart. She walks closer and closer without saying any words, then into my room. Don't tell anyone, but I am so freaked out.

"I love books," She says. Why she's telling herself that? Her's an adult. She doesn't have to read anymore—only kids are 'posed to read 20 minutes every night. Now She is sitting on the bed—MY bed—and I am very, very angry. Then She starts reading one of my books out loud.

"They suck blood by shearing away feathers on their prey and biting down. With ghoulish faces that would frighten the living daylights out of the bravest person, Vampire Bats have actually been completely misunderstood. This breed of bats are the only ones who will adopt their neighbor's babies if the mom doesn't survive. Vampire Bats teach us not to judge a book by its cover, but instead, they encourage us to discover more information for ourselves," She reads.

Why did she choose my other favorite book? How does she always know what books I like?

[I see you.]

"Another common misconception about Vampire Bats is that they are dangerous to humans. In fact, there has never been a report of a human death caused by Vampire Bats," I read.

"That's not real," a muffled voice corrects me from under the bed.

"Why is the bed talking? How weird," I joke, and keep on reading.

He slides out from under the bed, "The fact wasn't real. A Vampire Bat bited a man and him died because of rabies. But it only happened one time."

"So, I'm confused—are Vampire Bats good or bad?" I inquire.

Dallas stands close enough to lean on the bed. "Them are bad, because them look bad."

"What if they're good, but they just did a bad thing?" I suggest.

Dallas just stares at me, without saying a word.

I propose, "Why don't you grab some of your favorite books and we'll read them together?"

He shakes his head and stares at me a little longer, up close—but not too close.

"What's your name?" he requests. I'm 99.9% sure he knows this one. He might have trouble with memory recall, so I give him the benefit of the doubt. (Just kidding—I'm tired of all the excuses adults make for kids being shitty people sometimes.)

"My name is Donut—I thought you knew that?" I casually reply.

The left side of his mouth curls into a cute half-smile, and he tries really hard to keep his lips closed in a neutral expression.

"That's not your name," he confidently informs me.

I pretend to be surprised and say, "You're right! That's not my name at all. I can't believe I forgot my own name. My real name is actually Armpit McGee—nice to meet you!"

I extend my arm towards Dallas to shake his hand. He folds his arms, and this time, his mouth opens slightly, and he giggles. I can see him relax a bit, and he leans a little closer to me.

"You's name is Zoe," he grins, pointing his six-year-old finger in my face while speaking with his three-year-old words.

"That's right! You're the winner!" I announce, "And I don't know about you, but I'm hungry."

"Me too. I'm hungry," he agrees.

"Hi Hungry, I'm Zoe," I say in the most Dad-joking way.

Dallas hits his forehead with the palm of his hand, "No I'm real hungry."

"Let's go grab a snack," I suggest, as he leads me out of the room.

We walk into the kitchen, and Dallas opens a cupboard door, stands on it, and climbs onto the counter. He walks across its surface (right over the stove, mind you) to open the freezer and pull out some chicken nuggets. I stand back and watch it all unfold—I want to help him, but I resist. Dallas walks back with the bag of nuggets and gets a paper plate from a higher cupboard. He plops five nuggets on the plate, then opens the bag to get one more. He walks the bag of nuggets back to the freezer and returns to his paper plate. Opening up the microwave, he puts the plate in and presses a button three times. He sits on the counter and waits.

"Do you usually eat chicken nuggets for breakfast?" I wonder aloud.

"If I hungry I can eat them whenever I want," he shrugs, and I start to get the sense that he fends for himself a little more than I'd realized.

[I see red.]

Making food is easy, and only babies let other people get things for them. I know how to make two things, in case I get bored with one of them. I became like a chef when I was about four because Mommy stopped getting out of bed when I was hungry and I also didn't have a Dad anymore. She slept all day and was awake all night drinking wine that is red, and Dad moved to someone else's house. Her never talked to me and even forgotted to take me to preschool sometimes, but when I went, I was late, late, late. I teached myself to make nuggets and corn dogs, but here's the thing: there has to be these things in the freezer, or the recipes don't work. Sometimes I use them all up, and I have to wait for Mommy to go to the store and get more things.

If that happens, I just be hungry, and that's OK because my body can live on no things at all. When there are no pools, our bodies stay alive—like magic.

[I see you.]

"Can I have some?" I ask, retrieving the pack of nuggets from the freezer.

"On your own plate," he instructs. I open the cupboard and pull out three more plates.

Dallas looks confused and says, "You only need one!"

I put each plate on the counter, one at a time.

"I forgot how to count! Help me!" I pretend.

Dallas rolls his eyes, walking over to me. He points to each plate as he says, "One, two, three! You just need one!"

"How many do we need to put away?" I test.

"Two," he responds. I mentally revisit his report card and make some revisions.

"Silly me!" I respond, and put away the extra two plates. We hear three beeps and Dallas collects his nuked, processed chicken from the microwave. He sits on a stool by the counter and squeezes a giant blob of ketchup beside his nuggets.

"I used to have five when I was five, now I always have six," he explains. This is the first time in a long time that he's voluntarily shared information with me, and I have to decide not to look excited. I grab the bag of frozen nuggets.

"How many are you?" he inquires.

"What do you mean?" I question, confused.

"How many candles were on your last cake?" he explains, like I should have known what he was talking about already.

"Twenty-six," I reveal.

"You can't have twenty-six chicken nuggets because that's too many chicken nuggets. Maybe there isn't even that many in the bag," Dallas explains.

"Well, there's only one way to find out," I remark, before tipping the entire bulk-sized bag of frozen chicken nuggets on the counter. Dallas's eyes grow wide—apparently he was not expecting this. Pieces of loose breading fly everywhere.

"Um, you better clean that up. Jacob gets real mad when the house is messy," he admits. I lay the nuggets across the counter in four equal rows of five nuggets, then there's one left over.

"I bet you can't count all these. I mean really count them by pointing to each one as you go," I tease. Dallas is motivated by challenges, and I have to be smart about where to put them. He climbs up on the counter again and sits among the breading and bagless nuggets made from unidentified chicken product. His dirty feet are up close and personal with his food, and there's a bedraggled band-aid falling off his knee. He extends his index finger and points to a nugget.

"One," he says, moving to the next. His last report card states he can only count to twelve, and is unable to assign 1:1 correspondence to objects (e.g. one nugget is counted as one, the second nugget is counted as two etc.—each item has its own value assigned).

"Five," he declares, pointing to the fifth nugget. He keeps counting, and as we approach twelve I begin to expect some difficulty. I mentally note the following three things:

1. Dallas can assign 1:1 correspondence, at least to ten.
2. We have to remember that his brain is a three-year-old, so his academic abilities are unlikely to be higher than a preschooler.
3. It's common for preschooler's counting to go awry after twelve, considering teen numbers don't follow the same naming conventions as the rest of the numbers.

"Twelve," he counts and pauses. I see him thinking about this one, "Threeteen? No, fourteen?"

"Thirteen," I say, "Keep going. Thirteen, four-"

"-teen, fiveteen," he continues.

"Fifteen," I add. "What's next? S-"

"-ixteen, sebenteen, eighteen, nineteen, twenty, twenty-one," he finishes at the last nugget. "We got twenty-one nuggets, and you is twenty-six old."

"Is that enough nuggets for me?" I poke.

"No way! You're more many than the nuggets," he reminds me.

"What's the difference between twenty-one and twenty-six?" I challenge him.

"They're two different numbers because one says twenty-one and one says a six in it," he quite literally explains. This question was a stretch—the language is way outside his ability.

"Is twenty-one more or less than twenty-six?" I ask differently.

"It's not more," Dallas replies and goes back to his stool.

"I am going to have the same amount of nuggets as you," I say, piling six onto my plate. I put it in the microwave and press the button three times. As they rotate in electromagnetic waves, I open the giant bag and use my forearm to slide the sixteen remaining nuggets back into their home. I press the zip lock at the top, and hope that no adults will ever know or care that we played with our food. I wipe up the breaded bits, destroying the evidence.

I make more mental notes:

1. Dallas can count to at least 21 using 1:1 correspondence.

2. With the exception of "thirteen" and "fifteen," he can count fluently—possibly indefinitely.
3. He quickly completed (3-2 = 1) verbally, compared more/less between 21 and 26.
4. In this environment, at this moment, Dallas was able to demonstrate 10/18 social skills as per his report card. Granted, there were only two people present—none of which were children. Still—baby steps.

The microwave beeps, and I take out my steaming morsels. Dallas has already finished his nuggets, and jumps off his stool. He puts the paper plate in the trash can and goes back to his room. In fifteen minutes over "brunch," we've completed more academic work than he's done at school in a week.

CHAPTER EIGHT

Ramsay

[I see you.]

"Wanna see my trampoline?" Dallas yells from his bedroom.

"Sure," I say, and he leads me outside. A giant dog bounds towards me from an unsuspecting corner of the ridiculously small San Franciscan backyard.

"Who's this guy?" I ask, as the rambunctious hound licks my face.

"Ramsay," Dallas tells me. "Him's called after the guy who yells and yells so much. My Mom think's that cooker is so funny, but him says the F-word too many times, and that's why I only watched the one with kids."

"That's a great name," I giggle. "Why didn't you tell me you had a dog?"

Dallas shrugs, "You didn't ask." (I guess that's true)

"Can I come onto the trampoline with you?" I request.

"There's only a'posed to be one person at a time, but that's because me and Grey bashed our heads together one time because we jumped too silly," he explains. With this simple statement, the mood shifts like black clouds over a sunny day. On one hand, I'm thrilled that he's trusting me with these kinds of admissions, but on the other, the weight of his loss settles heavily in my stomach.

"What if," I suggest, "I jump with you, but we jump sensibly?"

"Silly is more fun," he replies.

"What if we give it a try?" I persist.

Dallas nods his mop of long, curly hair as I escape the licky tongue of Ramsay by climbing onto the trampoline. Dallas starts jumping as I fumble around like a newborn horse—somehow I remember trampolines being easier than this. I definitely didn't wear the right bra for this situation. As we jump, we both start laughing.

[I see red.]

For your big fat information, I still don't like Zoe. Listen to me; I'm telling you the real truth here. Her is on my trampoline, and it's super fun jumping with another person because I don't have a brother anymore (and my sister is a diaper-face baby who does nothing), and also I don't get to have any friends at my house. We are jumping a little at first, and then bigger and bigger. Uh oh! The silliest thing is happening! My stinky dog Ramsay just jumped on the trampoline with us!

"Ahhhhh!" Zoe yells, as Ramsay puts himself on her shoulders and now her is lying on the floor of the trampoline with him licking she's face. Ramsay has spit for days and days, and now it's all on Zoe's face.

"Help!" Zoe yells, but she's also laughing.

I am also laughing so much I might pee a bit in my pants. I open the trampoline net and throw one of Ramsay's toys out the gap (he's always leaving him's toys in the trampoline). The silly dog jumps out, and I make the net closed tightly. Zoe is laying on the trampoline with dog spit all over she's face. I sit down next to her, still laughing at what he did.

"Ramsay is a bad dog. I forgot to tell you about that part."

"He's not bad," Zoe says.

"He's not good!" I laugh, hitting my hand to my head. Zoe sits up.

"What if I said there was no such thing as good and bad?" she tells me, and her must be joking because that's not real.

"That's fake," I tell her, because she needs to know.

"Hear me out," Zoe says, "What if there are no good or bad dogs—just normal dogs who do good or bad things?"

"Like if white was normal color because it's no color, and red was for bad and green was for good—and a dog was just white, but sometimes it was red and sometimes it was green?" I ask her. Zoe's face has a big smile, and I wonder why her's so happy. We're not even doing gold stars.

"Yes! Exactly!" she says. I lay on the trampoline with her, but next to the edge with the door part. My dog is barking so loud for four barks.

[I see you.]

While Dallas is relaxed, I'm going to see how far I can get with testing his academic knowledge in a casual way. Rhyming is a vital skill that children must learn, as a way to increase their ability to read, write and spell. Also, rhyme teaches children to manipulate language and express themselves in more ways than just poetry. Since Dallas loves music, I'm having a hard time with the idea that he can't identify rhyme—mainly because most lyrics are built on rhyme.

We'll work more on the finer details later, but right now, I just want to know what he can do.

[I see red.]

"Dog. Dog, log. Dog, log, bog," Zoe says, and I don't know why. "Can you add more?"

"Dog, log, bog, big," I say, looking at the clouds.

"Ooh! Close!" she says, "Big, bog. Hear the difference? "Ig," "Og" Like this—dOg, lOg…"

"Bog!" I yell, "Tog, zog, fog!"

Zoe is smiling again and says, "Yes! That's called rhyming. This rhymes: tog, zog, fog, blog, frog!"

"Blog, frog, dog!" I yell, and I laugh because this is a funny game and I want to play again. I'm also looking at the clouds, and one is shaped like a bunny. Bunny, funny, runny.

"Do bunny and funny rhyme?" I ask.

"Sure do!" Zoe tells me, "What about this? Bunny, funny, lumpy, honey? Do they rhyme?"

"Do it again," I say because I am not sure and also forgot what her said.

"Bunny, funny, lumpy, honey," Zoe tells again.

"Lumpy is the odd one," I say, "Lumpy, bumpy."

"Want to give me a challenge?" she asks.

"Hmmm… Bag!" I yell.

"Bag, tag, sag, rag, flag," Zoe says, and she's definitely very good at this game. "Here's a challenge for you: cat."

"Cat, f…fat! Yeah, fat is a word! A mean word, but it's a word. Cat, fat, flat, yat, gat. Are them words?" I ask because I'm not sure, and being not sure makes me nervous.

"Doesn't matter. We can make up tons of words for this game—like daf, baf, maf," she goes on and on.

"Maf is a word. Like when you get numbers and do plusses and take aways," I remind Zoe because she must've forgotten.

"Almost! Watch my tongue—math," Zoe says, poking her tongue out her mouth. "Math is numbers. Maf—fff—is a made up word. Practice with me—fff, now thhh."

I bite my lip when I say f and I get to poke my tongue out when I say th. This game is so fun because my brain is getting so big with information, and I also get to poke out my tongue at Zoe, who I don't like yet.

[I see you.]

Mental notes:

1. Dallas can rhyme words.
2. His auditory processing is fine; he just needs to have things explained to him sensitively. I can see that embarrassment has played a significant role in keeping his academic learning at arm's length. He doesn't know why his ability to learn was stunted, but he does know that he's not as "smart" as the other kids.
3. Dallas is able to catch up on missed concepts with relative ease. He's also showing signs of readiness for new challenges.
4. Because of his home situation, Dallas lacks in cultural capital. (That is, access to non-financial social assets that promote him beyond his economic means. Yes, the family "lives rich," but they're drowning in debt. Dallas has never been to a museum, he's been to very few restaurants, and hasn't attended extra-curricular activities.)

We lay on the trampoline for a while, together but apart. I notice he's close to the door of the trampoline safety net, and I wonder if that's because he thinks I'll hold him again. Today I feel like I'm spending time with an entirely different child—a clear departure from the boy who threatened to jump off a roof just four days earlier. Finally, I'm starting to relax.

"Do you think this cloud looks like a bunny?" I remark.

"I was thinking that already!" Dallas stammers excitedly.

We first met during the summer, where we spent two weeks alone. With his family, he was a monster, but with me, he was great. He was this beautiful child, so free and for the most part, easy. Sure he had meltdowns and strong opinions on things, but he was accessible. Everything changed when we went back to school—he completely shut down—there's been a steady decline ever since. Today has been the first time he's been able to have a back-and-forth conversation with me in three weeks. Something about school doesn't bode well with this kid.

I look at my watch—12:30 pm.

"It's time for lunch," I announce.

"We already eated lunch!" Dallas remarks with a puzzled inflection.

"Humans need to eat every few hours," I reason.

"We can eat more nuggets," Dallas shrugs.

I dismount the trampoline, into the slobbery embrace of Ramsay, who has been waiting for the equivalent of a dog month for us to return. He furiously wags his tail, and it hits me right in the back. He's a sweet, sweet dog in need of some serious training. Dallas leads us into the kitchen and climbs up on the counters again. I hate that he subsists on chicken nuggets, but I'm also aware that changing too many things at once is a recipe for disaster. We've already made so many advances today—these chicken nuggets are the least of my concern. Dallas repeats his earlier process, making himself exactly six nuggets. I take a kale salad out of my backpack and set it on the counter. He stares at my food with the same disdain as I stare at his, despite the fact that I ate nuggets just a few hours earlier. Clearly, I was only eating those delicious nuggets for his benefit… it's called building rapport, people. They weren't delicious at all...

I see a kiddy painter easel in the living room, with a large pad of paper attached. I grab a marker and write Daily Schedule at the top.

"Do you know what times on the clock mean?" I ask, casually.

"There's numbers, and they mean things happen at them times," he says with nugget breading flying out of his mouth.

"Exactly! So, we're going to make a poster about what we do every day. That way, if we forget, we can look at the poster. Does that sound OK?" I suggest.

Dallas shrugs, "OK."

I grab the pen, and we get to work.

[I see red.]

Zoe and me made a poster. It is about times and clocks and things that we do at those o'clocks, also what the clock looks like when things happen. She's good at drawing clocks. Here is how it looks like:

Daily Schedule

Time	Activity
9:00am	Zoe arrives Dallas and Zoe eat breakfast
9:30am	Number activities

10:00am 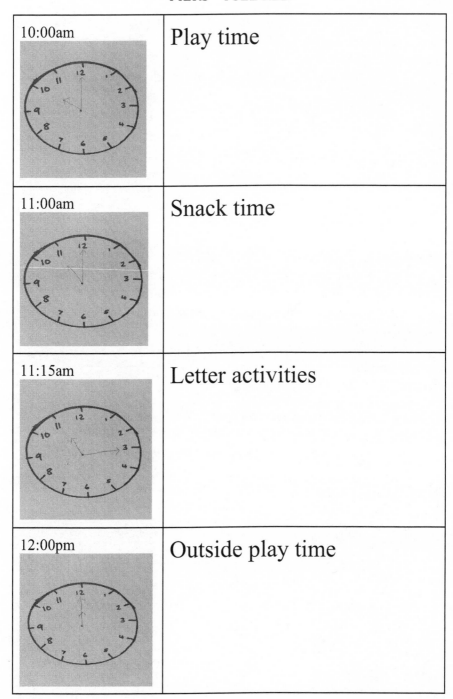	Play time
11:00am	Snack time
11:15am	Letter activities
12:00pm	Outside play time

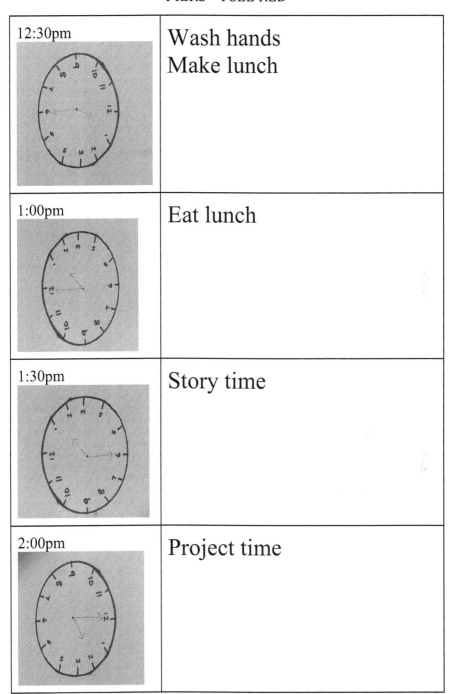

12:30pm	Wash hands Make lunch
1:00pm	Eat lunch
1:30pm	Story time
2:00pm	Project time

3:00pm 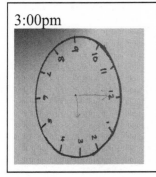	Jacob and Aurora come home Zoe leaves

I look at the clock on the wall and it looks like the long hand is on the five and the short hand is a teensy bit after the one. I never knowed how to tell time, and I still don't know how to actually do that, but I matched it with the shape on the schedule.

"If we look at the schedule, which activity would match one o'clock?" Zoe asks.

"We already eated lunch!" I laugh.

"Wow! We are really ahead of our schedule today, Dallas. When we work harder, faster and smarter we get free time. What should we do until story time at 1:30 pm?" Zoe says, and I think hard.

"Well, actually I don't like stories. Only information books," I remind her, because she forgotted.

"We can do information books, that's no problem at all," Zoe tells.

"Let's play with Ramsay again," I decide.

"First, we'll set an alarm for 25 minutes. When it's almost story—uh, information book time I'll give you a reminder. When it beeps, we go inside. Deal?" she says.

"Deal!" I agree, "Let's find that stinky dog."

[I see you.]

We walk outside, and Ramsay launches himself onto me again. This dog needs some boundaries—I really wish he had owners who gave a shit. I'm pretty sure he was an impulse buy before they had the baby. That happens so often—people acquire a dog, then when a baby comes along, they completely drop the ball with the dog. Without training the dog is out of control.

Subsequently, nobody likes being around him. Then the dog gets a bad rap for what humans neglected—and so goes the story.

"Does Ramsay know any tricks?" I ask, doubtfully.

"Him isn't smart. He's a bad dog, 'member?" Dallas replies.

"I thought dogs were white... red was bad, and green was good?" I recall Dallas's own words. "Ramsay is white. Sometimes he does red things; sometimes he does green things."

Dallas hits his forehead with his palm, "I forgotted. Everyone says he's a bad dog because him is too silly," he pauses and grabs the dog's face. "Ramsay—you are not good or bad. You just a doggy."

Ramsay dances around and whacks me once again with his crazy tail.

"I was thinking about our schedule—the one with the clocks," I interject.

"I know what's a schedule," Dallas replies with a sharp tongue.

"I was wondering what you'd like your project to be?" I ask.

Dallas thinks for a minute, "What means a project?"

"Well, it's something you work on for a while. It's something you carefully plan, it's something that means you do your best work and don't give up."

Dallas thinks a little more, as he grabs a dog toy and throws it to his giant, lanky, licky pet. Ramsay bolts towards the toy, rolls in the dirt, completely forgets about the toy, starts digging a hole, then runs back to Dallas. He stands there panting excitedly in his sweet, goofy, doggy way. He lets out a single, seemingly unnecessary bark.

"I wanna make Ramsay be green," Dallas concludes. "I want my project being about telling him how to have good manners and be kind to people."

I smile from ear-to-ear. I couldn't have planned this any better if I'd tried, and I thank my lucky stars I came here today with low/no expectations.

I smile, "Together we'll make him the greenest dog that ever lived."

CHAPTER NINE

Fatherless Day

[I see red.]

Jacob and the baby got home after the clock picture on the schedule said he would—halfway to the next number, actually. Zoe and I spent extra time making Ramsay behave gooder than him usually acts. She said it will take lots of days to get him to be green instead of red—we have to be patient and not give up. Patient is a new word I have, and before today I didn't know what means 'patient.' Today I learned it means waiting calmly, especially when it feels like no things are happening. When Jacob got home, him looked angry with Zoe. They are fighting now, and I am pretending not to listen, but really I am hearing all the words.

"Fix him yet?" he laughed, but not in a way that was funny.

"He's not broken," Zoe said in a serious, serious way.

(Trust me, I have seen her be serious.)

[I see you.]

Jacob is perhaps the least likable human I've ever met. Keep in mind: this statement is coming from someone who has spent the last three years with people who have tried to kill me more than once. Jacob… he's a thoroughly different animal. It would be validating to say he was a fat creep who had dried pieces of flaming hot cheese snacks all over his chest, and his hairy gut hanging down out of his shirt—but that's not Jacob at all. He's a remarkably well-kept man in his early 30s who took five months off work to be a stay-at-home dad to his first and only child. He treats Aurora the way any child deserves to be treated.

Dallas isn't his biological son; I get it. Dallas is a handful; I get it. Dallas probably has a personality disorder; I get it. Dallas can sometimes rival Jacob for the Worst Human Ever Award; I get that more than most. But the way Jacob treats Dallas, compared to his own flesh-and-blood child, is astounding. He looks at Dallas with hatred in his eyes, and each word exchanged is sharp-tongued and fear mongering. Whatever Jacob is hoping to achieve out of this relationship with Sarah, he didn't plan to achieve it with Dallas at home. It's not as if he thought the boy would disappear; I guess he just hoped the dad would take him someday, to give them a break from the constant mess that is Dallas. That day never came.

[I see red.]

Jacob walks away from Zoe, and I hear the garage door come up. I look out the front door, and Mommy is here in the black car with the four rings. Zoe gets all her things together, and then Mom walks in the house.

"Oh hey Zoe, I thought you'd have left by now. How did everything go?" Mom asks.

"We had a fantastic day, thanks for asking," Zoe tells her, then she looks at Jacob meanly.

"Thank you, Zoe," Mommy says, looking a little scared to say anything that might make Jacob mad. When Jacob is mad, things get real, real bad around here. Believe me.

[I see you.]

Sarah is a slight thing: small, skinny and almost rodent-like. She moves rapidly through space and time, with an inability to focus all of her attention on anything at once. She's pretty, in her own sort of way, but there's something about her inconsistency that weirds me out. One minute she's present, she's on board, she's supportive. Next minute, she's back to her old ways of ignoring, vacillating and retreating. She sides with Jacob more than she wants to, I know that for sure. I see where Dallas inherited his small stature, his attention deficit and hyperfocus, his blue eyes, and manipulation strategies. I guess he's an equal mix of his mother's physical features and her prenatal wine habit. I had often wondered if psychosocial dwarfism was partly to blame for the fact that Dallas wears size 3-4 clothes at the age of six. To grow, a child must be loved.

Jacob works in Wealth Management, with the ironic caveat that he, himself, isn't wealthy. He tries to act rich—I guess it's his way of keeping up with the Joneses. He wears insufferably expensive clothes, and must approve of Sarah's every outfit before she can leave the house. They met a little over a year ago in a douchey nightclub, while Sarah was completely unraveled by the loss of her son and her husband's subsequent rejection. Dallas's mother's savior was, and I suspect still is, the bottle. A one night stand gave them bouncing baby Aurora, and while she was pregnant Jacob moved in and out of the house at least three times. Because Jacob has shown himself to be so intelligent and considerate, he bought Ramsay, a $2,000 Purebred Irish Wolfhound, as a 'practice baby' and then proceeded not to train him. That's a 130lb dog, in a 300sq ft backyard with a 16sq ft trampoline. Real smart, Jacob. Now everyone resents Ramsay for being 'stupid,' simply because he was never trained to be 'smart.' Jacob could use a lesson in cause and effect, but he's too entitled for things like that.

Here's what gets me: they drive an $80,000 car, yet their fridge and pantry are a barren wasteland. Dallas's shoes are falling apart, the knees of his pants are threadbare—but Jacob has every new gadget on the market. Aurora is even well-dressed, at half a year old; because that's what you get when your dad is biologically your dad. Sorry Dallas, your fate lies in holey pants, frozen food, and worn out gym boots.

I'm repulsed by the vibe in this house. When everybody is home at once it's enough to make the hairs on the back of my neck stand on end. I get the sense we are wading through toxic levels of unprocessed grief—knee deep in things that will somehow replace Grey. The dog and baby being the most prominent of replacements. I wonder how Dallas can possibly grow and change in this environment, and I'm concerned Sarah doesn't realize the level of damage that continues to take place.

Any fool could see Sarah and Jacob are contributing to Dallas's condition, yet Sarah can't (or won't) assume responsibility. Giving her the benefit of the doubt, I'm not sure she has the ability to step up and give him what he needs. She can't see the forest for the trees.

[I see red.]

Zoe comes over to me and crouches down, so her eyes are near mine, and her tells me that her is leaving. Her doesn't say goodbye, I don't say goodbye, but I high five she's hand. Her leaves through the normal door.

Mom picks up the baby and says questions to her that she can't answer. She can't talk yet, at least I haven't seen her talk. Maybe her can, but she doesn't want to. Mom comes into the living room and sits with me.

"Sounds like you had a good day with Zoe," she says.

I shrug my shoulders, "We're making Ramsay green."

"What do you mean?" she asks.

"There's no such thing as good and bad. Just normal dogs what do good and bad stuff," I tell her.

"What? How is he green, though?" Mom says, all confused.

"If white is the color of all the things. Red is bad, green is good. Imagine Ramsay is white and sometimes he's red if he's a bad boy, and sometimes green when him's a good boy," I explain, and I'm pretty excited. "So Zoe and me are gonna make him green most of the time. We are going to teach him manners."

"I can't believe we're paying a glorified babysitter to train our dumbass dog," Jacob yells to Mom from the kitchen.

"I'm sure you're doing writing and math, too?" Mom says, like a question.

"Yeah, but mostly training Ramsay. Him can't do manners today. It doesn't happen that quick—you have to be patient," I let her know, because her might not know how long to wait. Her smiles, and takes the baby to the other room with Jacob. I go outside and see if Ramsay wants to go on the trampoline.

I jump up and down for fifty hundred times, and Ramsay doesn't know how him can get in. From outside I hear Mom telling Jacob something;

"She probably has a bigger picture plan with the dog training. I'm sure they're doing the regular reading-writing-arithmetic business, too. "

"The whole thing is bullshit," Jacob swears. "Expensive-ass bullshit."

"We have to be patient," Mom says, and I smile because that's our word for today.

"I'll give her a week," he growls.

Ramsay is still having trouble getting onto the trampoline. I open the net a teeny tiny bit, but not too much, and I call his name while tapping my knees. Him isn't sure about how to jump up here, but I remember what Zoe said today: We have to be patient. I keep jumping, I keep calling and calling his name. I wonder why he forgotted something he already knows how to do? I wonder when he might remember.

I lay on the trampoline again, and watch fog rolling in the sky. In San Francisco we don't get normal summer, we get the foggy kind. Zoe taught me a thousand things about the weather today—she said the season when school goes back is called fall but it feels like winter because of where we are on the map. I think it's cold enough for a snow man, but it doesn't snow in our land. Zoe also said that in a few weeks it will be Indian Summer, near Halloween time, which isn't for a while. Its month is October, and our month is called August—all the months have names, but none are called Dallas. When I look at the gray fog racing, racing, racing over the sky, I start to think about Grey. I wonder how loud I would need to yell for him to hear me? I just want to tell him I'm sorry for making him dead.

I've tried this so many times before, and he just doesn't listen. I whisper his name at first, and wait and see if his ghost is around. I don't know if ghosts are real, or if I want them to be real. I say his name a little louder, just to try again. I wait for a hundred minutes, and nobody says anything to me.

"GREY!" I say, loudly this time. Mom comes out of the house.

"Dallas, it's freezing out here. Come inside."

"I'm talking to Grey," I say, trying not to cry.

"Don't be ridiculous," she tells me. "Go inside before you catch a cold."

I cross my arms and stay where I am. I stare into her eyes and yell, "No!"

Mom reaches into the trampoline and grabs me by the arm. "Go inside!"

I jump off the trampoline and run straight to my room. I hide under the desk in my special tent, and I take out a picture of Grey that I keep in my hiding place. The picture is kind of fuzzy, but it's still Grey. Crying is for babies, but I can't stop water coming out of my eyes. I hold the picture, and Grey's favorite toy close to my chest. I wonder when I will stop missing him?

I hear Jacob ask Mom, "What's up with him? He was fine a minute ago."

"Nothing," she lies. "He's just playing a silly game. Make believe stuff—you know how kids are." Mom's voice sounds a bit shaky. I can hear her walking around a bit, then she says, "I'm just going to take a shower."

The water sound runs for a long time, and I get out of my tent. I walk by the bathroom, and I hear Mommy crying. The door is shut, but I know what crying sounds like because the baby does it all day long. Mom used to cry in her's shower after Grey died, so Daddy didn't know her was crying. When Dad saw, him would leave the house and one day he just never came home. He made a new family, and so did my Mom. I am the only one who didn't make a new family. I never choosed Jacob—and Jacob never choosed me.

I peek around the corner to the living room, and I see Jacob on him's computer. Aurora is in her's baby swing, going side to side while she falls a bit asleep. Jacob kicks his shoes off and does a big fart.

Him doesn't look like he's going to leave here anytime soon.

CHAPTER TEN

Playing Catch Up

[I see you.]
<u>7:13pm</u>

Julia arrives home with an enormous pizza and her younger brother Ezra. We open the box and sit around the proverbial "box" watching stupid reality TV shows together. The mindlessness of reality TV is addicting, and I let myself get totally caught up with the shows and forget about Dallas altogether. Ignorance is bliss, but it doesn't last long.

"How was today?" Julia asks.

"It went well, thanks," I say, with cheese dangling from my lips. I wipe my face on a napkin. "His step-dad is a dickhead, though."

Ezra laughs, "What did you do today?"

Julia's brother comes over about once a month or so, but we only technically know each other on an acquaintance level. He was a total baby when we were growing up, being two and a half years younger than Julia and me, so we never gave him the time of day. Though, I could always see how eager he was to be part of our conversations. We're trying to re-establish the relationship as adults, but I'm not quite as into the idea as he seems to be.

"I'm just starting to homeschool this kid," I say, to keep the conversation flowing.

80

"Wow, that's amazing—what's he like?" Ezra asks.

I shrug, "Meh."

We glue our eyes, again, to the box. The show is like a train wreck—I shouldn't be watching, but I can't look away.

10:45pm

"I'm going to bed," I yawn.

"I want to hear more about this job," Ezra adds, slightly desperately.

"Maybe some other time," I reply, grabbing my pillow and heading out.

"I'm moving to San Francisco next month," he quickly blurts before I leave. "You'll have plenty of time to tell me then."

Ezra smirks, paying me an uncomfortable amount of attention while I couldn't be less interested in making small talk. If I ignore these signs, perhaps I will escape my fate of being the object of his affection. I notice him noticing me, and my strategy is to pretend I haven't noticed. That makes sense, right?

"Goodnight," I yell. Julia mumbles the same words back at me, while Ezra perfectly enunciates his farewells. I would cringe at how hard he's trying, but I don't have the energy.

12:07am

Despite going to bed over an hour ago, I'm wide awake and desperate for sleep. Side note: today was a great day. I hope tomorrow is just as productive—I can see Dallas has a lot of untapped potential.

2:45am

I must've fallen asleep for a few hours, but it feels like I barely closed my eyes. I'm so frustrated that I'm awake, and my mind starts to wander as I try my hardest to count sheep. Ezra's unwelcome affection has me curiously anxious about my future. I wonder who I'll marry? I wonder if I'll know he's the right one when I meet him? Is 'love at first sight' a thing? What if I die alone? What if I never get married and I become a crazy spinster? I need to sign up for an online dating site. No—I don't. I seriously don't. I haven't got time for meeting random guys. What if he looks like a babe in the pictures and is a nerd in real life? I'm too young to sign up for a dating site.

<u>4:00am</u>
He's standing on the edge of the roof, laughing maniacally while his arms restlessly flail around his torso. I walk closer to him, and he stands with his back to the precipice. He looks me in the eye and says, "You were wrong about me. I see RED." He leans back and falls. I scream—looking over the edge to see his broken body bleeding the brightest red. He lays dead on the sidewalk as people walk around him like he isn't there. I scream and no sound comes out.

I sit bolt upright in my bed, shaking and gasping for air. Then, I hear three polite knocks.

"Zoe—are you OK?" Julia wonders, opening the door.

"Sorry…" I mumble groggily, "Bad dream."

"Um… do you need anything?" she asks, half asleep. Ezra awkwardly appears behind her, and I pull the covers over my head.

"I'm fine, honestly," I mumble, before realizing I need more oxygen. "Thank you."

Ezra and Julia close the door, and return from whence they came. I take a moment to die of embarrassment, then I get up to use the bathroom—tiptoeing past Ezra snoring on the couch. Looking outside the bathroom window, I see the pitch black of night, broken only by streetlights scattered evenly on the roadside. The one nearest our house is flickering. I wonder if we're all just flickering lights in this life, inconsistently swaying between brightness and desolation, productivity and stasis, good and evil. I hear creepy nocturnal birds squawk their pre-dawn songs— evidence that life exists at this hour, despite the fact that I feel more alone than ever.

I guess sleep will pass straight by me tonight.

#

[I see red.]
The long hand on the twelve and the short hand is pointing at the nine. At this very exact time, I look out the window and see Zoe walking up the stairs. I don't think I'll hide from her today,

82

but I still don't like her, so I just won't be the first to say hi. She knocks on the door, and Mommy opens it up to let her in.

"Perfect! You're here!" Mom says.

"Good morning!" Zoe tells Mom. I wonder what's inside her backpack today? I wish for blocks to build things, but I know they're bigger than her bag. I wish for books about dangerous, mean animals, and I know they definitely could fit in her bag. I wish for a guitar, but it's just a silly wish because them are too huge for a backpack.

Mom rushes around and says, "Sorry, I really have to go—ah—same food as yesterday, I might not be able to answer my phone today—meetings. Jacob has already left to take Aurora to daycare, and he'll be home around three."

"No problem, I've got this," Zoe brags.

Mom runs out to the black car with the four rings and the garage door goes up, up, up with a sound like drrrrrrrrr. Mom drives out too fast and the front bit on the car scratches on the driveway. The garage door goes down like drrrrrrrrr. Zoe sets her things down and doesn't say hi first either. Her looks tired because her is yawning, and she also has coffee. Kids can't have coffee because their hearts will beat straight out of their chest, but adult hearts need some fastening.

"I guess I'm going to have to eat pancakes all by myself," Zoe says out loud, to nobody in particular. I'm thinking about pancakes now. Oh man, I want pancakes.

"I'm not saying hi first," I yell.

"Oh, hi Dallas!" Zoe says with a smile. Phew—she said it first! Now, pancakes.

"I want pancakes, too," I say, running from the living room.

"I thought you'd say that!" says Zoe.

Her opens the bag and I can already tell she tricked me. It's full of little bags of white dusty stuff and some tins and boxes and milk and eggs.

"Liar!" I yell. "Them aren't pancakes!"

"They will be soon," she says, laughing. I still don't believe her.

[I see you.]

From what I know about Dallas, he'll agree to the activities on the schedule until, in reality, has to do them. I'm going to follow through on having him complete the scheduled tasks, but they're open-ended enough to be combined. So, we were scheduled to eat breakfast at 9 am and do number activities at 9:30 am? Today, we make pancakes—killing two birds with one stone.

"Let's see…" I feign discovery, waving a recipe above my head. "Oh! Look what I found!"

"Just a stupid paper," Dallas moans, in a brilliantly six-year-old way.

"This stupid paper is going to tell us how to transform this bag of ingredients into some delicious pancakes. We just need to follow the instructions," I exclaim, knowing full-well that following directions isn't one of his strong points. "First, we need a measuring cup."

"What means measuring cup?" Dallas questions.

I open a few drawers and cupboards. Jeez, looks like friggin' Halloween in here. Cobwebby as the dickens. I'm pretty sure nobody has cooked a meal in this house since Jesus was a baby. Luckily, at the back of the drawer, there's a pile of unused measuring cups with tags still attached. Also, I know that fractions are typically on second-grade curricula and Dallas is pre-K at best. Today we're focusing more on counting than fractions. Other goals include, but are not limited to: expanding his culinary repertoire past chicken nuggets.

"These are measuring cups," I reply, shaking the cups on their plastic key-ring. "Measuring is when you do an exact amount of something."

"I thought pancakes got maked by water in a shaking thing? We only made them one time at my house, but one time I got them at the cafe, but we can't go to the cafe if I am being bad," Dallas admits.

"Well, today, we're making pancakes from scratch."

"What means scratch?"

Jeez, this kid is cute sometimes. I giggle, "Scratch just means it's made from real ingredients ."

"Why don't you just say that?"

"Scratch sounds better."

Dallas scratches his arm, then laughs. "Yeah!"

[I see red.]

Zoe has paper that looks like this:

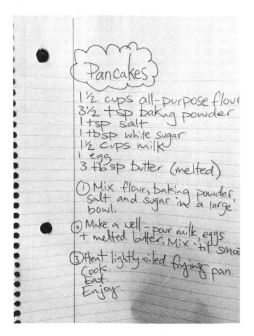

Her will turn the list into pancakes, and I'll help her. She got these cups from a cupboard I never knowed about, and we are measuring amounts of white things to a big bowl.

"One and a half cups of all purpose flour," she reads, then holds up a paper bag with words on it. "This says 'flour.' F-L-O-U-R. F says ffff—remember?"

"Oh yeah!" I say, practicing biting my lip. "Not my tongue out like thhhh. Them are different sounds."

"Those are different sounds, yeah! I can see you're learning a whole lot lately," she says. "One and a half cups—that means this one, and this smaller one. Let's fill this one first."

Zoe opens the bag and I dig the bigger cup into the flour. It's smooth and white, also a little bit cold. I tip the full cup in the big bowl; then Zoe hands me the littler cup. I fill it up and do the same into the big bowl. Her shows me two special spoons; one is bigger, one is smaller.

"This is a tablespoon, this is a teaspoon," she says.

"Them are—those—are different spoons," I tell her.

We add all the dry ingredients; then we have to crack an egg, which I have never done before. Eggs are hard on the outside and runny on the inside, and them have clear and yellow bits. Now we stir, stir, stir. But not too much! Zoe told me the gluten gets tough if you do that. Now we get to cook and flip, and cook and flip—a hundred times until the batter is all used up.

[I see you.]

"Wow! We have a lot of pancakes. We must have fifty!" I exaggerate.

Dallas smiles, and uses his finger to count each pancake individually, "We have thirteen!"

I get out three plates again.

"No, Zoe! Too many plates, put one away," he says, exasperated.

"How many do you want?" I ask.

"Six, silly! You can't have twenty-five. Have six like me. Ramsay can have two, because him is two," Dallas reasons.

"*He* is two?" I kindly correct.

"Yeah! He is two," Dallas reiterates, using the correct pronoun.

"It was nice of you to think of Ramsay, but dogs shouldn't eat pancakes," I explain.

"It will hurt him's tummy?"

"Yes, it will hurt *his* tummy."

"*His* tummy can only have dog food."

[I see red.]

I look over at the schedule—oh no! It's longer than breakfast time. Maybe Zoe didn't remember to do math? Maybe she did? I hate number activities, and I am not doing anything like school work. Nuh uh. No f-word way. Doesn't Zoe know it's too hard for me? Doesn't she know I'm not smart like other kids?

Everybody else knows, I wonder why she didn't remember.

[I see you.]

Dallas suddenly gets up from the stool at the counter, and runs into the bathroom. He slams the door behind him, leaving a plate of piping hot pancakes waiting. I wonder if nature was calling? Better leave him for a minute. Wait—I've been stung by bathroom disappearances two too many times before. Suddenly I'm anxious again.

"I'M NOT DOING NUMBERS ACTIVITY!" his voice echoes from the bathroom.

"You already finished numbers, dude," I laugh. "We are eating pancakes, putting things in the dishwasher, then playing for an hour." He cracks the door ever so slightly.

"What numbers did I do?" he interrogates me suspiciously.

"Measuring ingredients, counting pancakes..." I list.

"Are you being real?" he questions, skeptically.

"Definitely," I promise. "I'm going to eat my pancakes now. Come out when you're ready."

I walk away, willing to keep my promise, but nervous that today might still turn to shit. Were there any windows in the bathroom? F-word. I forgot to check. My mind flashes briefly to Dallas standing in traffic, hair blowing in the breeze of trucks zooming by. He's victorious, he's smiling, he's tempting death. Adrenaline surges through my body. Should I go outside and look? What if the window is up high and he falls to the ground? Why did I think he was fixed? Clearly, his calm behavior is temporary. It always is. OK, I need to think fast. Just as I make a beeline towards the back door, Dallas calmly walks out of the bathroom.

"I want the pancakes," he asserts, casually, climbing onto the stool again. Is he up to something? What's he going to do next? My breath is shallow; cortisol levels feel high.

"Are you gonna eat yours too? You have six. Do we have syrup?" he questions, like everything is fine. "Why are you by the door?"

He's fine, Zoe—pull yourself together. He didn't run away; he's right here and he's safe. I force breath into my lungs, grabbing the syrup from the bag. I exhale as deeply as my body will allow, and paint on a smile. Pulling up a stool on the outside of Dallas, I instinctively place my shoe on his foot rest. I've positioned myself to avoid elopement, feeling confident I can reflexively catch him if he tries anything while we eat. I help him pour syrup over his long stack, and he smiles accordingly. For better or for worse, sugar is the currency of children.

"You know what?" Dallas laughs with sticky lips. "Ramsay farted on me yesterday."

I giggle too. Dallas giggles more... and now we are laughing like kids. I am friggin' delirious from lack of sleep, high as a kite on maple syrup, and he's all about fart jokes right now. Man, these pancakes are delicious.

If I can't have sleep, I can at least have a sugar rush.

#

[I see red.]

The clock said, "Long hand twelve, short hand three," and Jacob didn't come home yet. When the long hand was about to be on the twelve we saw him's—his—car drive by the house but he didn't stop. Zoe and I kept playing with Ramsay and making him green, but Jacob just drived around again.

We are teaching Ramsay how to sit. We got a bag of treats for him, and we give him a treat when he does the right thing because treats are like gold stars for dogs. I say, "Sit!" and if he sits, I hold out the treat and he licks it off my hand. If he doesn't sit, I am not allowed to say, "Bad dog!" because Zoe said he's not bad. Instead, I can say, "Let's try again."

Long hand is on the four; short hand is between the three and four. Jacob drives into the driveway and brings the diaper baby inside. I see Zoe look both happy and sad that he's here, but I don't know why. Jacob and Zoe seem to not like each other.

[I see you.]

"Did you fix him yet?" Jacob repeats, like a carbon copy of yesterday's passive aggressive comment. This time, I can't let it go, and I feel my ability to filter my response slipping through my fingertips.

"He's not a problem to be fixed," I hiss with unwavering eye contact.

"Zoe, let's be real. He's fucked up beyond repair, and we are paying bank for you to train our dumb mutt. There's a hole in the bucket with Dallas—anything you put in comes out the other end just as fast," Jacob growls, giving back the same level of intense eye contact.

"Can we at least step into another room so he can't hear this conversation?" I plead. If there's anything worse than this conversation, it's the idea of Dallas hearing yet another episode of Jacob ripping him to shreds.

"So you agree with me?" he huffs, with a greasy smirk.

"I really, really, disagree with you," I retort, hoping by some miracle that I can stay professional through this confrontation. I can't let anger—even righteous anger—take away my access to Dallas. As soon as Jacob knows how much I want to be with Dallas, he'll use him as a pawn to manipulate me into doing whatever he wants.

Jacob stands up and looks me right in the eyes.

"I'm against this whole homeschool fiasco bullshit. What are we? Like, Mormons in the middle of butt-fuck Utah? It's bullshit. He should be in school with kids. Look, I'm sure you're doing your best with him," he adds, with false praise, "but the ship has sailed."

"He's only six years old! The ship certainly hasn't sailed—it's anchored in rough, stormy seas waiting for a captain," I say through my teeth. "Lead him, or he'll lead himself—and we both know he's not developmentally able to cope with that."

"And how long is this process going to take?" he yells.

"How long is a piece of string?" I yell back.

"That—right there—is why I don't trust you as far as I can throw you," Jacob seethes, looking like he's about to throw me. I'm suddenly feeling very unsafe here, and the thought of leaving Dallas in this environment sends shivers down my spine.

"This isn't about money. It's about making something beautiful out of that little boy, who is grieving for the life he had before he even knew to appreciate it," I plead, hoping Dallas can't hear me.

"To be clear, I don't want you in our house. I don't want that psycho child in the house either, but Sarah insists you're both fixtures for a while. I'm counting down the days until he's placed in Juvie, because we all know that's his future," Jacob snarls. "Paying you to sit around here and play with the dog, acting like you're 'fixing' our biggest problem, is like throwing cash down the toilet. Dallas will never amount to anything."

My extremities are tingling, and I feel rage inside me like nothing I've ever felt before. Like a moment hanging in time: we're on opposing teams battling for good and evil. The evil side has always had a head start. It's always been the easier team for Dallas to align himself. The good side is an uphill battle; I wish I could perch this little boy on my shoulders and climb the hill for him. I wish I could take his hand right now and leave this place and never come back. I wish he knew how wonderful, how valuable, how treasured he is.

On the precipice of my explosion, the garage door sounds. Sarah is home. Jacob is keenly aware of my lack of response and wears a smug, self-important half smile around the kitchen. I hear Sarah open the car door. I have mere seconds to respond to the beast.

"I can't wait to see your face on the day he proves you wrong," I reply. Jacob laughs sarcastically, then we both paint on a smile for Sarah's arrival. I greet her quickly, then plot my swift exit. At least now, with Sarah home, I am not afraid of Jacob being violent toward Dallas. She's a shitty Mom, but I have a good feeling she wouldn't let him lay a hand on her son.

[I see red.]

After she talked a hundred years with Jacob, Zoe comes outside.

"Time for me to go, Buddy," Zoe says. "See you at nine in the morning."

I stay outside with Ramsay while watching Zoe leave. I hope Jacob didn't be mean to her, because I know how bad it feels when he's mean. Zoe is nice, and her doesn't deserve that.

When she's gone out of my seeing, I start to think about homeschool. Did you know I actually kind of like it? I wish I could fast-forward from now until 9 am. The 'Zoe' parts of the day are so much better than the parts without her. I wonder what kinds of things we'll do tomorrow? I wonder if I can teach Ramsay a trick before then?

I need to have patience. That's our new word.

CHAPTER ELEVEN

March We Onward

[I see you.]

As of today, Dallas and I have been on the homeschool bandwagon for a month. Four whole weeks have passed by, and Ramsay can finally sit on cue. Sure, we've had our ups and downs—but nothing like what was happening at school. I am irrevocably convinced that Dallas was not made for conventional schooling, nor is our state's traditional education made for him. This month has been a testament to early intervention, albeit through the muddy waters of dysfunctional parenting.

Apart from my obvious disdain for all things Jacob, my greatest challenge in Dallas's intervention is the fact that his life is built on a house of cards. His mother can't handle her own life, let alone the lives of a baby and an emotionally disturbed six-year-old child. If I've learned anything these past few years, it's that one surefire way to lose your child's trust is being unreliable. If you say you'll be home at three, you should be home at three (I'm looking at you, Jacob). If you threaten a child with a consequence or promise a reward, follow through. Do you want to know why you feel like you're talking to a brick wall? There's no weight behind your words—say what you mean and mean what you say. I know this family is bleeding, but it's time to stop the blood. Dallas's life depends on it.

Looking back on Dallas's report card from last year I can see an insane amount of progress. He can count anything and everything, to any number he likes. He can hold a pencil, and he's starting to trace letters. He recognizes his name when written down, identifying letters in the writing he sees all around the place, and can write DALLAS with magnetic letters. His speech is becoming more mature and clear, with his vocabulary expanding every day—particularly since he's starting to like storybooks. We haven't left the house yet, but if we continue on this upward trend I'm thinking of adding small field trips to the park, the library, or the store.

To me, the most meaningful part is knowing he's capable of stability within himself. He might refuse the occasional math problem or writing activity, but with a little coercion, he comes around quickly. The consistency of homeschooling has been key for Dallas—every day I arrive, and he knows there are specific expectations. We have breakfast, we get shit done, we eat lunch, we play, we connect. Every day is painful, boringly similar because that's how his healing will come about. He looks at me and sees, for the first time, an adult in his life who expects something of him and isn't afraid of his meltdowns. He sees someone who will love him beyond his behaviors, even if I struggle to like him at times.

Jacob and Sarah have a rocky relationship that gets rockier by the day. They are in vehement disagreement about Dallas's intervention, and I know that causes a lot of tension. Sarah vacillates between supportive mother and a total trainwreck, but at least she tries to be the kind of parent Dallas requires. I know she loves him, I know she wants the best for him, but she doesn't seem to have the right ingredients to make that happen. Her top priority lies with preventing Jacob's explosions.

Sometimes I think about baby Aurora, and I wonder how she processes all of this. If Dallas's intervention is pursued, he gets a second chance at life. On the flip side, this little baby is likely to lose her father, and therefore her family unit, in the process. Jacob will never stand by Sarah as long as she's genuinely supporting Dallas's growth. So, are we robbing Peter to pay Paul? Are we choosing to heal Dallas at the expense of Aurora's primary attachment experience? In a perfect world, both kids could thrive, and all parents would step up to the plate. But this isn't a perfect world, and these parents will choose which child will flourish, and which will wither. Aurora will be the lucky one, yet she will never know the half-brother she was born to replace, and she will never know why her mother cries every night.

One child has two parents, one child is rejected, and the other is forgotten. There's not a single photo of Grey in the house, yet they all live with his ghost.

[I see red.]

Today me and Zoe will start on a new trick for Ramsay. He can sit now, so we get to choose another thing for him to do for treats. I have been thinking it would be good to have him learn to roll over—I've seen a doggy do that before, and he looked cool. When I was super little, I used to like dogs, and we always wanted to have one. Grey would ask Mommy every day, and she always said no. Then him died, and we got a dog.

The clock says almost nine o'clock, so I watch for Zoe out the window. I see her, so I run to open the door. Jacob runs after me, grumbling something, but I pretend he didn't talk. A thing about Jacob—if I pretend he didn't talk, the mean things he says can't be powerful to me. I always win, not Jacob. Zoe is coming up the stairs, so I hold my hand out for a high-five.

"I remembered the thing what we should teach Ramsay today," I say, loudly and fast.

"What is it?" she says, looking puzzled. I learned that word from an old times book about a bear who loves honey and his friends are a tiger and a kangaroo. Also, it means like, "What?"

"Let's teach him to roll over," I say.

"That's a great idea!" Zoe agrees.

"Let's start now!" I am absolutely too excited to wait.

Zoe puts her stuff in the house and crouches a little bit. "I can see you're super excited, but we have a few things to do first," she whispers. "If we get breakfast and number activities done extra fast, we can start with Ramsay at play time."

"But I wanna do it now!" I yell and run away to my room.

Zoe talks to Mom, which I can hear from under my bed, and the normal talk they do before school starts. Mom always is busy, busy, busy and Zoe is always like, "OK, you can go now." Mommy works at an office and has a computer (also a plant on her desk). They have lunch for free and every snack ever. She took me once, but she will never take me again because I didn't behave.

The garage door goes up, and the black car with rings drives out backwards—too fast. Scraaaaape goes the car on the driveway. Door goes down. I'm hungry because it's breakfast time. "Rumbbllle…" says my belly, and I know I can't wait under the bed for too much longer.

[I see you.]

Ignoring Dallas is a tactic that works every time, except when he runs away. Incidentally, ignorance has a zero percent success rate during those times. He hasn't run away all month (as we've been basically under house arrest), but I can't shake the feeling we might be sitting on a landmine. The longer he controls the urge, the crazier the outburst will be. That is, unless he's done with running away? Developmentally, he's getting towards the old end of elopement. I've had previous clients grow out of running away, so it's not impossible to believe he's beyond that behavior.

Having said that, he just ran away and hid under the bed, so…

[I see red.]

I'm too too hungry for hiding. Something in the kitchen smells really good, so I try to guess what it might be. I walk out of the bedroom, and I see what Zoe has. I love blueberry bagels, so I climb up onto my stool and wait.

[I see you.]

There he is! I make a mental note—

9:01 am—ARRIVAL/BREAKFAST
Antecedent: ZF arrived, D wanted to train the dog early, disregarding the schedule in place. ZF said breakfast and math were first.
Behavior: D expressed that he wasn't interested in waiting, and ran to hide under his bed (?)
Consequence: Behavior put on extinction. D returned to kitchen at 9:05 am.

"Ready for your second favorite breakfast?" I ask confidently.

"I like pancakes first, blueberry bagels second and then the third favorite is scrambled eggs," Dallas says, with a full breakfast analysis. "Did you bring cream cheese?"

"Of course!" I remark, feeling like my primary intervention has somehow just been breakfast related. "Can I ask you a question?"

"What is the question?" he returns.

"Why do you run away sometimes?" I ask, nervously hoping we're not opening Pandora's Box. He remains on the stool, visibly thinking about the question. Then, he shrugs.

"I wonder if it makes you feel powerful?" I continue.

He shrugs again, and mumbles, "When can I have the bagel?"

The toaster pops up, and the sweet aroma of hot blueberry bagel fills the air.

"Right now, Buddy," I say, smiling. I spread the cream cheese for him as he waits. "Want a glass of milk with that?"

"Mmmhmmm," Dallas nods while taking a bite of the bagel.

"Want some real blueberries on the side?" I suggest, rattling a pint of organic blue superfoods. The food nerd within me waits with baited breath.

"Yep!" Dallas yells, as he puts six of them on his plate.

"You can have more, you know?" I laugh.

"Six is enough for me. I can have six more later," he reasons.

We sit down for our twenty-second day of breakfast, thinking back to the school days—I'll gladly accept our current fate. There's an epidemic in education, where schools set up kids like Dallas for failure. I can tell by the look on the teacher's face that she either doesn't like or doesn't understand the kid. There's a sting in the way educators say Good Morning to a child they despise—almost imperceptible to the naked ear, but I pick it up on my radar every time. Very nearly monotonous, with a lowered inflection at the end; I notice the eye contact they make with other staff, I notice anxiety levels rise before anything has had a chance to go wrong. I see them asking kids with Tourette's to stop their tics; I see them punishing the little ones consistently rolling on the floor during circle time instead of recommending Occupational Therapy for sensory issues. I see them angry at children with Autism because they're well… Autistic. Nothing will change in the school system until all people are treated with respect. I'll take the proverbial house arrest over the prison escape, any day.

I look at Dallas's little face with his missing front tooth, realizing he's growing up before my very eyes. His chin isn't quite so pointy anymore, his legs must have grown three inches since we met, and he recently got a more grown-up haircut. His arms used to flap and flail as though they were a separate entity, and I haven't seen that at all during the homeschooling period. House arrest feels like a process of detoxification; he's losing the poison and being replenished with nutrients. The detox has been both figurative and literal, given that his dietary repertoire was exclusively nuggets, and now he's accepting three different kinds of breakfast (FYI: He isn't a fan of oatmeal, oh how I've tried). He still eats chicken nuggets or corn dogs for lunch, but I'm all about baby steps. A carrot stick here, a cherry tomato there—I'm trying new veggies with him every day.

If we get through this week without any running away, I'm going to ask his parents if they mind us going on short field trips. In the spirit of baby steps, I plan to walk him to the end of the block (I'd prefer this to happen with a leash, but I guess that's not kosher for a six-year-old) and back again. The next day, we can walk two blocks. If we can go out for a week without any running, we'll go to the park—the one with a fence. If he runs on any of the days, (depending on the severity of elopement) we take a break from field trips, then start again from the ground up.

After all, slow progress is better than no progress. (I think I first saw that quote on a shitty decorative throw pillow, and I'm embarrassed to admit it was meaningful to me.)

[I see red.]

The blueberries in my bagel taste different to the ones on the side. The side ones are more wetter and, did you know that fresh blueberries are actually white on the inside? A whitey clear color. I didn't know that before, and now I do because I discovered it for myself. Also, I do feel powerful when I run away, for your big fat information.

Breakfast is my best food of the day.

#

[I see you.]

> *2:20 pm—PROJECT TIME: TRAINING RAMSAY*
> *Antecedent: D prompted Ramsay to sit—instead, the dog jumped on D's shoulders with muddy feet.*
> *Behavior: D expressed frustration, saying that R was a bad dog, and he'll never be good. D cried because his shirt was dirty, and then he hid under his bed.*
> *Consequence: Hiding behavior put on extinction. D came back to ZF and R after a 3-minute break. ZF encouraged D to try again—and R sat this time.*

"I can see Ramsay really upset you when he didn't listen," I observe.

"He knows better," Dallas sniffles, "I already saw him be able to sit, and I want him always to be sitting when he's told."

"Why is that important to you?" I wonder.

"For being safe."

"What do you mean by 'being safe'?"

"What if the baby is outside and Ramsay jumps on her? She will need safety. I can't always protect her from Ramsay if he doesn't get to be good," he struggles to admit. "Ramsay is nice most of the time, but he is too big to not listen."

"Are you saying that having rules helps people, and dogs, to stay safe?" I suggest.

"I don't want the baby to go to heaven," Dallas whispers while petting Ramsay.

"I wonder if you're thinking about Grey right now?" I whisper back, making sure I don't make eye contact. In my peripheral, I see his head hanging low, and I hear him sniffling.

"I know you don't like coming too close to me, but if you want a hug, I'm always here for you," I stammer, nervously. He cries a little more and shakes his head.

"No arms," he sniffs.

"What do you mean?" I ask.

"I want a hug but don't put arms on me," he requests, still with his head down.

He sits in my lap, leaning his head on my shoulder. My hands are on my knees, as I sit motionlessly. At least twenty minutes go by, as we say nothing.

"If you ever feel like you are too angry, too frustrated, too sad, or too confused—you can take a break without running away. I will listen to you every time, as long as I can trust you. You can say, 'I need a break,' and then go to a safe place that we'll make for you," I suggest.

"I already have a space," he began, "There's a tent under the desk in my room. It's made of my old bed sheet hanging down."

"That sounds fantastic," I remark, "Can you show me?"

Dallas leads me into his room, where I've barely spent any time. I guess it's a matter of dignity and respect—people don't let just anyone into their bedroom. I consider bedrooms to be extremely private spaces, and only to be entered when invited. Kids are no different. Dallas climbs under the tent, constructed from a blue and white spotted bedsheet.

"Look inside," he commands, "But don't come in."

"I don't think I'd fit," I laugh. Dallas has piles of books inside the tent, as well as some stuffed toys and a music player with headphones.

"I lied to you," he whispers, looking down as he untangles the headphones.

"What about?" I ask nervously.

"This isn't my old bedsheet—my old bedsheet has red spots. The blue spotty one was Grey's because we have bunk beds. I'm on the bottom because he is older, and we made tents from his sheets," Dallas continues untangling the headphones as he speaks. "When he went to heaven, Mommy wanted to sell the bunk beds and wanted to throw the sheets in the trash, but I said no. I throwed out the red ones, and I kept the blue ones."

I sit with my knees crisscrossed under my chin, at the threshold of the tent. I take a moment to make sure he's finished speaking, respecting the weight of what he's just said.

"This is a perfect tent," I reply. I let the sheet fall down, and I leave him alone with his memories. He pokes his hand out the side, and I hold it without saying a word.

CHAPTER TWELVE

Another Brick in the Wall

[I see red.]

Here is a list of lunches I like:

1. Pasta and Pesto and Parmesan (All start with P)
2. Alphabet Soup (I write my name D-A-L-A, no that's not right—try again—D-A-L-L-A-S)
3. Picnics at the park. We take pretzels (the big crunchy ones), lots of colorful veggies, some dip that's called hummus and sometimes even a juice we make in the blender, which is from a crazy fruit called a pomegranate.

Ramsay can walk on a leash now, and he sits before we cross the street. We say, "Sit," and he sits, then we give him a treat that's just a little bit of kibble. He adores kibble, and adores means love, love, loves. He is still crazy and silly, but less crazy and silly than he used to be before we trained him.

Here are things I can do now, that I couldn't do when I went to school at school:

1. I can do my name with a pencil (or a pen if I can't find a pencil) and I don't need any dots like this:

(That's for babies.)

I do like this:

(2) I can count to every single number in the whole wide world, even one hundred. You can ask Zoe if you don't believe me.

(3) I can read little words like a, at, cat, rat, map, app, and the. I can't read books, though, but I hear good stories after lunch all the days at homeschool.

[I see you.]

So, we made it through another month—sometimes crawling, sometimes walking and other times it felt like we were running. We're finally out of the house and mobilized in the community. Every day we go out somewhere, which helps with the monotony of daily life. Dallas is working towards a new behavioral goal, which is a trip to Discovery Country—a theme park outside the city. There has been so much water under the bridge, so many behaviors left behind that if he earns the field trip, I believe he'll be able to handle it responsibly.

The relationship between Sarah and Jacob has rapidly gone downhill. In fact, it's gone wildly downhill and crashed into a tree. Jacob and I had a… disagreement….about ten days ago. We were at the end of one of Dallas's best days yet, and Jacob found every reason to (in his words) 'bring us back down to reality.' After he had stood there telling Dallas, yet again, that he was nobody and would amount to nothing—I fought back. Retrospectively, I shouldn't have yelled at Jacob in front of Dallas, but I would have felt worse if Dallas saw me doing nothing. One thing led to another, and Jacob fired me. Dallas chased me as I was leaving, and luckily Sarah drove into the driveway at the same time. I told her what happened, and she reinstated me on the spot. This event was the catalyst for their breakup. Who knows what went down in their home that night, but the next day Dallas stayed under the bed until noon, then wouldn't leave my side until his Mom returned.

Jacob officially moved out last weekend, and they're in the process of working out a custody agreement for Aurora, but I don't think he'll be very successful (I think he might have been violent towards Sarah, but I'm not sure). Subsequently, I have worked longer hours with Dallas, and at times, I have also taken care of baby Aurora so her parents can meet at the lawyer's office. I barely see Julia anymore, and I haven't been on a date in half a year. As the days get better for Dallas, life closes in a little for me. This job is swallowing me whole; the fear of becoming a spinster cat-lady strengthens with every day. This revelation is not the only thing that awakens me in a cold sweat.

I am embarrassed to admit that I am suffering from frequent nightmares related to Dallas on the rooftop, Dallas on the road, and Dallas with access to firearms. By day, I'm seeing a brand new child, but in my dreams, I'm stuck with post-traumatic stress. I feel pathetic even alluding to PTSD when I'm the adult here. This is all part of a job for which I willingly signed up—and to be honest, I've seen it all before. Dallas's antics (while severe) are nothing new. When I close my eyes, I see the shine of a switchblade in the hands of a child, and I hear myself discouraging him from what he's about to do. When someone is choked or tortured in a movie, I have to look away, because I remember being held against the wall by a teenager—breath stuck in my lungs. I'm embarrassed about these flashbacks, like cracks forming in an otherwise structurally sound human. My job is the only thing I have going for myself right now, and if I stop for long enough to be afraid of my clients, I'm nothing.

After all, Dallas is the one who saw his brother drown; he's the one who loses his sense of agency in the midst of grief and sadness, he's the one who has been kicked while he's down. I am called to put my life on hold to make this child whole again, yet I pay a price of nightmares — and without adequate sleep, I feel more anxious during the day. I remind myself that he's safe now. He hasn't run away (at least outside the house) for three months, yet, in the back of my mind, I doubt his ability to remain this way. Out loud, I declare that he's on an upward trend. In my heart, I prepare for doomsday.

This is one time I don't want to be right.

#

[I see red.]

At four o'clock the garage door goes up, and Mom drives the blue car with a golden shape like a plus sign into the driveway. We don't have the black car anymore because it cost too many moneys, and Mom is running out of dollars. She said that there's a guy who helps us stay safe from Jacob, and he will help us, but he costs too many dollars if we keep the expensive car with four rings. I don't mind selling a car and buying a 'No Jacob' House in exchange.

Jacob moved out on a day that's called Saturday after he held my Mom's neck for a little bit of time. The Police cars with their lights and sirens came to the house, and Jacob isn't allowed to come back here because we have a piece of paper that's a Straining Order. I made friends with the baby because she can do more things now but she is still a diaper baby. I played with her while Mom talked to the Police Man, and I found out that she loves green toys. All she sees is green, green, green.

I whispered a secret to her ear, "My Daddy moved out too."

[I see you.]

Sarah walks inside with Aurora on her hip. The baby smiles at me and extends her arms. I'm not sure whether to take her or not, when her Mom hands her over. She's adorable for someone whose father is a complete dick. She looks like Dallas, but her eyes are slightly more innocent. I don't doubt she's seen some shit in her life, and I worry for her future. I smile at her, and she nuzzles her head into my shoulder, leaving a snotty mark as a souvenir.

"He's trying to get weekends with her," Sarah says, throwing her hands up in the air. "Screw that, I mean seriously, that's bullshit."

I nod awkwardly, wishing that I wasn't so involved in this dysfunctional family's shit storm.

"I guess you just need to fight with everything you've got," I conclude, knowing that this is the most evident and general statement I could make.

"Anyway, thanks again for coming. We'll see you in the morning," Sarah says.

"Oh, by the way. Dallas needs 100 stars to go to Discovery Country with me, and as of today, he's got twenty. Just thought you'd like to know, he's progressing well."

"Good boy!" she says, as I'm caught between a cringe (I hate it when parents don't separate behavior and child) and a smile, knowing that she's acknowledging effort. I kiss Aurora on her sweet little head and hand her back to her mother. I pick up my bag, saying goodbye to Dallas. He jumps onto me and gives me the biggest bear hug of my life.

He whispers in my ear, "I wish you were my Mom."

I have no idea what to do with this. I just hope to God that Sarah didn't hear what he said.

[I see red.]

Zoe sets me on the ground and gives me a high five; then she leaves really quickly. She usually talks to my Mom for a while, but not today. I run outside so Ramsay and I can wave goodbye to Zoe as she walks to the bus.

"BYEEEE ZOEEEEEE!" I yell through the fence. Ramsay barks one time, and we watch her walk away until she's gone. I sit on the ground by the fence, wishing that Zoe never needed to leave. I wish she brought a sleeping bag and stayed here every night, or took me home to her house. I climb onto the trampoline with Ramsay, and we watch the clouds.

It's sunny today, and kind of hot—Zoe said it's called Indian Summer. I roll my shorts up, so they look like underwear, and feel the warm sun on my white legs. The clouds are changing slowly today, and I start to wonder if Grey can see them too since he's in the sky. He would see them close up, with the world underneath. I wonder if he sits on the clouds? I wonder if he ever tried to eat clouds? Also, I wonder what the clouds tasted like?

"Grey," I whisper. "Grey, can you hear me?"

Nobody talks to me, so I guess his ghost doesn't want to play on the trampoline again, today. I still don't know if ghosts are real, but I try to talk to Grey's ghost every day, just in case he's listening.

"GREY!" I yell, and Mom comes outside with an angry face.

"Dallas! Come inside. It's too hot out here; you'll get sunburnt."

I fold my arms and say, "No. I'm busy."

"The minute Zoe leaves you transform into a demon," Mom yells. "Every day."

"Leave me alone," I yell back at her. "Let me play outside!"

Mom stares at me, then turns around and goes inside. I lay back down on the trampoline and whisper Grey's name again, hoping the ghost would listen.

[I see you.]

When I get home, Ezra is sitting on the couch using his laptop.

"Needed some free wi-fi?" I quip.

Ezra straightens and laughs. "Sorry, Julia will be home soon. She left a key under the doormat for me, and thought you'd be out until late."

"Nope, I decided to have a night off partying," I say, walking to my room. I throw my backpack on the floor and lay face down on my bed.

I feel dirty. I didn't grow Dallas in my womb; I didn't give birth to him or raise him. I'm not worthy of his wish that I was his mother. Why did he have to go and make the moment weird? I can't tell Sarah what he said, but I can encourage her to be more involved with him. I give him the kind of attention and boundaries that he needs, because; (a) I'm paid to do so, (b) I have no attachment to Grey, and (c) I understand the severity of Dallas's mental state.

I need to train Sarah to reconnect with Dallas, to bond with him again—I only wish they were able to work through their grief together. Grey's loss has left a festering wound—one that has been untreated for three years. Sarah tried to fix it with material possessions, fancy cars, a giant dog, a relationship with a guy who belittles everything she does, and a sweet, unsuspecting baby girl. None of these things have fixed the wound like Sarah had hoped, and without treatment, infection will kill them all.

Ezra knocks on my door, "Coffee?"

I lift my head and sweep my bangs from my eyes. He's holding a French press and my favorite mug, with a hopeful expression on his face. Hopeful that I won't turn him away this time; hopeful that one of these days I'll give him the kind of attention for which he's vying. I'm not on the same page, but I relent.

"Of course," I respond. Ezra looks elated, and I realize that I could throw him a bone every now and again. Not being attracted to someone doesn't give me the right to be a bitch—sometimes I think I use all my 'nice' up on Dallas, and at the end of the day I'm a grumpy hermit. I walk out to the kitchen, and he pours two cups of coffee. Grabbing the creamer from the fridge, Ezra takes it from my hands and completes the coffee-making process. He carries the mugs to the couch and sets them on the coffee table.

"Appropriately named table, don't you think?" he says.

I half-heartedly laugh by exhaling through my nose, the way children do when their Dad makes a joke. Ezra pushes my favorite mug towards me, and drinks from the other.

"I know you like that one," he smiles. "You use it every time I come over."

My heart skips a beat, and I don't know why. I guess it's been a long time since someone really cared about my preferences, or looked after me in any way. I've become so used to being the caregiver.

"What are you working on?" I ask, gesturing towards his laptop.

"Just some code," he shrugs. "I start my new job on Monday."

"Typical San Francisco tech guy," I joke.

He looks slightly offended, "Why?"

"Fashionable haircut, beard, t-shirt from a hackathon, hoodie, skinny jeans, boots… all the vital ingredients of a San Franciscan. All of your Santa Cruz is gone," I smile (all of my Santa Cruz is gone, too.)

"I was never really into surfing or skateboarding. You know me, I was the kid who stayed inside," Ezra laughs.

"Yeah, I remember that. You were super into video games."

"Were? I still am!" he announces, raising his coffee mug in the air. "Here's to growing older, but never growing up!"

I oblige, picking up my cup and gently tapping it to his. I grab the remote control and turn on the TV so we can watch one of the million reality shows on offer. Kicking off my shoes, I curl myself onto the couch. Ezra closes his laptop and unlaces his old-timey leather boots.

We relax together, and for the first time, I realize Julia's little brother is a fully fledged adult. He's not so bad after all.

CHAPTER THIRTEEN

For the Love of Dog

[I see you.]

It's Indian Summer here in San Francisco—a season invented to explain why it's only hot near Halloween. While the rest of the country prepares for Jack Frost, we're making s'mores on an open fire. For this brief window of time all is well in the world. It's 8am and I'm already sweating, walking from home to the bus stop—I peel off my cardigan and throw it in my (already overflowing) backpack. My skin warms in the sunlight as I bask in the ephemeral, vitamin-drenched rays. As the bus arrives, I squeeze into the diverse crowd of sweaty commuters, where unluckily, my nose is level with a teenage boy's armpit. Unexpectedly, I start my day spending way too long deciding if it would be socially inappropriate to hand him a stick of deodorant.

Dallas is hovering on seventy-five gold stars. That means we're twenty-five stars away from my terrifying plan of taking him to an amusement park. I wonder if I can plead insanity and get out of this? Oh boy. I mean, I'm really underestimating him right now, because he's doing great. He has been for a while.

We're now two months and two days into homeschooling, and his progress has been exponential. Despite an ever-changing home environment, it seems the consistency of Monday through Friday is creating a safety net for Dallas. In many ways he has grown three years in less than three months. He's finally mastered pronouns, and tackled many of the giant educational obstacles that have been standing in his way.

Walking from the bus stop to his house, I don't see him waiting at the fence (as per his recent custom). I peek through a gap in the fence, and he's on the trampoline, but without Ramsay. That's odd. Maybe Ramsay is captivated by a new chew toy, or he's being fed. I walk the steps to his front door and knock. Sarah lets me in, but doesn't seize me in her regular frantic spiel.

"Jacob took Ramsay," she says, with tears in her eyes.

My heart sinks. I expected Jacob to be brutal in this time of separation, but I never expected this. The worst part is that Jacob didn't even like Ramsay until he started to be trained—heck, I'm not sure if he even likes him now he can do tricks. I'm sure Jacob realizes he can't have access to Aurora, so he's using Ramsay as a pawn in his sick little game. All the while, the person who loses out most is Dallas. Small wonder, since Jacob blames Dallas for the breakdown of the relationship.

"I don't know what to say," I stammer in shock. "Does Dallas know?"

"Yeah, these last few months he plays with Ramsay... well, I guess he *played* with Ramsay... every day when he wakes up— woke up? God, I hate past tense," she stumbles, in a stunningly human moment. "Today, he went outside and the dog was gone. He ran into my room, and I had to tell him the truth. He just lay beside me and cried."

"I'm so sorry," I sigh. The one glimmer of hope that sparkles in this tragically shitty upheaval is the fact that Dallas is responding in a completely age-appropriate way. I feel like a bitch for finding the silver lining, but if he experienced this kind of loss three months ago he would have run into oncoming traffic. He cried, he sought adult comfort (which, to my knowledge, was given) and took himself outside to the trampoline for a break.

"I know this is a setback—I hope this doesn't ruin his day," she says, avoiding eye contact. "God, we just can't catch a break lately."

She puts Aurora on her hip and walks out to the car. I walk outside and see Dallas on the trampoline with Ramsay's favorite toy.

"Can I join you?" I ask, with low expectations, and to my surprise, he nods. I climb through the safety net to lie beside him.

Dallas sighs, staring blankly at the sky with puffy eyes and a vacant expression.

For a while, we say nothing.

[I see red.]

I feel like Ramsay is dead. I know he's alive, but I also know I will never be able to see him ever again. I miss feeding him kibble when he does tricks; I miss his stinky breath and shaggy fur. I even miss his poops in the backyard. I'll never have another dog like him, never ever in my whole wide life. Zoe and me lie on the trampoline for a hundred years without talking, then I feel ready to tell her something.

"Jacob is an asshole," I say, staring at the sky.

Zoe laughs a little, then her laugh gets a bit bigger and it makes me laugh, too. Then we are both laughing so big that we roll into the middle of the trampoline and bump our heads together.

"I agree with you, buddy," Zoe says, "He's a big, fat asshole."

Zoe hugs me with her arms, which I am OK with these days. She does a little kiss on my head, just like my Mom used to do before Grey went to heaven. We lay outside for a hundred more years, watching the wind make clouds into shapes. I see a duck, and Zoe sees a sheep. I tell her that saying it's a sheep is cheating, because sheeps already look like white and fluffy. Zoe pulls her phone out of her pocket, and the numbers say 10:34am.

"It's way past breakfast time, little one," she says.

"Sometimes when I'm sad, I am also not hungry," I tell her, sitting up on the trampoline. She sits up, too. "But I'm less sad now that you're here, so I think I could eat some pancakes."

Zoe smiles, "Of course! But, we have one problem."

"What is it?" I ask.

"We need ingredients. We'll have to walk to the corner store," she says.

I remember that Ramsay used to walk with us when we went to the store, and the park, and the library. My tummy feels less hungry. My eyes feel like they are filling with water, and I am embarrassed to cry because I'm almost seven. I can't help it; my tears come out even though I want them to stop.

"I know it's hard to go to the store without our best friend Ramsay," Zoe says, hugging me with arms. I sniffle, and cry again. I stop, then I start. My nose is putting snot on Zoe's shirt.

"When will I stop missing him?" I cry.

"When the time is right," she says quietly, "Every day you'll miss him a little less, and then some days you'll miss him even more. One day you might be having fun, and then remember how his tongue felt when he licked your face—and your fun might stop for a while. Another day you might feel sad and his memory will cheer you up. Maybe you'll always miss him, but it gets easier."

I want pancakes—but I also want Ramsay.

"Maybe we can have pancakes tomorrow," I say.

"Today, we can just look in the fridge and pantry to see what we can find," Zoe suggests.

I shrug and say, "OK."

We walk inside and Zoe brings out my sticker chart.

"I know these stickers don't mean much to you, but I want to let you know you have shown a lot of bravery today. You've made some really grown-up choices," Zoe says, peeling a sticker from its paper. "You've earned three gold stars today—one for self control, one for using words, and the other is for taking a break when you needed one. Congratulations, Dallas."

I smile, but not too much. I walk over to the pantry to see what's inside. Ugh, there is just a can of corn and some dry things.

[I see you.]

I open the fridge—slim pickings. The pantry is basically the same, which leaves me wondering what in God's name his mother feeds him. Aurora is just starting to eat solid food, so there's a few cans of baby food hanging around. No eggs, no milk—I'm being careful in case a tumbleweed rolls out. I spy a loaf of bread! I go back to the pantry and raid the barren wasteland.

"I'm going to make you something delicious," I exclaim.

Dallas looks confused, "We don't have any stuff— *ingredients*. We don't have the ingredients to make something delicious."

I take his face in my hands and look him in the eye, "Buddy, we can make something beautiful out of this. Trust me."

The toaster's lever clicks into place, as Dallas watches the inner walls glow with orange heat. I take some butter out of the fridge, and heat water in a saucepan. I fish two peppermint teabags out of my backpack, and grab two mugs from the cupboard. I remember there's a decorative teapot on the shelf in the living room, so I wash off the dust and dry it with a towel. The toast awakens with a pop, and Dallas puts two pieces of bread on each plate. The water bubbles in a rolling boil as I shut off the flame, open the tea bags, and pour the water into the teapot. While it steeps, I spread butter on the toast and sprinkle it with cinnamon and sugar. I cut the toast into quarters (triangles, because I'll never hear the end of it if I serve him square quarters—believe me, I've tried) and set it on the counter. I bring the tea, and the mugs.

Dallas climbs atop his stool, and I sit beside him. I pour some peppermint tea into his cup, along with some tap water to cool it down. I pour hot tea into my mug, and we sit together, looking at our breakfast.

"Something out of nothing—that's what we do," I say, raising my mug.

Dallas raises his little mug of lukewarm tea, and says, "To Ramsay."

"To Ramsay," I echo, as we clink our mugs together.

"To becoming green," he exclaims proudly, with a huge grin.

He takes a bite from his small, triangular cinnamon toast, and I can tell he likes it. He eats all eight quarters before I go through three, and that's when I know he's going to be just fine.

\#

[I see red.]

Today we aren't sticking to the schedule. Zoe told me it's only for today, because all people sometimes need to take a break. Also, we are supposed to be training Ramsay right now because it's project time… but I don't have a project anymore.

"What should we do instead?" Zoe asks.

"Let's lie on the trampoline and look at clouds," I say.

We climb onto the trampoline again, and I grab one of Ramsay's old toys. It stinks real bad, it's all chewed up—but it reminds me of my good old dog. We lie on the trampoline and stare at the sky full of white, fluffy clouds. They're extra high today, and I bet that's so Grey can get a better view. I scoot over towards Zoe, so our bodies are touching. My ear presses against her chest; I close my eyes and listen to her heart.

"Do you believe in ghosts?" I ask.

[I see you.]

Considering Dallas wishes I'd be his mother, I'm mildly uncomfortable with how close he's becoming. The problem is, without my affection—he has none. I'm replacing the maternal puzzle-piece missing from his life, but consequently closing the gap so his *actual* mother has no place in his life. So much of this intervention is about choosing the lesser evil, when it doesn't matter which way you go—a lesser evil is never good. I have a snap decision to make, and selfishly keep the affection meant for Sarah. I hold him close, because I know he will look back on his life and remember who comforted him when he needed love. I kiss him on the top of his head; his hair smells like a guinea pig.

"I wonder if you're thinking about Grey," I question.

Dallas nods, "But… are ghosts real?"

If only I knew, kid. I have asked myself the same question so many times before, but never with the same curiosity as this little boy.

"I don't know, Buddy."

"Sometimes I talk to Grey's ghost, but he never talks back," he whispers. "Maybe ghosts aren't real, or maybe he's still mad at me."

"Why would he be mad?" I ask.

Dallas screws up his face and looks at me suspiciously. He says, "You know why."

I wonder if he told me something and I've forgotten. I rack my brain, but find nothing. We lay together without speaking, staring at the clouds. Dallas repeatedly throws Ramsay's disgusting chew toy up in the air and catches it again.

[I see red.]

At 2:45pm, Mommy comes through the normal door with a normal baby on one hip, and a furry baby on the other. She gives Aurora to Zoe, and gives me the furry little thing. It all happens so

114

quickly, but I realize, this guy is actually another dog. He is wiggly and licky, and a whole lot smaller than Ramsay. He licks my face, and I laugh so much.

"Do you like him?" Mom asks. She's also smiling and laughing with us.

"I LOVE HIM!" I yell.

"What do you want to call him?" she wonders.

I think for a minute, looking at his reddy brown fur, then I say, "Cinnamon!"

CHAPTER FOURTEEN

Ninety-Nine Stars

[I see you.]

Now that Cinnamon is part of the family, there's all types of canine bodily fluid surprises waiting for me to clean. Every pair of shoes in the house has been chewed through, and that cute little dickens just sits there wagging his adorable tail. Don't get me wrong: I think the puppy was a good idea, but I'm a little salty that she bought a new dog so quickly. In my humble opinion, letting go of Ramsay was a teachable moment. We finally started to process through some of the grief Dallas felt about losing Grey, and I think it was cut short by the introduction of a new puppy. I guess his Mom had a hard time with past tense, so she went into replacement mode—I guess some patterns are harder to break than others.

We've got ninety-nine stars done and dusted. In my opinion, this intervention has been an outstandingly successful, albeit an exhausting, journey. If everything goes according to plan, I'm going to take Dallas to Discovery Country next Friday. When I arrive at Dallas's house, he's waiting on the steps for me, with Cinnamon on a leash.

[I see red.]

"I have a surprise for you!" I yell as Zoe walks up the steps. She looks very surprised already, and also a bit suspicious (that's a word that means not sure if it's good or bad). I bring Zoe into the house, and I show her inside the fridge. We have eggs, milk, yogurt, fruit, vegetables, and even some muffins. Zoe is smiling, and she looks very happy about this. Mom walks out of her room and joins in our fun.

"I finally went grocery shopping," Mom says, a little bit like she's embarrassed.

"Looks great!" Zoe says, "This is a brand new season for your family."

(It's called Indian Summer.)

"It was all Dallas. He's been bugging me to buy real food for weeks. He won't even touch a chicken nugget these days," Mom explains (that's real), then she leaves in the blue car with the baby, and Zoe opens her backpack.

"Dallas, today is a very special day. For taking care of yourself, your body and others, I am awarding you your one-hundredth star," Zoe beams, pinning the star to the chart. I can hardly believe it! We are finally going to Discovery Country—a place I have wanted to go for my entire life and I have never been allowed. Our special day is really, actually going to happen! I jump up and hug Zoe (with my arms) and say thank you a hundred times.

"You worked very hard for this opportunity, Buddy. You should be really proud of your effort," Zoe says, just like a thing grown-ups say to other kids that aren't me.

"When can we go? Now? Can we go now?" I beg. "Pllleeeeeaassseee?!"

"Not today, sorry Bud. We can't leave Cinnamon alone; he's too little," she explains. "We can go next week on Friday. We'll get him a babysitter."

"Dogsitter," I correct Zoe because he's not a person baby.

#

[I see you.]

Halloween is on Monday, so we are making all kinds of creepy crawly things today. Of course, I have an educational agenda behind everything that I'm presenting as random fun. There's plenty of cutting, tracing, threading, and play dough manipulation for extending his fine motor skills. He's classifying objects according to their attributes, making patterns and performing simple math. Right now he's writing a description of a play dough monster, all with best guess spelling (e.g. "The mnstr hav fr iz, it is gren, it is skry" = "The monster has four eyes, it is green, it is scary").

Dallas suddenly stops and looks at a Halloween themed book we borrowed from the library. He opens the pages and fixates on a cartoon ghost which is evidently a child with a sheet over their head.

"Maybe ghosts are real," he whispers, touching the illustration with his index finger. I decide not to comment, and soon enough Dallas goes back to sticking googly eyes on cardboard.

[I see red.]

If ghosts are real, Grey is mad at me. If ghosts aren't real, I have to go into the sky to talk to Grey, but that's too high for me. If I dress up as a ghost for Halloween, he might recognize me, and we can jump on the trampoline together.

[I see you.]
3:20pm

Another wildly inconsistent time for Dallas's mother to arrive home, throwing her baby at me like a European Gypsy. I am starting to feel too old for this odd hybrid between being a nanny and being an educator, when in fact, I'm neither. I'm a Behavior Specialist, and a badass one at that. I hurriedly walk to the bus stop while Dallas yells goodbye to me through the fence—I'm stoked to be done for the day.

3:32pm

A kid on the bus is flipping his shit, and I'm judging his Mom so hard. For Pete's sake—if you're feeding your kid cola and blue candy, how can you expect any better behavior out of him? He reaches out and hits his mother, as she sits there and takes it. He kicks her shin and screams, "I HATE YOU!"

My mind flashes back to the days at school when Dallas would say that to me. There's a knot in my stomach as I remember the exhaustion, the bruises and tears that meant one thing then, and something completely different now the dust has settled. I lift up the sleeve of my jacket to see the scar from where he stabbed me with a pencil. Although it's shiny, pink and healed, this scar is stuck with me forever.

4:00pm

I arrive at the mall and head to the electronics store. If we're going to a theme park, there's something I need to buy first. I ascend the escalators, as the bright lights and ambient noise begin to drive me crazy. Reaching into my bag, I extract some headphones, which are tangled to hell and back. I take a minute to bring this chaos into order when I hear something out of the ordinary.

"Zoe!" a voice calls. Turning around, I spot Ezra waving and running towards me. In my mind, Ezra will always be a lanky eleven-year-old nerd with glasses halfway down the bridge of his nose. Yet, before me is a breathless, man-sized man—sans glasses, plus chest hair. Somehow in public, he seems even more grown-up than he does at our house, and against my better judgment, he's really growing on me.

"Oh, hey Ezra."

"I saw you from where I was sitting at the coffee shop, and thought, what are the chances? Two malls in this entire city, and there you are," he laughs nervously, then smiles. I'm not about small talk, and I get the sense it's not Ezra's forte either.

"What are you doing here?" I ask.

"A quick pit stop before heading home to Santa Cruz. It's my last visit to San Francisco before I move up, so I was just checking the classifieds for apartments."

"You know rent is astronomical here, don't you?"

"Yeah."

"You know it's impossible to find anything bigger than a shoebox, right?"

"You sound like you're trying to talk me out of moving," Ezra speculates.

I laugh, "I'm just trying to keep you realistic."

"And... off your couch?" he adds.

"You saw straight through me," I smile.

"I like your couch," he laughs. I avert eye contact, trying not to let him see that I'm smiling. I think he knows the awkward direction in which he has steered the conversation. He looks at me and says, "April Fools!"

"Ezra, it's October 28," I reply, confusedly.

"Therein lies the joke," he laughs. We both begin to giggle until we can't stop. When he's not so nervous, Ezra is a giant goofball.

"Well, you can always buy a tent," I reason. "Living on the streets is all the rage here in San Francisco."

The conversation dries up, and I wonder if he's judged me for making light of the homelessness epidemic. Now we're standing there awkwardly trying to think of things to say to one another; the cogs in our minds are grinding overtime, yet to no apparent avail. It doesn't seem appropriate to part ways yet, so I further rack my brain for some common ground.

"How's—"

"Well—"

We both speak at the same time and stop. Ezra giggles and I push my bangs out of my face.

"How's the homeschooling?" he says.

"It's going really well, actually. The kid is doing really well."

I start to wonder why I can't come up with any descriptors other than 'really well.'

"You must have the patience of a saint," he exhales, shaking his head.

"Yeah, Saint Augustine. He was, like, a really shitty Saint," I stumble, awkwardly. If I had a dollar for every time someone said that I had the patience of a saint, I would have at least ten dollars by now. I realize I've completely forgotten how to have an adult conversation; I've been stranded on Planet Dallas for far too long. Ezra laughs for the hundredth time, and I half expect him to walk away now that he realizes I'm not the smart, confident woman he thought I was. I figured the antidote for his unwelcome advances was to show him simply the 'real me.' For some strange reason, he stays here, complete with a sweet, goofy smile on his face.

"You want to grab some coffee?" he asks. I choke (not literally, thank God).

120

"Like… now?" I sputter like a middle schooler who can't stop saying like. Also, he was just at a coffee shop, which leads me to believe that this guy has a caffeine problem.

"Sure—I mean—unless you have something else to do?" Ezra remarks, nervously.

"Actually," I confess, starting to chicken out.

"We can meet up another time if you like?" he calmly maintains. "I'll be living in my street tent in a week. We can share a can of beans on the sidewalk or something."

Relieved that he wasn't upset by my tent joke, I laugh by uncomfortably puffing air out of my nose at a rapid pace. That's not even a real laugh, so now I'm worried that I'm acting condescendingly. Going from one offense to the next, I see my insecurities spiraling out of control, and I try to remember that I am a strong, independent, badass woman.

"Actually, I was going to say that I was on my way to the Gadget Emporium," I recover. "I need to pick up something. Want to come with me?"

"Sure," he says enthusiastically, as we walk to another escalator. "Aren't malls the worst?"

I giggle, "The worst. Especially the lighting and the smells—I swear I picked up Sensory Processing Disorder from these kids."

He looks confused, "I think I have that—but I wasn't aware it was contagious. Hey, you're the expert!"

I have noticed that when I'm with a child who has sensitivities to certain sensory input, I begin to pre-empt what kinds of lights, sounds, smells, textures, and tastes will invoke a meltdown. Subsequently, these things begin to make me anxious by association, and after years of fearing the sound of coffee grinders and dreading fluorescent lighting, I am a nervous wreck at the mall.

"Only by proxy," I catch myself talking shop.

"I want to know what we're buying at the electronics store," Ezra questions, as we walk into the gadget wonderland. I walk him over to one of the display cases and point to the item in need.

"A GPS tracker for kids?" he asks. I nod, then he continues, "What are you, like, keeping someone under house arrest?"

(I wish there was a tasteful way to say yes.)

"I'm taking a six-year-old to Discovery Country next Friday," I mumble, with a furrowed brow. Why did I do this to myself?

"Say no more," he agrees, as he throws his hands up in the air. "It looks like a watch."

"That's the point," I admit, "Otherwise he'll take it off."

The salesperson approaches and notices my eye on something.

"Lost your kid?" he quips. Haha, very amusing, I forgot to laugh. The struggle is real, ass hat.

"Well, I'm planning to take him to an amusement park next week, and I want to prepare in advance," I explain politely. "I don't want one with short distance connectivity; I need something with real-time GPS. Also, I want one that looks like a watch."

The salesperson looks at Ezra and chuckles, "So the kid takes after his mother?"

"Yeah, she's a wild one," he lies. "Our little guy is just a chip off his old mother's block."

I shoot Ezra a death stare, as he smiles widely back at me. Calling me old? I've only got twenty-six candles on the cake, kid. Then, for some reason, I play along. (Why am I smiling?)

"How old's the boy?" the salesperson asks.

"Six and a half," I inform, "The half totally matters at this age."

"You guys look very young to be parents of a child in grade school," the salesperson judges.

Ezra looks him up and down, before saying, "I don't think our family planning is any of your business, sir."

He's killing me, seriously, this guy is a character. One of those characters you love to hate. I quickly point to the device that I'm after, and state, "He's all about dogs these days, so I think this brand will be best. I'd like the brown dog style, please."

"Of course. We also have a red one in that style," the salesperson obliviously suggests.

"Not red," I assert, "We're just coming out of a red phase and have no intention to return."

"OK, so let me walk you through the features. We have a GPS tracker that works in real-time, which sounded like a strong priority for your family. There's also an alarm if he takes it off. This links to an app on your phone that will alert you when he's outside a set boundary, as well as give him the option of pressing a panic button," he continues. "When you give it to him, explain that—"

"Oh, no. We're not going to tell him it's anything more than a watch," I interrupt.

"This one doesn't have the capacity to make phone calls—is that OK?" he asks.

Ezra threads his arm through mine and rests on the glass counter. My heart beats a little too fast, and I hope he can't see my face turning red. Part of me wants to run out the door, the other part of me loves pretending to be his lady. Ugh, pull yourself together, Zoe! He's Julia's little brother. Liking him would make my living situation even more problematic than it is now. Julia always complains that I am not making enough time to hang out with her—imagine if she knew I was spending my spare time with her brother.

"That's fine," I hurry. "We'll take it."

The salesperson processes my purchase at the register, while Ezra makes the most of pretending to be my significant other. He holds my hand and points out the highest rated baby monitors, monologuing about the benefits of digital video versus digital audio. As we walk out of the store, I shrug him off with a half smile.

"OK, joke's over," I remark. "You're creeping me out."

Ezra laughs, "I want to take you out to dinner. Not with Julia—just me and you."

"I'm super busy at the moment," I start, as he interrupts.

"Well, once I'm settled in San Francisco things might have slowed down for you," Ezra shrugs. 'Slowing down' is virtually impossible when it comes to Dallas.

"Who knows?" I add, "Try me when you're back."

"I'll see you soon," he smiles. We look at each other, then look away.

I'm keenly aware that the best moments of life usually start out as the most awkward. Vulnerability hits me like a ton of bricks, feeling as if someone just pulled my pants around my ankles. In an instant, I reach down and pull them back up. If I was fast enough, nobody has to see that I was exposed. Nobody has to see that for a moment, I let my guard down. I am a confident, self-sufficient, badass female—I don't need to be swooning over a twenty-three year old at the mall. If, by chance, this becomes something of a 'best' moment in my life, we're still trudging through the awkward stage. I have a feeling it'll be awkward for a while yet.

"Well, I gotta go," I lie, weaseling my way out of this insane situation.

"I'll call you," he promises.

I walk away from Ezra with a smile on my face, yet mortified that I might have a small, tiny crush on Julia's little brother. This isn't an optimal time for crushes—I've got a job to do.

CHAPTER FIFTEEN

Scare, or Be Scared

[I see red.]

Today is Halloween, and I am dressing up as a ghost when we go trick-or-treating with Mommy in one hour (long hand on the twelve, short hand on the five). Ghosts are made of see-through. They aren't people, but instead, they are what's leftover when a person dies. At least, that's what I think they are.

"Mommy," I say, but she's not listening. "Mom. MOM. MOMMY. Mom-"

"Yes! Seriously, stop. How would you like it if I said, 'Dallas! Dallas! DALLAS!' so many times?" she growls. Actually, I would love it if Mommy said that.

"Mom!"

"YES, what do you want to tell me?"

"What are ghosts made of?"

She rolls her eyes back into her head and breathes out of her nose.

"Enough with the ghosts!" Mom says, then goes back to looking at her phone.

"Mom!"

"What?!" she yells, this time with a very angry face.

"Are ghosts real?"

"For God's sake, Dallas. Ghosts are not real. I'm not going to talk to you again until you can think of something different to say."

I think for a minute. Mommies are supposed to always tell kids the truth, so ghosts must be fake. I try to think if she ever lied to me before, and I remember the day she said that we didn't have ice cream, but we did. That was a lie. I wonder—are there different kinds of lies? Are some lies badder than others? Can there be good lies?

"Mom!"

"WHAT?"

"Is Grey a—"

Mom stops me before I finish what I'm trying to say. She yells, "STOP!"

"Let me finish!" I yell in her face.

"I know what you're going to say, and the answer is no. Grey is not a ghost. Grey is not an angel. Grey is not with us or watching us. Grey may or may not be in heaven, depending on whether or not heaven exists. Grey is dead."

Mommy gets up from the table and goes into her bedroom. She starts the water running in the shower, and I hear her sniffing tears back into her nose, and trying to cry quietly. I wonder how long she will cry in the shower? I hope it's not more than one hour. Then Aurora cries and Mom stops the water. She wraps up in a towel and picks up the baby.

"Where's your costume?" she yells.

"In my room," I say.

"You're almost seven," she sniffs. "Put it on yourself. I need to help the baby."

Mommy sets Aurora down on the floor and gets a Bumble Bee costume from her room. When she gets back, she yells at me because I didn't get my outfit on yet.

"I swear to God, Dallas—if you don't get ready immediately, we're not going. Aurora doesn't care if we stay home, and neither do I."

I run away into my room and grab the blue sheet from my tent. I cut two eye holes with scissors and feel bad because I'm ruining Grey's bedsheet.

"Sorry Grey," I whisper.

I put the ghost outfit on and wait for Mom in the living room. The stupid baby looks at me and cries, holding her arms out to stupid Mom so she'll pick her up.

"You just don't know when to quit!" Mom yells. "You're not wearing that."

"No!" I yell. "I'm a ghost."

"Dallas! Take that off!" she screams.

"It's my Halloween costume!" I scream back. "I made it!"

"You have a thousand dress up outfits, and you have to go and make a new one? Give me that sheet. I'm throwing it out," she says, grabbing at my ghost outfit. It's hard to see through the eye holes, but I run back to my room and slam the door. I hide under the bed and listen to Mommy yelling at me, deciding if I deserve to go out trick-or-treating tonight.

"Unless you change into a different costume, I can't take you trick-or-treating. It's your choice."

I think about my bucket overflowing with candy, and I quickly decide that I can be a Ninja kind of Turtle instead. I roll the ghost outfit up into a ball and shove it behind my bed where Mommy will never find it, and never ever throw it away.

[I see you.]

I've agreed to let Julia host a small Halloween Party at our house tonight for a few of our friends. When I get home from work, she's setting up the house—running around like a chicken with its head cut off. She's squeezing the stuff from glow sticks into mason jars when I wonder what the heck kind of party is about to go down.

"These are for the window sills," she justifies.

I raise my eyebrows and feign a smile, "Cool!"

Throwing my backpack in my room, I open up three envelopes and swiftly toss all contents in the trash. I've had it with my bank, so I vent to Julia.

"I told the bank seven years ago that I wanted paperless statements. Seven years! And I'm still getting physical mail, can you believe it?"

I hear the toilet flush in the bathroom, and it dawns on me that we're not the only ones home. The bathroom faucet sounds before the door opens, as Ezra walks into the living room. His face lighting up when he sees me—my heart skips a beat against my will. I feel my cheeks flushing an embarrassing shade of watermelon.

"I thought you were back in Santa Cruz?" I choke.

"I went home for the weekend, and then I got a call from someone with a spare room in an apartment, so I came right back to check it out," he stammers.

"You guys seem to be getting on famously," Julia remarks, with squinted eyes, as she pours bags of candy corn into even more mason jars. My face goes from flushed to an embarrassing shade of fuschia, and I avoid the topic.

"Need some help?" I ask.

"Yeah, need some help?" Ezra parrots.

Julia hands us a bag of hot dogs and a can of pastry. She pulls up a picture of some gross hot dog mummies, and gestures, "Can you wrap these?"

Hot dogs make my stomach churn, and not just because they're made of mystery meat. I think back to the days at school, armed with a walkie-talkie and the code word I almost always used. My mind flashes back to the principal, scolding me for saying the wrong words, and Dallas running halfway to China in the meantime.

"Ezra can take care of those," I say, pushing the hot dogs in his general direction. "I'll put frosting on the cupcakes."

He shrugs and goes to grab the can of pastry at the very moment in which I choose to pass it towards him. Our hands touch for a moment, and he keeps his fingers on mine for just a second longer than would seem natural. He's smiling with his friendly green eyes, and I look away as fast as I can. Dammit, Ezra—just make the stupid hot dog mummies. All the while, Julia buzzes around the living room filling an inordinate amount of mason jars with God-knows-what. (You'd think mason jars were the only vessel on this planet, according to online pinboards.)

"How was your day?" Ezra interjects.

"Halloweeny," I shrug. "You know how six-year-olds are." I want to talk to Ezra, but at the same time, I kind of want to crawl into a hole and die. The older I get, the more I discover how little I enjoy surprises, specifically ones that involve males of interest.

"Six and a half. The half really matters at that age," Ezra adds. I raise my eyebrow and throw him a half smile. With a bit of luck, tonight I'll realize that I only find him attractive because he's the only guy in the room right now. Once this place fills up with eligible bachelors, I'll see that this outrageous, minuscule crush for what it really is.

[I see red.]

I throw my bucket of candy onto the pavement so I can see how many I have.

"Dallas! Why did you do that?" Mom asks, and I ignore her because I'm busy. I have thirty-five chocolate candies and forty-three colorful ones. I've eaten twenty-seven candies while we have been walking, even though Mommy said I'm only allowed three. I love, love, love candy, and I am thinking about how many I will eat this week. I will get so fat in my tummy—I might explode! Also, now that I am bigger, I am the world's best at counting. I can even count to one hundred if I wanted to.

"Does Aurora have more candies than me?" I ask Mom. "You both have the same," she says. "She can't even eat candy, so who cares? Now get up off the ground."

"Sorry Mommy," I say, and watch the gazillionth person tell her how sweet Aurora looks in her Bumble Bee costume. I look good, too! I could have looked gooder in the ghost outfit. We are outside a house with an open door, and just then I notice a ghost waving at me. It's about the same big as me, and just for a second, my breaths go away. I wonder if kids look like ghosts, or like see-through kids when they are dead? Does Grey look like himself, or like a sheet with eye holes? I drop my bucket of candy and run up the driveway to the door.

"GREY!" I yell.

I reach out my hands to touch the ghost, and he feels like nothing. I put my hand in front of him, and the ghost's light goes on my skin. I wave back at him, and whisper, "Grey—is that you?"

Mom follows me, with the Bumble Bee on her hip. She pulls my arm so I stand up, and points my head to an electric thing on the roof.

"Dallas—it's a projection. It's not real," she says. "You have to stop with the ghosts."

"They are real!"

"They aren't real! I don't know where you got this ridiculous ghost obsession—did Zoe do this to you?"

I pull my arm away from Mommy and yell, "No!"

"I wish she wouldn't encourage you to talk about your brother," she says. "He's not coming back, Dallas. Not now, not as a ghost, not ever. Do you want your candy or not? It's strewn across the driveway, and it won't be long before other kids are going to take it."

I look at Mommy, and my lip starts shaking. I don't want water coming out of my eyes—I don't want to be a baby and cry in front of everyone. I shake my head and look down.

"You don't want your candy?" she asks.

I shake my head again, and a tear goes onto the ground. I watch a second one land beside it.

"We seriously only came out trick or treating because you wanted candy," she says. "You can't take Aurora's candy if you leave yours on the ground."

I keep my head down, and Mommy yanks my hand. Some kids are already picking up chocolates from the driveway before they melt, and Mom tells them to go away because it's not theirs. She puts ten chocolate candies and thirty-five colorful ones in my bucket.

"Are you OK?" Mom says, and I say nothing back. "Dallas, I'm sorry. I miss him too."

I put the Ninja Turtle hood over my face and stop talking until the end of the day.

[I see you.]

By the time the sun goes down, our living room is filled with people in ridiculous outfits—including Julia dressed as a piece of sushi (and somehow still trying to make it look sexy) and Ezra wearing a suit, holding a sign that says SORRY (he's dressed as a formal apology). I'm sporting a onesie with a glow-in-the-dark skeleton printed on black spandex, feeling a little more exposed than I intended. The hot dog mummies seem to be staring at me from the food table, leading me to decide I'm not quite ready to make peace with highly processed sausages just yet.

Small talk is the bane of my existence. After an hour of trying to discuss something other than the weather, rent prices, the election, and where I bought my skeleton onesie, I escape to the back steps. As I look to the city skyline in the distance, I remember the day Dallas climbed on the school roof; I look away. Sitting in this breezy city stairwell quickly loses its appeal, so I consider going inside. Then the door opens.

"Oops. Sorry, I didn't know you were out here," Ezra stumbles.

I pat the step beside where I'm sitting, "Join me."

Ezra sits down, with a giant smile enveloping his face. We say nothing for a while, and I wonder if I should be regretting the extension of my invitation. I was never good with awkward moments, but somehow a relationship with Dallas has helped me come to terms with silence. I dread the idea of Ezra opening his mouth and saying something small-talky, I want nothing less than having him ruin the moment with a statement about the view, or the warmth of Indian Summer.

"Just so you know," he says, clearing his throat. "I think you're incredible."

His compliment has caught me off-guard. Before I have time to respond, the door flings wide open again, and a guy from Julia's work comes to sit beside us. He smells like the whiskey he's guzzling from his stupid mason jar. The ice clinks as he lifts his drinking arm up to the sky and slurs, "Nice night, isn't it? Indian Summer, hey? Amazing view of the city from here."

I have never before been so repulsed by three fragmented, questionable sentences in my life. I look at Ezra and stand up, "Um, thank you. You too."

I awkwardly stumble into the house from the back steps to find somewhere I can be alone. This time, I find solace in the bathroom, where nobody will find me.

CHAPTER SIXTEEN

Discovery Country

[I see red.]

I wake up extra early today because today is the day that we finally get to go to Discovery Country. I already have the map—I slept with it in my hand last night, so I don't lose it. Zoe gave it to me a couple of days ago. She printed it from her computer. She also wrote me a book, which is about what to do in public, in case I forget. It looks like this:

DALLAS AND ZOE GO TO DISCOVERY COUNTRY

We are going to Discovery Country on Friday!

Zoe and I will leave at 8am, and drive to the amusement park. It will take about an hour, and there might be some traffic. I need to stay with Zoe at all times, which will be easy, because she will wear a special bracelet that links through my belt loops.

There might be long lines, and that's OK, because I am learning how to wait patiently. Zoe and I can play together while we wait.
If I feel tired, hungry, thirsty or frustrated I can ask for a break. Zoe will find a quiet break space for me as soon as possible. Because it's a special occasion, I can eat some treats, but I still need some real food.
There will be lots of things to buy at Discovery Country, and I might wish they were mine. Zoe and I have agreed that we will only spend money on entry and food.

Even if I'm disappointed, I will understand when Zoe says we can't buy toys.

If I lose Zoe, I will ask an adult to call her. I will have her number on a lanyard around my neck, under my shirt. If I am lost, the safest adults to talk to are ones with kids. I will stay with the adults until Zoe finds us.

I earned this trip by showing safe, kind, trustworthy, brave and honest behavior for three months.

I can't read the words of this book yet, but Zoe read it to me three times yesterday. We acted out all the situations like we were in a TV show. We had pretend conversations like, "Hello lady, I am lost from my Zoe and I need you to talk to her phone. The number is on my neck." We also got this thing that looks like Ramsay's—I mean Cinnamon's—leash. One part clips on my pants; the other part Zoe wears on her wrist. She was very serious that I can't take it off.

I absolutely can't wait to go. The clock says 6:20 am and I am ready with my clothes and shoes on. I am learning to do shoelaces but I'm not so good at it yet, Zoe taught me a hundred times but it takes two hundred times to be good at shoelace tying. I am hungry, so I eat a yogurt from the fridge and also a muffin that wasn't homemade but bought from the store. Ugh, I have to wait a hundred hours until Zoe gets here.

[I see you.]

My alarm sounds, as I shoot my arm to the nightstand and press snooze... maybe three times. Today is November fourth, the very day I have planned to take Dallas to Discovery Country. It seems like I have a degree in catastrophizing, so I need no encouragement to think of all the things that may go awry. Throwing off my blanket, I sit up in bed; today will be a good day.

I have been sleeping pretty well lately, especially knowing Thanksgiving and Christmas break are coming up. The holidays bring the hope of a little break from Dallas, despite the fact that I have absolutely zero plans for Thanksgiving, which is paradise for my introverted self. Come Christmas time, I'll be back in Santa Cruz with the family. Ezra made the move to San Francisco yesterday and texted me to hang out this week. Between you, me,

133

and the deep blue sea—I am trying to forget what happened on the stairs at the Halloween party. Even if I were able to admit that I have feelings for Ezra, I would never be able to tell Julia. Herein, my strategy with Ezra will revert to ignorance.

I have woken up feeling confident about today, for three significant reasons:

1. Leash
2. Lanyard
3. Locator

(I have made an alliterated list for your reading pleasure.)

Call me "over the top" if you must, but these three items give me immeasurable peace of mind. Sure, I'm nervous, but I have to remind myself to place fact over feeling:

FEELING: Everything about this day is terrifying.

FACT: Dallas has a history of running away, but hasn't run in three months. He has displayed exemplary behavior since leaving conventional schooling. He has proven himself to be trustworthy, and mature enough, to handle a trip to an amusement park.

8:00am

I arrive at Dallas's house, and his greeting reminds me of a pre-green Ramsay. He leaps from the third step, catapulting himself into my arms. Short of licking my face, he's a picture of the old dog to whom we taught new tricks. I catch him, and he looks at me with a gap-toothed grin. If he had a tail, it would have whacked me in the legs by now.

"It's today Zoe! It's really today!" he yells and hugs my neck as I realize that this is the kind of choking I could get used to. I hug him back and set his wiry little body on the stairs.

"I have something for you," I announce, opening my backpack.

"Is it a present for being good?" he asks.

"Nope. It's a present that has no strings attached—that's a saying that means 'no matter what.' This is a gift from me to you, because I want you to know you're important to me," I explain. "Close your eyes and hold out your hand."

Dallas squeezes his eyes so tight and holds out his little arm. I take the location tracker out of the box and fix it to his arm.

"Open!" I exclaim. Dallas's eyes grow wide, and he hugs his new "watch" to his face.

"I love it!" he yells, with a huge grin. "Now I will always know the time. I'm never taking it off!"

His sunny mood is contagious, and I realize that today has the potential to be wonderful. He runs inside to show the watch to his Mom, and I overhear her telling him how lucky he is to get all these treats in one day. As I walk inside, I see that Dallas is showing the watch to Aurora and Cinnamon. I take a moment to talk to his Mom.

"That was really generous of you, getting him a watch and all," she says, looking down. Since Jacob threatened to take custody of Aurora, she has been working really hard to spend wisely so that she can afford the legal fees. I know for a fact that she stopped buying Dallas so many presents, and this is the first time I realize I've truly stepped into her place. She looks like a kid coming second place in a 100-meter sprint: exhausted and disappointed. She's been given the consolation prize—the full responsibility of Dallas, without any of the perks. Here I stand, showered in affection from the boy, giving him things I can afford to buy.

"It's a GPS tracker," I admit. We both laugh awkwardly, in this rare moment where I'm not trying to hold her life together with masking tape. "Don't tell him, or he'll take it off."

"I don't think he'll run," she infers, in the kind of tone parents use when they are afraid someone else is taking their job. "He hasn't run away since that day on the roof. Jacob didn't believe you could fix him; thanks to you he's practically a different kid. I don't know where we'd be without you."

"Thank you," I clumsily accept the compliment. An uncomfortable moment passes where I realize that she thinks I've fixed her broken son. We haven't even dealt with the core issue of grief, and the truth is, until she's ready to acknowledge the role of trauma in Dallas's behavior, we're all just chasing our tails.

Dallas and I pack ourselves into the car, as Aurora and Sarah wave at us from the driveway. We're finally on our way.

#

[I see red.]

The line is long, and the sun is sunny. Zoe and I practice being patient while we wait a hundred years to walk inside, but after only about fifty years, we finally go inside. We walk into Discovery Country, and it's everything I already hoped for, but bigger! There are rides everywhere, and families, and foods that I don't see many times.

"What's that?" I ask.

"Funnel Cake," Zoe says.

"What means Funnel Cake?"

"Cake poured through a funnel."

"What's that?"

"A turkey leg."

I laugh, "A leg? Like a turkey's actual leg?"

"Yeah, I guess that's pretty weird," Zoe says, and we both laugh.

I have a list of some rides I'd like to do, and I wrote it on paper. It looks like this:

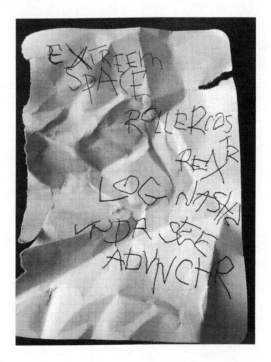

(Zoe makes a hundred lists every day, so I learned to list things too. I couldn't do a list when I didn't know how to do writing; now I know how to do both things because I'm nearly seven.)

I heard that Extreme Space is like a rollercoaster inside space, but you don't leave the Earth to go there. I wouldn't mind if we left the Earth, but I'd like to try it out anyway. When we looked on the internet, I saw this GIANT T-Rex next to a ride, and Zoe said its name was Rollercoaster Rex. I want to go on that one, because it looks like an awesome ride for tough guys like me. Then, also, I want to do Log Nation, because Zoe said it's the most fun thing here.

"Where should we go first?" she wonders, and I show her the list.

"It's not in order," I tell her, and we take a look at the map. Zoe says we should do the Under Sea Adventure first because it's closest. We can even see it from where we are standing, and I want to run there, but I walk. Also, I am connected to Zoe like a dog and a human, and I get to be the dog, which is very fun.

The line is a little bit long, and Zoe pulls a granola bar out of her backpack for me. We eat a little picnic in line, and before too much longer, we are getting in the ride. It's like a fake submarine, and there are no seatbelts. I don't think I have ever been on a ride before, at least I can never remember, especially if it was before I was three. Nobody remembers baby memories, but I do remember Grey. He liked under the sea things; that's why his bed sheets were blue like water. He had some goldfish, too, but they went down the toilet after he died at the pool.

[I see you.]

I really hyped up this ride for Dallas, and I'm glad we are doing it first. We're completely enclosed in a fake submarine, so he can't possibly run away, meaning less stress for all involved. I let the leash fall to the ground as we pile into the submarine, and just like that, he's free. The cabin smells like diapers and kid farts, as well-meaning moms and dads speak condescendingly to their toddlers. If I had a dollar for every time, someone said, "Fishy!"

137

I'd have enough money to buy an overpriced funnel cake. Jeez, I forgot that this ride was for babies and their stupid baby-talking parents. Kill me now.

Dallas is glued to the window, completely enamored by the fish swimming by. Some are real, some are fake, and I'm not sure he knows the difference. With his toothless grin and button nose pressed against the glass, I see this sweet, introspective boy enthralled by a baby ride. I see a wounded kindergartner experiencing the moments he missed as a preschooler. I see the gaps in his development closing like doors on a bullet train, zooming off into a new season. I suddenly feel embarrassed about the leash on his belt buckle. The parents on this ride must think I'm the worst.

[I see red.]

The clownfish was Grey's best fish because he liked the movie with a clownfish family. He had a stuffed toy of a clownfish that he cuddled when he went to sleep. I see a hundred of them on this submarine adventure, and also a shark! The shark is smiling, and he looks like a cartoon, but most fish look like real in an aquarium. But this isn't an aquarium; this is actually under the sea.

I am almost seven; I would know.

[I see you.]

When the submarine door opens at the end of the ride, I subtly pick up the leash and lead Dallas through the gift shop and outside. He hasn't stopped smiling this whole time, and he even kept his agreement not to ask for toys. He wants to ride the submarine again, and I remind him that there are dozens of other rides here. We take another look at his list and choose the Rollercoaster Rex.

I'm a little concerned that we've gone from a baby ride to big kid ride, so we'll see what he thinks once we see the coaster in person—plus—he'll need to be tall enough to ride. There's a giant fiberglass T-Rex reigning over a mildly scary rollercoaster, and frankly, I think the dinosaur gimmick might be the scariest part. The ride is fast, though—the kind where passengers legs dangle as they zip through an outdoor zigzag of sorts. Dallas's face lights up even more, and I remember that I've never seen this child afraid of anything in his life—except maybe Jacob. He speeds up, pulling like a dog on a leash. (I'm getting some disapproving stares.)

[I see red.]

T-Rex looks really real, and it freaks me out for a second, but I can't let my face know to look scared. I get measured to make sure I can ride safely, and I am zero inches bigger than I need to be. I didn't tell anyone, but I standed on my toes for measuring, because I hate being little for my age. Zoe and I wait in line for fifteen minutes, and we play the hat game, and this is how you play:

1. Say a name of a kind of hat (e.g. Police hat, baseball hat, helmet, etc.)
2. Take turns and don't repeat the same hat two times.

When it's our turn, Zoe helps me onto the seat because my legs are a bit short for a six-year-old who is almost seven. She does the harness for me, checking it a hundred times so that I don't fall off. She tucks the dog leash behind my butt and sits in the seat beside me. The people who work there check to make sure we don't fall out, and I put my hand out for Zoe to hold. The people who work there tell me that I have to keep my hands to my own self, so they don't get cut off. I listen to them because I want both of my hands forever.

It starts moving faster than I have ever been, and I feel like my face is melting off. The breeze in my hair is better than when cars rush by on the road. My body feels like I'm flying, and I wonder if we can go, just for a second, up to heaven to tell Grey about this. He would love everything about today.

[I see you.]

The ride slows down as I feel my hair fall completely on my face. Dallas is beaming, cheering like he's at a football game. We come to a stop, as the staff member opens Dallas's harness before mine. He jumps down while I'm still stuck in the seat—I immediately expect him to bolt, but instead I watch him wait patiently for me. He doesn't even try to walk away, he just waits. I guess I have been overreacting a little today.

I take Dallas to get lunch and unclip the leash. I think we have well and truly gone beyond leash territory—especially since there's a lanyard and GPS locator as backup. He chooses a hot dog with fries, and I eat the same so we can match. Today seems like an appropriate day for me to make peace with a hot dog, like a confident declaration that everything is going to be OK. Jeez, it's been friggin' years since I've eaten processed crap like this, and it lures me with its strange brand of deliciousness (I think it's called MSG). After lunch, we take a break, and I let him use my phone to play a few games—after all, we don't want to see our hot dogs again on the next ride.

While he plays games, I take a moment to look at the map and plan our next moves. The two remaining items on his list are Extreme Space and Log Nation. Extreme Space is closer to where we are now, but I'm not sure it's a good idea straight after lunch. If we walk the other way, we can visit a petting zoo, then head to Log Nation.

#

We made our way through the petting zoo, with the goats being Dallas's clear favorite animal of the day. He said they reminded him of Ramsay, and we took a bunch of photos together. He walked beside me the whole time, so I started to feel a little embarrassed that we'd begun the day on a leash.

Arriving at the Log Nation, we're happy to realize that the line is almost non-existent. This ride is a childhood classic—one of those water amusements, where you float through different scenes inside a fake log. At the end there's a drop and everyone gets soaked—and that's the very moment they take a photo. When I was a kid, I loved to pretend that Log Nation was real. We were really in the Wild West, spectating from a log boat. We were really part of finding the outlaws and making the world a better place.

I hope Dallas likes it just as much.

CHAPTER SEVENTEEN

Log Nation

[I see red.]

We get into this log that has been carved in the middle to become seats. I am sitting in front of Zoe, and there are no seatbelts like the Rollercoaster Rex. We start to float like the log is actually a boat, going into a scary, wet cave which I didn't expect. It's super dark in here.

"How are you doing with the dark, Buddy?" Zoe whispers from behind.

"I'm OK," I say, which is kind of lying because I feel scared.

"You can hold my hand if you need to," she says.

"I can do it. Let me do it by myself," I tell her because I'm almost seven.

We float into this room, and BAM! There; that lightning and thunder! I let out a little scream, and Zoe lets me hold her hand. It's raining, but we aren't getting wet in the logs. A man with a big mustache comes out and explains that he's looking for a rabbit who stole some gold. He has a long gun called a rifle, and I am super nervous that he might use it like Jacob said he was going to use his gun on me if I didn't become a good boy. He didn't have a gun, at least I never saw him have a gun, and he told me not to tell my Mom he said that. I never told her, even though I wanted to, just in case he shot me. I want to get off the ride, but I can't tell Zoe or she'll think that I'm a baby. I throw her hand away.

"Are you OK, Bud?" Zoe questions. "I'm sorry, I didn't remember it being scary like this when I was a kid. It'll be over soon—you're going to love the ending."

"Don't touch me," I grumble, "I'm almost seven, and I can do this by my own self."

We keep floating, and now we are in a room that is very bright. Phew! I can see everything, and this nice bunny is hiding from the man with the gun. The bunny land is so colorful, and everyone is happy in this place, so I want to stay a while. I'm OK, and I'm not scared anymore. We float a little longer, into a darker room that the bunny ran inside. He's a thief, which means a stealer.

"Rats! He's back!" the bunny says, with his words not matching how his mouth moves. He's a bit like a robot. The bunny jumps into the river to hide from the man with a gun, and his body goes totally under the water. My heart is beating extra fast because maybe the bunny doesn't know how to swim? All the other kids in the logs are laughing and yelling, "He's in the water!" I'm not yelling; I'm only worried the bunny can't swim. If he can't swim, and we keep floating in this log, he might stay under the water. I keep thinking about this, as we sail into another super dark area.

Bunny is totally under the water in here, and his ears are poking up above the surface like a submarine's periscope. The kids in other logs are laughing at him, telling the gun guy where to find him because he's a thief. I don't care that he stole something, I care that he can't swim. It's completely dark now, so I climb out onto the huge, slimy rocks beside the water. I have to help the bunny, or he'll be dead like Grey.

[I see you.]

It's pitch black right now, and I'm a little worried about how Dallas is handling this ride. He seems tense, but I am trying not to touch him since he asked for some space. There's something beautifully relaxing about floating along a river in the dark, so I enjoy the weightless sensation of buoyancy, coupled with momentary blindness. I revel in the part of the ride where you can only hear the characters, where you get to imagine the hilariously cartoony situation when the gold thief is finally put in jail. From memory, it stays dark for a while, then comes the drop.

142

"Get ready for the drop, buddy! We're gonna get so wet!" I laugh, trying to warn him. Dallas is going to lose his mind when he experiences the freefall—food for his sweet, daredevil soul. I can't wait to see the picture at the end! As the daylight emerges at the end of the tunnel, I feel my heart skip a beat. The blood drains from my face. The seat in front of me is empty, and I have no idea where the hell Dallas has gone. The moment is caught in suspension: frozen and hanging in the air, waiting for me to solve the problem. I can't look at my phone because it will be ruined by the splash as we drop. If my phone dies, I can't see where he is on the GPS, and now I realize, that stupid dog "watch" just paid for itself. I try to call for help, but nobody hears—my screams join a chorus of everyone else in this God-forsaken amusement park.

The log pauses on the precipice, taunting me with the undeniable reality of my situation. Dallas could be in any of these one hundred and thirty five acres of land if he hasn't found the gates to the parking lot yet. The mechanism releases, as I fall alone and terrified: screaming with everything that is within me.

[I see red.]

It is hard to find my way back to the bunny in the dark, but I am not letting him get away from me. He can run from the hunter, but he won't run from me. I am the winner: I will save him from the water, and I will save him from all the kids laughing at him. I want to tell the bunny that kids laughed at me too, and one time I punched a kid in the face for doing that. His tooth came out, and he had to go to the dentist with a lot of blood in his mouth. I was never allowed back at that preschool ever again.

The bunny can't die today. I will find him, I will rescue him from the water and I will keep him safe until his Mommy comes and hugs him tight. His Daddy will stay at the house, and they will still be a family tomorrow. That is how it works when you're a winner—winners save the day.

[I see you.]

I jump over the line partitions, sprinting back to the staff piling people into logs.

"Help me!" I scream. "Help! I lost a six-year-old boy in the ride. He was right there, and then—"

The pimple-faced ride attendant interrupts me, "Where did you lose him?"

I fumble through my bag for my phone, opening the GPS app. A geotagged dot pulsates at a point inside Log Nation. I hand the phone to the attendant.

"He's wearing a GPS tracker," I confidently report, knowing that I'm more prepared than most people faced with this situation.

The attendant grimaces sympathetically, "Ma'am, with all due respect, we've never had this happen before."

Shit. You mean I am the first person in the history of Discovery Country who has lost their kid on the inside of a ride? You mean to say, since 1982, nobody's child has ever climbed out of a ride in the dark and ran away into oblivion? Dallas, you win this time. I'll make you a trophy, I'll give you a medal, I'll bake you a cake—just come back to me.

"I need you to stop wasting time, and start finding my child," I assert, zooming in on the real-time geotag. The dot doesn't seem to be moving, and I'm concerned that we've lost connection. "Please!"

"I've got to be honest, that's not a very accurate location. I mean, there are multiple levels in Log Nation. You see above and below, but there's underground and ladders everywhere," he mumbles. An older staff member steps up to the plate, overhearing the tail-end of the conversation.

"We have a 920C inside Log Nation. Code two—I repeat—Code two," he calmly announces through his walkie-talkie. "Ma'am, I assure you, we'll find your child as soon as possible."

Three extra staff members run to Log Nation, and the older attendant directs them to the places that may match the GPS.

"We need a description of the child—do you have a photo?" he requests.

As I find the picture, I mumble, "He's six and a half, sand colored hair—longer on top, he's wearing cargo shorts, a black t-shirt... OK, here's a photo of him from this morning."

Staff members run off into the distance. I stare at the wall, praying that God will protect Dallas again this time. I think of

144

everything that could hurt him—the mechanics, the pyrotechnics, the water...

What if he drowned?

[I see red.]

I find the bunny with his ears sticking out of the water. He hasn't come up for breath yet, and I am really worried that I've found him too late. I jump into the water—even though it's dark, even though it's scary, I have to make sure he breathes. I always have a plan, and today I need to do what I couldn't do with Grey, which means today I will save a life. I will pull him to safety, I will put the breath back inside of him, and I will stop him from leaving to heaven.

The water is cold, cold cold, and smells like a pool. I put my arms around the bunny, so I can try to get him out—but he's too heavy. He's bigger than I thought, and I'm really scared I won't be strong enough to get him to safety. I feel his ears and head, but below, where I expect him to have a body—he just has a stick. The plan suddenly falls apart, because he's supposed to be real. If he's not a whole bunny, can I still save him? I'm scared to death, and I scream as loud as I can go.

A log is coming, with a Mom and two kids inside. They are pointing and laughing at the bunny, yelling, "HERE HE IS! CATCH HIM!" but I won't let him be a loser. I jump out of the water and onto the rocky land, where I pick up a fake rock and throw it at the kids. They didn't see that coming! The stupid lady screams for help so loudly, about a hundred times, and nobody helps her at all.

See? Losers don't get help. Who's the loser now?

[I see you.]

The attendant's walkie talkie amplifies an almost incoherent mumble, "...920C Found, ahh.... we also have a 240...same guy..."

"What do those codes mean?" I plead, the younger attendant looks awkwardly at, the older staff member. "Please! You have to tell me what's going on!"

"We've reported a lost child, asking staff to look for him ASAP," the older attendant volunteers with hesitation. "But, your child's just been reported for assaulting passengers inside the ride. We're not 100% on details, but it appears he's been throwing rocks at people and messing with the animatronics."

Taking Dallas on this ride was the most ridiculous idea I've ever had. No—actually—bringing Dallas to a theme park was the most ridiculous idea I've ever had. I want to crawl into a hole and die—please Lord, let the Earth swallow me. Take me home on wings like eagles. If I start running now, I can start my life over in some place new. I'll lay low, assume a new identity, marry a bricklayer from the suburbs and spend my days making meals in a crockpot. I swear I'll never leave the house—and God knows—I won't have children because I'm really shitty at taking care of them. I'll live a quiet, simple life if I start running now and don't stop until Mexico.

The walkie talkie mumbles again, "10-97…. 920C found….ah, there's no code for this."

The older attendant walks away to a more private location, and I overhear only two words—run and ladder. I look at my app, and the pulsating GPS dot is moving again. The younger attendant urgently runs to the front of the ride, while oblivious passengers queue for Nightmare Nation. He places a hand on his forehead, shading his eyes from the sun. He looks atop the gigantic barn-like structure that houses the water ride, and runs back to his supervisor.

"The man hole!" he yells.

"He's on the barn roof?" the supervisor clarifies, with sheer terror in his eyes.

I run outside to the nearest trash can and reunite with my hot dog of regret. I throw up twice more, for good luck. I lift my eyes to see a wiry little silhouette climbing on a rusted, fake barn roof.

You won, Dallas. You won.

CHAPTER EIGHTEEN

Life's Short—Run Fast

[I see red.]
The roof at Log Nation is not flat like the one at my old school. It's pointy like a barn, and there are rusty nails hanging out because whoever made it didn't do a good job with a hammer. There are some holes in the roof where the tin part got very thin, and when I peek through the hole, I see people having fun in the logs. The bunny must be dead by now, and something I know for sure: you can't bring a dead thing back to life, unless his name is Jesus. I know, because Rachel told me. I don't care if I die from climbing on this roof, because then I can tell Grey all about the Under Sea Adventure. He is going to be so jealous.

I climb even higher, to the most high point which is like a chimney. I can see the entire park from here, even cities and seas. I've never been somewhere this tall, and I wonder if Grey can touch my hand if I reach up high enough. I stand up on the chimney, and lift my arms as far as they go.

I cup my hands around my mouth to make my voice louder, "I'm sorry I didn't save you." He doesn't yell back.

"GREY!" I yell. "Can you hear me?"

I will keep yelling until he answers.

[I see you.]
My eyes are glued to Dallas's silhouette atop the highest point of the barn. As he lifts his hands, I fall to my knees. My gaze is fixed; I'm stealing the privacy of his last moments. What I'd give just to know why he snapped—I want to rewind time and keep him inside the safety of his home. I'll be held responsible for

147

this, maybe even put in jail. Once the internet gets a hold of this story I'll be a global laughing stock at best—a purely incompetent human in the public eye. There goes my career as a Behavior Specialist, flushed down the toilet of shame. As Dallas threatens to end his life, he takes mine with him.

I hear the sound of helicopter blades chopping through the sky, with a rescue paramedic dangling precariously on a rope. So it's come to this? All of the intervention, the effort, the input, the days I've spent as a punching bag… and it's come to this. What if Dallas jumps before he's rescued? They have no idea what they're doing. They don't know how to deal with him—he's not like other kids. I should be in the helicopter, but I'm right here on the ground like a sitting duck.

In a mix of terror and relief, I watch as he collects Dallas like a swinging pendulum—but I know we're not out of the woods yet. Doesn't he know how strong Dallas can be when he's angry? What if he drops him in mid-air? I scream his name into the sky, while a sickeningly entertained crowd that gather like vultures. They record the so-called rescue on their cell phones, while Dallas's life literally hangs in the balance. I want to hit the phones out of all their hands, but the little of my sensibility remaining tells me that would be a bad idea. I am not about to throw fuel on the 'crazy lady who lost her kid' fire. Instead, I turn around and yell, "Have some respect!"

A dad-aged guy puts his phone down and encourages the others to do so as well.

They don't.

[I see red.]

A man in a helicopter catched me, and he's trying to kill me in the middle of the sky. If I can just wiggle outside his grip, I will fly like the blue car. I wonder if arms work like wings? Will I glide? Will I fly if I flap them up and down? I could try, if only he wasn't holding me so tight. The helicopter man chokes my breath, and my screams are like whispers when I mean them like yells.

"GREY!" I whisper-yell.

This helicopter guy won't win! I am the winner, every single time! He climbs us into the helicopter which has no doors and connects me to himself with a special harness. Another very,

148

very muscley guy holds me still while the harness goes on. If I try my best, with all my strong, I can still jump outside the helicopter. After all, there are no doors.

"Shit—he's a force to be reckoned with," the rescue man says. (He sweared!) "I'm going to need one of you to buckle us into the seat somehow. We need to be anchored."

The other big man pushes us back away from the door hole and threads a seat belt through both harnesses. I hear it click in place, and the second strong guy stands in front of us. My legs kick at him, before he uses his giant arms to stop me.

"A force? More like rabid," the second guy says. I know what that means, because the Vampire Bat killed a man from rabies. "Do we need to sedate him?

"Is that even legal for a child this age?" the first guy, the one who connected me with a leash, says. I don't know what "sedate" means, but I have a feeling it means for them to kill me. I start kicking and screaming all over again.

"We're close to the ground—medical crew can make the call. Hopefully, they'll get the mom to the hospital as soon as possible,"

[I see you.]

The Police arrive, parting the crowd like the Red Sea. They whisk me away, while the relentless pack of vipers snap pictures in my face. We get in the back seat of the police car, driving with lights and sirens out of the parking lot and onto the freeway. News crews are pulling up, and I use my sweater to block my face.

"Where are you taking me?" I ask, terrified of the answer.

"The boy has been taken to the hospital," the Police Officer replies.

"Is he alive?" I stammer.

"He's physically fine—apart from a few cuts and bruises. I mean, it's a goddamn miracle," he explains. "Mentally, though... well, we have a few questions."

"He's been going through a rough time, and he's improved so much. I thought he was able to handle this now he's catching up, but he obviously can't. I shouldn't have brought him here. Am I in trouble?" I rant, words falling from my mouth like vomit.

"No, you're not in trouble—we're just taking you to the hospital," the Police Officer answers. "We have a lot of questions."

"Did you call his Mom?" I ask, cringing.

"Wait—you're not the child's mother?" he roars.

"No, I'm his Behavior Specialist. I brought him here today as a reward that he had to earn—three months—no, four whole months without running away. Then out of the blue, he takes off on a ride," I rant again, wishing my mouth would stop moving. The shock causes the floodgates to open, and the more I verbally throw up, the more I hate Dallas all over again. I have never felt such deep love and equally deep disdain for another human being in all my life.

"You do realize his Mom has probably seen this on the news before she's heard from you," the Officer reveals. "We need to contact her immediately."

I know this, but it still punches me in the gut. To add insult to injury, I'll never get another client ever again. I guess it's time to acknowledge this kid has ruined my confidence, kindness, and career. There's no harm in kicking a horse while it's down—so let's call his mother and make sure she knows I'm a giant, irresponsible failure.

A glorified babysitter is all I ever was, a huge waste of money—Jacob was right.

[I see red.]

I whizzed to the hospital in a helicopter, and they ran me inside to a bed. I stopped trying to get away, just to trick them. When they stopped trying to catch me, I jumped off the bed again. I always win! I ran through the halls, and then banged to the floor with a big man nurse holding me down. They took me back to the bed, and the big man held me tight while a doctor squeezed medicine in my arm like a shot.

The medicine is making me… NO! I WILL WIN! But the medicine is making me feel… so… sleepy.

[I see you.]

I rush into the hospital, while the police officers call Dallas's mom. I find him out cold in a hospital bed with a six-point restraint. The sight of his seemingly lifeless body stops me in my tracks, as I wonder what on Earth preceded this restraint system. The rescue team briefs the medical staff, and I try to hear what they're saying.

"I don't know the child's history, but I'm not sure he's mentally stable," one says.

"He didn't speak at all—maybe he's nonverbal?" the other adds.

The team notices me standing beside Dallas's bed, and their conversation grinds to a halt. They descend on me like a pack of wolves.

"Why is he unconscious?" I ask.

"Ma'am, are you this child's caregiver?" the Doctor asks.

I nod my head, "I am his Behavior Specialist. I brought him to Discovery Country today the police are calling his mother."

"We had to sedate him—he ran away several times," the Doctor explains. He holds a clipboard and a pen, and curiously asks, "We're unable to move forward with his case until we solve some of the mystery surrounding what happened. Can you give us some background? Name, date of birth, diagnosis, family situation?"

"Dallas Jensen, 2/28/2010—no formal diagnosis, but suspected conduct disorder... amongst other things," I report, at which point the Doctor's pen writes furiously. "Trauma in the child's third year of life, broken home. Doesn't attend conventional schooling, I have taught him at home for three months."

The Doctor writes like his life depends on it, and I know every word out of my mouth falls to the ground like lead. The weight of Dallas's problems can no longer be pushed under the rug. He's not fixed; he's not healed—heck, the jury's out on whether or not he's even improved. Congratulations, Zoe, you've successfully ruined a human and now he's bleeding out before your very eyes. The Doctor walks away as the police approach.

"We have a few questions. Please step into the hallway," they request.

I look over at Dallas. He's lying in a bed for mental patients who shit their pants before murdering the neighbor's dog. This tiny child with floppy hair and missing bottom baby teeth, this little boy with a passion for pancakes and puppies—in a bed for grown adults deemed unsafe for society. In this split second I decide that even on the off chance this fiasco hasn't ended my career, I've served my last client. I always knew Dallas would be the death of me, and beyond this moment I just need to focus on my personal resurrection.

I don't know who I am with or without him, or who he is without me—but I guess we're about to find out.

#

<u>11:49pm</u>

I walk through the door of my house, throwing my keys on the counter. Eight hours have passed since the incident, and I've been rushed from pillar to post ever since. After the hospital, I went back to the park to get my car, again to the hospital to see Dallas's mom and finally home to bed.

I take a shower, lathering myself in soap to wash the filthy stench of failure from my skin. My phone is blowing up; I haven't answered a single message since this nightmare began. I stand under running water for longer than I should, staring straight ahead at the foggy glass before me. I replay the conversation with his mother in my mind, wishing with all my heart that I could turn back time.

I don't know what I was expecting her to say—I guess a little, "Good job with the GPS," or, "I totally understand," would have been nice. Words wash over me like rain bursting from thick, gray clouds.

"I trusted you."

"He could have been killed."

"I have already lost one child—how could you be so irresponsible?"

"You have no idea how it feels to be his mother."

I drug myself before bed, with the heavy prescription kind I got from the doctor when I was suffering from insomnia. There are so many emotions to feel, and right now I don't feel anything. I stare at the roof, waiting for sweet sleep to take me far, far away from here.

CHAPTER NINETEEN

Star Light, Star Bright

[I see red.]
I wake up slowly; I'm in a bed that smells wrong, in a place I've never been before. I'm thirsty, so I look for someone who can help me get some water—but I'm all alone. I get up and try to open the door, but it's locked. What happened to Funnel Cakes at Discovery Country?   What happened to Zoe?

[I see you.]
I greet the day with a sleepy hangover. I try to listen to the birds and seize the moment, but I just don't feel it. Reality crashes down on me as I struggle to put one foot in front of the other. I get dressed and eat breakfast; I go through the motions like it's just another day. Another day with Dallas and Cinnamon, another breakfast on the trampoline, another mind-numbing book about dangerous animals. But I know I'm fooling myself.

There's no breakfast before I make my way to the children's' psychiatric ward—the creepiest place on Earth.

[I see red.]
A lady walks past me, and I call out to her. She's coming into the room to see me, and I don't even mind that she's a stranger. I am so lonely I don't know what to do, my body feels so weird and tireder than I have ever been. I rub my eyes and sniff, sniff, sniffle because I am crying and I don't know why.

"Hey Buddy," she says. That word is only for Zoe to call me—this is all wrong.

"Where's Zoe?" I ask, my voice still a little husky.

"I'm not sure who that is, honey," the lady says.

"Call Zoe," I say, and tears come a little bit down my cheek.

"I don't know her number," she replies, while touching my hair. I want her to stop.

"It's on a thing around my neck," I say, trying to grab the lanyard, but it's gone. I sit on the floor and cry.

[I see you.]

Arriving on the fifth floor, I retrace my steps from the day before. I pass through security and walk towards the ward where Dallas was moved last night. I walk into his room and the bed is empty. I guess they downgraded him to a lower security part of the hospital, so I check in with a nurse to find out.

"Zoe Fletcher? Dallas Jensen's mother left a note for you," the nurse reports with a sorry expression. She hands me the letter, and I rip open the envelope. It reads:

Zoe,

There's no easy way to put this: Dallas has been moved to Starlight Children's Residential Home in Wyoming. With permission, the Department of Family Services removed him from my care last night, and he will remain in group home care for the foreseeable future. I'm completely overwhelmed, but also relieved he is safe. I just can't take care of him right now.

I have given permission for you to contact Dallas at Starlight, but for the time being, I cannot handle knowing about his state. He has hurt me beyond forgiveness, and I need some time and space before I can be near him. If you contact him, please don't give me any updates. I trust that you can handle your relationship with Dallas without my interference. I hope that in time, I will be able to see him as my son again.

I have failed both of my sons, and I plan to make things better for my daughter. Aurora and I are going to move away from the city and start our lives over. I hope to be able to give to her what I was unable to provide for Grey and Dallas. You have always seen

Dallas as someone capable of healing, and worthy of love. I wish I were able to see the world through your eyes.

Maybe one day, when the time is right, I will see you again. Thank you for the time you've put into our family. I will be eternally grateful for the three wonderful months we spent with the Dallas we once knew.

- Sarah

I sit down on the couch behind me, trembling as I re-read the letter. I knew things were going to change, but I hadn't anticipated this level of plan alteration. Jeez—Wyoming? He's all alone in another state, far away from everyone he's ever known and loved. I don't know what to make of this. I look at my GPS tracker app, and the dot pulsates in Wyoming. This nightmare is a reality, yet at the same time, it feels like just deserts.

I take my letter and go home.

[I see red.]

The lady lets me out of the room and shows me the kinds of things to do here at this place. I don't understand where I am or why I'm here. I wonder if this is real, or part of my dream? I wonder if I fell asleep in the car on the way back from Discovery Country and I'm stuck in a bad dream about a hospital with crazy people.

Two kids are playing table tennis, and one of the kids lost the game, and he is yelling and screaming about it. A man who works here is trying to calm him down, and he's holding him like when Zoe used to try to kill me. There's a girl who looks like ten or eleven, and she is walking to the window and poking it, and walking back to the couch. She keeps doing that, and I don't know why she still thinks it's fun because it looks boring.

"Dallas," the Lady says to me, "We need to have a little chat about why you're here."

I follow her into this room with soft furnitures like beanbags, and there are colorful paintings on the wall. I thought kids shouldn't paint on walls? It looks like that's allowed here. The Lady who works here has a blue outfit on, looks like the pajamas that doctors wear in hospitals. She has dark brown skin and a necklace with a picture of herself and her name (not a picture of

155

her name, just the writing of her name, which reads like "Alicka"). She sits on the beanbag closer to the door, and I sit down too.

"My name is Alicia, and this place is called Starlight Children's Home. You might not remember what happened at the Discovery Kingdom yesterday, but something very, very dangerous occurred, and you ended up at the hospital. Because you ran away from the doctors, they gave you some medicine that made you fall asleep."

I start to remember, and now I feel really embarrassed that Alicia knows that I ran away. I put my head down and look at the floor. She continues, "When you were asleep, the doctors flew you to Starlight to keep you safe. We are in a state called Wyoming, which is very far away from California."

Alicia shows me a map of America, and the new state is in the middle and down a bit. I am having trouble believing her words, because so many things happened when I was asleep. I think about Discovery Country, and I remember the bunny who was drowning. I put my head down again and cross my arms in front of my body; I am done talking to Alicia.

"I know this is a lot of information, Dallas," Alicia explains, "But you need to understand something before I can stop talking. You're going to live here for a while, with people who can keep you safe. Your mom isn't able to take care of you at the moment, and it might be a while before she visits."

I bury my head in my arms, closing my eyes tight. I mumble into my sweater, "What about Zoe? Can she visit?"

"We have to wait and see," she replies.

"What about Zoe just becomes my new Mom?" I say, muffled through my sweater.

"Honey," Alicia says. "That's not how these things work… I'm sorry."

I lift my head, "Her can take care of me! Her has taken care of me better than my Mom!"

"Right now, you live here," Alicia says, trying to touch my shoulder. I shrug it away and give her an evil look. "Dallas, your only job right now is to get used to Starlight. You don't even have to join in any activities yet, or talk to anyone. It's going to take a while for this to feel like home. I'm sorry, Buddy."

I start to cry, but I don't want her to know. I feel like I am on an island with no people and no food, and I have to wait for someone to rescue me. I don't like how this place smells, I don't know any kids, and the kids that I saw were scary.

I want Zoe.

[I see you.]

I don't know what to do with spare time. It's been so long since I've had a minute to do anything that I love, I have forgotten what it is I'd like to be doing. It's Saturday afternoon, a time slot I usually fill with planning the upcoming week of homeschool. I spent the morning on the phone with my parents, trying to iron out the ideas they have about Dallas which were put into their heads by the media. No, he's not a psycho. Yes, he's in a mental institution. No, I do not have him as a client anymore. Yes, I know I can come back to Santa Cruz if I want. No, I'm not going to do that unless I have a hard time making rent. Yes, I love you both very much, and I appreciate your support.

Ezra has only called me eighteen times in the past day, and I want to return his phone calls, but I worry about Julia overhearing our conversations. I pick up the phone to text him— perhaps it will be easier to meet face-to-face instead of literally talking behind his sister's back.

"Sorry for disappearing. Meet for coffee?" I text.

A reply fires back within seconds, "See you at at 5 pm."

A weight lifts off of my shoulders, a moment which is broken by a yell from the living room.

"ZOE!" Julia screams as I run out to see what's happening. There's a crate with a note on top, and a shaggy red-brown puppy inside.

"Cinnamon!" I yell, while my roommate scratches her head in confusion.

"What the hell is going on?" Julia asks. "Whose dog is this?"

I read the note, and I smile, "Mine."

#

5:00pm

Despite the fact that it's late afternoon, the sun has fled the day and night consumes us like fog rolling in from the sea. Fairy lights clothe the sidewalk trees, flickering as residual raindrops fall intermittently from branch to branch. I walk into the coffee shop holding a large tote bag, trying to look inconspicuous—spotting Ezra on a warmly lit sofa. We greet one another as awkwardly as two people who like each other can possibly manage: a fumbling hug, a kind of high five, a secret handshake not yet mastered.

There is so much discomfort in the genesis of a relationship, filling the space of your beloved with the face of a virtual stranger—even though I've known him all my life. Vulnerability rises, and we're left pretending that none of this matters... we're just two people (and a dog) meeting for coffee. Ezra has a steady, constant way about him, which some could mistake as robotic. I'm sure he feels nervous but has an almost supernatural ability to ignore anxiety. Where I respond with emotion, he acts on practicalities. I've spent a long time ignoring that we may just be complimentary puzzle pieces, built from the same piece of clay, and I want nothing more than to just know for sure.

Unfortunately, that's not the way life works. All we can do is bravely wade through the waters of uncertainty until the mud turns to dry, stable land. The warm light flickers in his kind, hazel eyes and the fortresses I've built so robustly around my heart fall like dominoes. A furry head pokes its nose from my tote and Ezra's eyes light up even more.

"Whose dog is this?" he whispers, laughing.

"I have so much to tell you," I say with a vague, overwhelmed expression.

\#

My finger circles the rim of the plastic latte lid, as Ezra hides Cinnamon in his hoodie. The pup snoozes patiently in his jacket, buying us time to discuss a few of many thousand items on the evening's agenda.

"I don't think you should do this job anymore, Zoe," Ezra says, plainly. I have been a single, independent woman for the best part of the last twenty-six years, and receiving advice like this tends to rub me the wrong way. If I hadn't already come to this conclusion by myself, I would have chewed him out with an assertion of my own choices. That's another thing about Ezra; he's kind, but he's not subtle.

"I know," I say, defeated. "I really loved it, though. You know—parts—of what I did were fulfilling, to both my clients' lives and my own. But other parts of what I did have really messed me up."

"I know," Ezra agrees. "You're on edge about things that most people ignore. I mean, I'm not one to speak about what is emotionally normal, but you never seem fully off-duty."

I have felt this niggling sense of anxiety creeping into my life at an alarming rate, almost exponentially since taking Dallas on as a client. It's a tough pill to swallow: a sense that I'm not as strong as I thought I was, not as resilient as I claimed. There's a feeling of fraud, a sense of defeat, a knowing that I've let people down. I carry the weight of promising what I couldn't complete, like a true bait-and-switch tactic; all I ever wanted to do was help people, but I've spent all my compassion. I guess it's true—you can't give what you don't have.

Ezra says, holding my hand. "Life can be fun, remember that."

All these Friday nights I've spent in sweat pants, too exhausted to go out and act my age. All these Saturdays I've avoided adventures for fear of being behind the eight-ball for the next week—fear of losing control of my organization or my nutrition—the things that seem to be holding my life together with safety pins. I'm a cautious old lady before my time. Ezra takes my hand, as Cinnamon rouses. He leads me out of the cafe, setting the dog on the sidewalk with his leash.

"Where are we going?" I say, with my feathers ruffled.

"Just follow me," he smiles.

"I need to go home and do laundry—and my room is a mess," I say, planting my feet on the sidewalk.

"It's Saturday night, Zoe! It can wait," Ezra reasons, grabbing my hand.

"Tell me where we're going!" I protest, taking my hand back into my own possession. He's trying to control me, and I won't have it.

"No," he laughs. "It's a test. Give up the idea that you have to be in control of everything, and trust me."

I stop dead in my tracks. Ezra keeps walking, and I observe his shoulders hunch with a sigh before he stops to turn around. That's it; he's had enough of me—I knew he'd give up once he realized these kids have broken me.

"No," I assert. "Stop acting like you can make decisions for me."

"I'm not trying to take away your choices, Zoe," he explains. "If anyone is telling you what to do, it's Dallas."

"Real funny, Ezra. Dallas is over a thousand miles away—how could he possibly be dictating my actions?" I snap, seething with rage. I knew it! He sees me for who I am, the sum of my experiences, and knows I'm unable to sustain a relationship. Ezra sees straight through me, and he's right on the edge of giving up.

"Everything you've done in the last few months has been for his benefit. He's your puppeteer, and he sure as hell doesn't deserve to be. You need time to be young and free, and you know it," Ezra assumes. A tear rolls down my face, and I don't even have the strength to wipe it away. I didn't give myself permission to cry, and I'm deeply ashamed of my weakness. I want to turn around and walk home to safety, forgetting I ever tried to be vulnerable. I want to be in the sanctuary of my room, with Cinnamon, alone without company—except—I know Ezra's right. He leans in to hold me, and I make an embarrassing smudge of makeup and snot on his hoodie.

We walk for miles, as Cinnamon leaps with excitement at all these new adventures—if only I could feel so free. I take a long, deep breath, pulling air into lungs that have long been frozen by anxiety. My hand holds Ezra's loosely at first, as my mind races to think of all the ways I plan to justify why setting out on a spontaneous adventure was a bad, terrible, stupid idea. With each step my grip gets a little more firm. My thoughts a little less loud. We arrive at Yerba Buena gardens, beautifully adorned by a warmly lit waterfall. Ezra takes Cinnamon and me through the walkway behind the waterfall, and we watch the aqua cascades from front row seats. It's loud in here—just loud enough to wash out the sound of fear holding me back from a life I should enjoy. We say nothing for a long while, as Ezra pulls me close to his chest. I hear the white noise of the waterfall in one ear, and his beating heart in the other. I've never been this close to complete surrender, and the precipice scares me like never before.

"I want to be your boyfriend," Ezra's voice cuts through the waterfall.

"I want to be your girlfriend," I reply. Then we sit, letting it all sink in.

"So… we're official?" he confirms.

"Yep," I say, leaning into his chest.

CHAPTER TWENTY

Cinnamon Rolls

[I see red.]

Today is the third day I have lived at Starlight, and I have talked to Zoe on zero of these days. I guess she was lying when she said she would like me every day, no matter what. This man with a chin beard (he's called Dr. Martinez) takes me into a room with bean bags and soft blocks for building, and he asks me questions about my life. I have answered zero of his questions.

"I heard you earned a trip to Discovery Country in California a few days ago," he says, pretending he's not questioning me. "That must've been awesome."

I sit in the bean bag with my hood over my face. My knees are under my chin with my arms hugging them tight. No, Martinez, I will not talk to you today. I know that if I sit here for long enough, he will get tired of talking to me, and he will go away. He walks out of the room thirty minutes later, and I listen as he speaks to a different doctor.

"Third day in a row that he's said nothing," Martinez tells.

"He's one of the most severe cases we've got here. Remember when Eli arrived last year? It took three months for him to open up," the other doctor says.

"I'm interested to know why he hasn't asked for his Mom. He keeps asking for Zoe," Martinez interrupts.

"She's his Behavior Specialist, right?" the other doctor replies. "I guess she provided the stability that Mom wasn't able to give."

The doctors say more things, but I can't hear them anymore. I take off my hood and start playing with the blocks. They let me play, so I build, build, build.

[I see you.]

Cinnamon jumps into bed with me and licks my face. He barks and runs around like crazy—it seems we didn't have enough time to make this one completely 'green.' I run a quick internet search for puppy training classes in the area before I stop and look this fluffy little shit in the eyes. I've got the skills; I've got the time—so it's only natural that I should train this dog myself.

I leash him, and we walk to the store to buy some treats, which is the exact time I realize how walking a puppy is a unique kind of madness. Ezra had handled him so well a few nights ago, but today Cinnamon is not obliging. He zigzags across the sidewalk as he pleases, almost tripping me with his wanderlust. His puppy legs don't follow any conventional walking pattern, they each seem to be operating independently. As I watch him, no matter how mad he makes me, I can't help but smile. Cinnamon is obsessed with experiencing all life has to offer, exuding joy to all he meets. I have been thinking about what it would take to be more like Cinnamon, and less caught up in myself.

Little by little, I will learn to let go.

#

[I see red.]

Today is the seventh day that I have lived at Starlight, and I have talked to Zoe zero of these days. Seven days equals one week, even if you start on Saturday, not Monday. I am starting to forget how Zoe looks like and how her voice sounds. The same thing happened when I wasn't allowed to see Rachel from church anymore—I just forgetted her a bit more every day. Now I just wouldn't know her face if I even saw it. I wonder who is taking care of Cinnamon, and I hope that Jacob didn't come back and steal him, too.

Dr. Martinez asks all the questions:

"What happened on the log ride?"

"Who is in your family?"

"Do you believe in ghosts?"

"Do you know why you're here?"

I tell him nothing. Zip, zilch, zero. My life is none of his beeswaxes, because it's for Zoe and me only. We are going to start a new life with Cinnamon, in a new house in San Francisco. We are going to move out of this stinky hospital house, and be a family that never ever breaks apart. We will be the family who eats pancakes, and most importantly a family who never gets any more dads or babies. I stop talking altogether, always thinking about what kinds of toys we'll buy for our new house. I wonder if Zoe and me will have bunk beds, and if she will want the top because she's older. I bet she'll have green sheets because she's the goodest person who ever lived. She will always jump on the trampoline with me every day; she will never go home at 3 pm, and she will help me talk to ghosts.

The more I think about it, the more I know that Zoe will come for me, even if I have to wait a long time for her to get here. Zoe is gooder than Rachel, who never even came looking for me when I was gone. Zoe will rescue me from this house, and she will come take me home.

[I see you.]

The more I think about Ezra, the more butterflies gather in my stomach. I want their wings to calm down, yet I am carried away with their beating. I swallow my pride and my fear, knocking on Julia's bedroom door.

"Jules—are you home?"

"Yeah, come in," she says, "I'm just painting my nails." I open the door to see her sitting with her fingers splayed, waving her hands as red nail polish slowly dries. The room smells of acetone, but she seems not to notice. I sit on the bed with my legs crossed.

"I need to tell you something," I confess.

"You're in love with my brother?" she says, with a half smile. I tilt my head and squint my eyes as if to say, "How did you know that?" She laughs.

"Jeez Zoe, he's been talking about you non-stop for months. I called it when he was like, fifteen," she admits. "He's loved you since forever."

"But he's had other girlfriends," I defensively retort.

"Because you've always dismissed him," she shrugs. "He's a good guy, even if he is my baby brother."

I grab the bottle of nail polish and swipe a coat onto my left hand. I should be relieved that Julia is into the idea, but somehow I feel awkward about being out of the loop, like when you're in middle school, and you find out your friends had a party without you. Cinnamon jumps up onto the bed, and I catch the nail polish before it spills on the blankets.

"So Dallas's Mom didn't want the dog anymore?" Julia says, petting him carefully enough, so her nails don't smudge.

"She doesn't want Dallas anymore either."

"How does someone not want their own son?"

"It's messed up, Jules."

I paint the fingernails on my right hand, as Cinnamon chews the sock on my foot. I realize it's time to get serious about training the dog, so I blow air on my hands to set my nails and get ready to leave Julia's room. Unsurprisingly, I manage to smudge 4/10 nails in the process.

"And yes, I am pretty sure I'm in love with your brother," I stammer, leaving the room like a shy schoolgirl. Julia smiles.

[I see red.]

It's still the seventh day at Starlight, and I am still waiting for Zoe to come to my rescue. Miss Alicia said I didn't need to join in with the activities going on here, but it looks like the other doctors and adults didn't hear when she said that. They keep coming up to me and talking, so I hide under the couch and roll myself into a ball with my knees under my sweater. Turtles hide in their shells, and I pretend to be a turtle. My home is on my back now, too, just like a turtle. Nobody brought me anything from my home, except the sweater I had with me at Discovery Country.

This is my only thing now; I don't want anything new.

[I see you.]

Cinnamon has learned how to sit and follows through 90% of the time. His favorite rewards are these bacon wrapped sticks of mystery meat, which are a huge step up from those disgusting dog treats made out of a bull's man-parts (yes, that's a real thing and yes, they smell like pee).

> *9:05 am—Morning Walk*
> *Antecedent:* *Squirrel runs across the sidewalk.*
> *Behavior:* *C races to catch squirrel, is prevented by leash.*
> *Consequence:* *ZF pauses walk until C is calm.*

When we arrive home, I decide that it's high time this guy learned how to roll over. I begin the process with a hand-over-hand prompt, physically rolling his body before giving him a treat. I do this five times, then introduce a hand gesture with the roll. After five more times, we practice with Cinnamon rolling independently. He masters the trick on the one hundred and fifty-seventh try, as I look outside and see the sunset.

I can't believe I spent my whole day making Cinnamon roll.

[I see red.]

Today is the tenth day that I have lived at Starlight, and I have talked to Zoe zero of these days. When I close my eyes, I see the house that we will own together. It's a tall one, connected to the houses on both sides. We have nice neighbors—one is a music teacher who will teach me every single instrument ever, and the other owns a bounce house company. His backyard is full of bounce houses and so is ours, because we were nice enough to let him store some in our yard. Zoe and I jump from one side of the fence to the next, from 9:00 am to 9:30 am, because it's written on our schedule.

We have a hot dog cart outside our new house, too. Whenever we get hungry, we just go outside and get a fancy hot dog wrapped in bacon, which is called a Mission Style Hot Dog— everyone in San Francisco knows that. We climb on the roof after we eat hot dogs, and Grey comes down from heaven for a visit. We play zombie games on Zoe's phone, and she never ever gives us a time limit. Grey tells us all about heaven, and explains how God's face looks like. Grey says that God is the nicest guy who ever lived, and when you look at God's face it's so bright that you can't see. Grey tells us that God isn't scary, and he's the kind of Dad who stays at your house and never leaves. He's the kind of Dad who plays baseball with us, and teaches his kids how to swim properly so they never drown. Grey says he can't stay on Earth, but he will visit us every day as long as we are on the roof after we eat hot dogs. They're his rules.

Suddenly, someone's hand is on my back. The turtle pokes his head from its shell, and sees Alicia.

"It's lunchtime, Dallas."

"I'm not hungry," I say, going back to my house with Grey and Zoe.

"You have to eat, or we're going to need to give you an operation where we put a feeding tube down your nose. Your body needs food for fuel," she says.

"No!" I scream.

"You want to know how to win this one? Eat. Winners eat food, Buddy," Alicia explains, leaving a plate with a hot dog beside me. She walks away, leaving me to complete the challenge. It's not Mission Style, but I can't expect Wyoming to have San Francisco things. I am hungrier than ever, because I haven't eaten in lots of days. I reach out for the bun, and take a quick bite. I tuck my head back into my sweater like a turtle, then poke it out for the next bite. By the end of the hot dog, I walk out of the room to find Alicia.

"Can I have more hot dogs?" I whisper in her ear.

She smiles, "Of course you can!"

I sit down at the table with Alicia and one other crazy kid. My hood is over my face, but at least I'm out of bed.

"Dallas, this is Louis," she says, pointing to the stupid nutso kid. He's flapping his hands and goes to grab my fork.

"No!" I yell, "You don't even need forks for hot dogs!"

Alicia swipes the forks, and puts them in her pocket. "You're right Dallas—we don't need any silverware, Louis."

I close my hood over my face so that there's a hole only for my mouth, and it's the size of a hot dog. This turtle only eats hot dogs, but dreams in his head about climbing on the roof with his new Mom, to visit with his ghosty brother.

[I see you.]

"Have you made any contact with Dallas yet?" Ezra asks.

I shake my head, "I will... but not yet."

I sip cola through the straw of a supersize cup, as we wait for our movie to start. It's been years since I have had soda, and the carbonation burns my tongue. I reach into a bag of pick 'n mix candy and pull out a sour gummy worm. I haven't had this much sugar for a long, long time.

"I can't believe I'm eating these," I laugh. "We have gum, right? For straight after the candy? I can't afford a dentist right now, and these guys are just cavities in the making. Not to mention—"

Ezra places a hand over my mouth, "Just enjoy the moment."

I make eye contact with him to establish dominance, and shove a handful of candy into my mouth. I laugh with my mouth full, regretting the calories ingested, but proving that I can seize the day.

"What are you doing for Thanksgiving?" Ezra asks.

"No plans," I shrug.

"Will you come spend it with my family?" he stammers.

"Sure," I smile, knowing that my Mom is going to die if I go to Santa Cruz without seeing her. "We might need to visit my parents for a minute, though."

"You're asking me to meet your parents? So soon!" Ezra jokes, considering he's known them since the day he was born. I elbow him in the side, and he puts his arm around me as the lights dim.

And so, the movie begins.

CHAPTER TWENTY-ONE

What Are You Thankful For?

[I see red.]

Today is the nineteenth day that I have lived at Starlight, and I have talked to Zoe zero of these days. Today is also what's called Thanksgiving, where people eat turkeys and say thank you to guys with belts on their hats. Zoe and me would be eating turkey on the roof instead of hot dogs, and I would say a BIG thank you to God for letting Grey visit us every single day. Grey growed up in heaven, and now he's nine, and he has big boy teeth. I would show him how my grown up teeth are growing too, and we can be twins, but born on different days. I am older than he ever was on Earth, but I'm pretty sure he's still the big brother. You don't stop growing when you get to heaven, except when you're old. Then you have to stop growing, or you'll die of being old when you're already dead, and dying only happens one time. I think Grey will get twenty-five and just stay that many.

I am outside on the trampoline in my mind, but at Starlight in real life. Alicia taps me on the shoulder.

"Dallas," she says. "It's time for the special Thanksgiving Dinner."

"Dinner time is six," I say through my hood.

"Thanksgiving is a weird kind of dinner. It's like dinner food at snack time," she explains. "Did you ever have Thanksgiving with your Mom?"

I nod my head.

"What kinds of things did your family do?"

I shrug, "I don't remember."

"I wonder if you had turkey?"

I poke my head from my sweater, and say, "Duh. Everybody has turkey on Thanksgiving."

"That's not true," Alicia replies. I sit up and look at her face.

"Poke out your tongue," I demand.

She laughs, "Why?"

"Because if you're lying, your tongue will be black—or forked like a snake!"

"Who told you these things?" she giggles, and pokes out her tongue. I take a very long look at it, and it's pink. Also, it is not forked, it's only normal.

"OK, so who doesn't eat turkey on Thanksgiving?" I ask, still a bit suspicious.

"Vegetarians," Alicia smiles.

"That makes sense," I agree. "Are you a vegetarian?"

"No, but I used to be."

"Well, what did you eat on Thanksgiving?"

"Enchiladas," she says. I make a face with one eyebrow higher than the other, and then we start laughing. I am laughing so much that I almost pee on myself.

"Oh, Dallas," she says. "I don't think I've ever seen you laugh."

Uh-oh. If I act happy, does that mean they'll keep me here because they think I like it? I throw my hood back over my face and run to the couch. I slide myself between the wall and the back of the couch where nobody can ever find me. I close my eyes and get Grey down from heaven as fast as I can.

"GREY!" I yell in my imagination.

"Dallas!" him says and squeezes me so tight he picks me up.

"Don't leave me again," I say. "I don't like the Earth without you."

Alicia pulls the couch away from the wall. "Dallas?"

"GO AWAY!" I scream.

"I don't understand what made you upset," she tells me. "Can you help me know what's wrong so I can say sorry?"

"I DON'T LIKE YOU. YOU'RE MAKING MY LIFE WORSER!" I yell so loudly. Alicia sits on the couch and waits.

"We can talk when you're calm, Buddy," she says.

"YOU. AREN'T. ZOE!" I scream. "STOP TRYING TO BE ZOE!"

I cry so much that my tears and snot go through my hood and onto my hands. As fast as I can, I run into my imagination, so Grey doesn't go back to heaven before I say goodbye. When I get to the roof I'm all by myself again—even Zoe is gone. I can't find my people, even in my mind I am all alone. I made Grey die; I am bad, I made my parents stop loving me. I did this to my own self.

[I see you.]

We set out at 9 am, with hopes to reach Santa Cruz by noon. Ordinarily, we can make the trip home in less than two hours, but there's usually heavy traffic on Thanksgiving. I just hope it's not too long for Cinnamon to hold his many bodily fluids on the inside—he's still working on his ability to ride in cars without accidents. Ezra smiles like the Cheshire Cat as his perfectly crafted playlist unfolds, revealing a string of songs he's been saving for the drive. Each one is ever-so-subtly telling me that he's madly in love, and I blush a little more with each new track.

"Your parents know I'm coming, right?" I ask.

Ezra laughs, "Not unless Julia blabbed."

"What?" I yell, punching him jovially on the shoulder. "That's so awkward. You're supposed to RSVP for guests. Basic social skill, Ezra Holmes."

"I do this kind of thing all the time, my parents expect it," he justifies. "Once I brought a friend to my cousin's wedding without RSVP-ing a plus one. We pulled up a chair to the bridal table."

Oh. My. Word. I bury my face in my hands, "Ezra! That's so awkward."

"Yeah, he's in jail now," he shrugs. I want to laugh, but I don't know if it's appropriate. Ezra is an unusual mix of oblivion and fun: two things I severely lack. He holds my hand and kisses it.

[I see red.]

I poke my head above the couch and Alicia is still there.

"Why you didn't leave me alone?"

"I was waiting for you."

"Don't wait for me," I sniff. "Eat the turkey."

"I don't want turkey without you," she says, and she sounds more like Zoe with every word.

"Then starve," I whisper.

"Bud, that food tube operation will still happen if you give up eating. It's not a punishment; it's just a consequence. Without food, you'll get very sick. Look at how your bones stick out of your chest."

I look at my ribs, and they really poke out too much.

"You could play the guitar on those ribs, boy," she says with a straight face. I try not to laugh, but I do... then I start playing air guitar on my ribs. She laughs, and I laugh too.

"I didn't know how skinny I got," I say, looking at my arms and legs what are just like sticks now. I look like a skeleton with skin on.

"If you want to be a winner, you need muscles. You get muscles from protein like turkey," Alicia says. I look at her with a suspicious face.

"Are you real?" I say, and she nods. Then I agree, "I'll eat, as long as it's just you and me."

Alicia holds out her hand, and I don't take it. I can't make myself be close to her because she's not my person. I don't look at her face, but I give her my pinky instead, and she loops it in hers. We walk to the kitchen to get turkey and bring our plates outside. We sit together in the cold outside air, looking over the huge, huge Earth with snowy mountains. I forgot the name of this land, which is so big, and we are so small.

"Alicia," I say. "What land are we in?"

"Starlight?" she replies.

"No, what land?"

"Lovell?"

"No... like California is my land. What land is this?"

"Wyoming."

172

Wyoming and the whole wide world is so big, and we are just so small. Maybe I am only a little bit alone today. Maybe Alicia is nice. Maybe I need to eat the whole turkey so my ribs go away and my muscles get big. I finish the food on my plate, and Alicia has only taken a couple of bites.

"Can I get more food?"

"Sure," she says, as we go inside together. She leaves her plate outside, and we pile more things on mine.

"Come on!" I say. "Let's go back to our picnic."

I hold my hand out, and Alicia takes it. For a second, I forget that she isn't Zoe. I forget that Zoe left me here in Wyoming land. I forget that I am absolutely scared of being a little kid who is all alone in a weird land, with hundreds of weird kids who pee the bed.

"How many are you?" I ask.

"What do you mean?" she says.

"How many candles on your cake?"

"Oh, twenty-three."

Twenty-three is less than twenty-six, which is how many candles Zoe has. There are a lot of sames, and a lot of differents about Zoe and Alicia. For sames, them both are very patient without yelling. For differents, their hairstyles are not alike. Zoe's hairdo is like brown with some bangs on her face, and mostly, all her other hair is rolled into a ball on top of her head. Alicia's hairdo is like a thousand little ropes, and her always wears it hanging down.

"I almost have seven candles," I tell her.

"Ooh, did you know that seven is a lucky number?" Alicia says.

I shake my head. It seems a little less lucky when I remember I will live at this land for the entire year that I will be seven.

"When's your birthday?" she asks.

"February 28th," I tell.

"So you're six and three quarters," Alicia figures out. "You can stop telling people you're six and a half now. You've grown up since six and a half; you're becoming a whole new guy."

I wonder about what she's said. I wonder if I change being who I am, will Grey still recognize me when I get to heaven? If I let Alicia be my Zoe, then if Zoe comes back, she won't be my new mom if I replaced her. Zoe doesn't deserve me to be nice to her. She made me come to this land, and she left me here. I want to be mean to her by being nice to Alicia. I reach out my arms and hug Alicia, and as I do, I feel like I have been punched in the stomach.

I scream and run back to my bed. Alicia's plate flips over and turkey flies everywhere, as not-Zoe runs behind me.

"Wait! Dallas!" she yells.

I get to my bed first and roll my body into a ball, tucked into my sweater. I pull the blankets over my head and cry a loud, loud cry.

"Dallas," she says. "I'm right here for you. Let's talk when you're calm."

"NO! NO! NO!" I yell from under my hood, under the sheets, under the blankets.

Alicia says nothing; she just sits on the end of the bed. I kick my legs so she'll get off MY bed, off MY sheets, off MY land. She sits beside the bed and waits. I pull the sheets down and look at her stupid face.

"You're not Zoe!" I scream.

"I know," she nods. "Zoe is your favorite."

"No! She is the worst. She put me in here! Zoe bringed me in a helicopter and leaved me in a weird house where nobody likes me!"

"Can I tell you something?" she says.

"NO!" I yell, before wondering what she wants to say. Alicia says nothing, she just waits. She doesn't look sad or annoyed, and she's more patienter even than Zoe. "Fine! Tell me something."

"Zoe didn't bring you here."

"Well, for your big fat information, who else could have bringed me? I was at Discovery Country, then I was at a hospital and they sleeped me with medicine, and next minute I have no home or family."

"It wasn't Zoe."

"Who was it then? The boogeyman? Him isn't even REAL, Alicia."

She looks mad and embarrassed. She lets me yell at her, but she is having a bad time being able to tell me who bringed me here. "Your Mom."

"What?"

My stomach hurts again. Moms don't send their kids away. Moms don't give away their kids. Kids aren't like presents—families are supposed to be together forever.

"I wasn't supposed to tell you that," Alicia tells me, as she looks behind her shoulder. "Don't blame Zoe. Don't blame your Mom either—I don't think you're able to understand why she sent you here. She didn't have a lot of choices."

"Why she didn't have a choice? Moms should keep their kids!"

"Can I treat you like a seven-year-old for a minute?"

"Yeah," I say, with my arms crossed and chest puffed out.

"Your Mom wants you to be safe. She isn't able to keep you safe anymore. So her choice to have you live here was made so that you would live a long, meaningful life. You can grow into an amazing, incredible man—you know how I know that?"

I shake my head, with my arms crossed tightly over my chest.

"Because you're like an acorn," she says.

"You making zero sense," I mumble with closed angry teeth.

"Hear me out," Alicia says. "See those trees out the windows? They're oaks. Do you know how oaks are made?"

"What is this relevant?" I yell, because I learned the word 'relevant' from Zoe.

"Get on my back," she says, and I go like a piggy back. She brings me outside and gets something off the ground. It's about an inch big, round and pointy with a little brown hat. She sets me on the ground.

"Acorns become oaks," Alicia explains.

"No way," I reply.

"From little things, big things grow. Seeds have to break before they become big trees, Dallas. You can take your acorn of a

175

life and throw it in the dirt, or you can dig that same dirt and plant the acorn deep in the ground. You can take care of it, or you can let it die. The choice is yours."

"What if I already breaked but I'm not planted?"

"Then let's get a shovel, some fertilizer, and water. You are at Starlight so you can grow, and I'm here to help you."

I hold the acorn tightly in my hand, and I don't know if I should plant it or throw it in Alicia's stupid pretty face. I think for a minute and put it in the pocket of my cargo shorts. I walk back to the house, and Alicia follows.

[I see you.]

"Zoe! What a surprise!"

"Hi, Mrs. Holmes!" I stammer, red-faced. Suddenly I'm twelve years old again, except this time I'm in love with Mrs. Holmes's baby boy. My stomach churns.

"Oh, please—call me Janelle," she insists. "And what a sweet little dog!"

"Mom," Ezra announces without making eye contact. "Zoe is my girlfriend, and she's having Thanksgiving with us."

Janelle looks flabbergasted, as Ezra takes my hand and barges inside like nothing consequential has occurred. I'm mortified listening to Janelle process the news with her husband, Mr. Holmes (who I might be able to call by his first name, too. Everything is happening so fast.) Julia is outside laughing at her parents.

"Well, he's always had a soft spot for Zoe," Janelle whispers.

"I never thought she'd go for him though," Mr. Holmes replies. "I've never seen a girl less interested in a guy."

"Kevin, she was seventeen last time you saw them in the same room for any substantial period of time," Janelle reasons.

"Why didn't he tell us she was coming?" Mr. Kevin Holmes asks.

"Does Ezra ever tell us anything? Remember that odd fellow he brought to Kyle's wedding?" she poses. 'Kevin' shrugs and they walk inside. Julia records the entire thing on her cell phone for later use.

#

As we down the last morsels of Pecan Pie, the family gets ready to loosen their belts and watch football in a horizontal position. I offer to help Mrs.—I mean Janelle—to clean up, but she kindly refuses my gesture. Julia is swiftly roped into the kitchen to consolidate leftovers into plastic containers and put cling wrap atop the food on plates. She throws me a stare that says, "How did you get out of this so easily?"

I try to help, but Janelle shoos me away like a fly. Ezra summons me instead, taking me outside with Cinnamon on a leash. We walk around his parents' suburban beachside neighborhood, all the way down to the boardwalk. The Pacific Ocean sings its calming lullaby with every wave crashing on the shore like clockwork. The dusky sun sets behind the cluster of amusement park rides, with glimmers of gold shining through rollercoaster beams. There are faint ghosts of children's laughter from the day that has passed, as families make their way into their cozy homes. The echo of sea lions' barking sends Cinnamon into a tailspin, and I suddenly remember Dallas.

"You're quiet," Ezra states.

I confess. "I wonder what Dallas is doing today. Holidays must be hard without family."

"Speaking of which—we should head back soon so we can go visit your parents," he justifies. I worry he's missed the reason I mentioned Dallas. I worry that my vulnerability wasn't well received, and that Ezra has no idea how much the Dallas issue is eating me. I'm racked with guilt that my past actions put Dallas in an asylum and my current actions are keeping him there. I'm deathly afraid that in trying to give Dallas a normal life, I took it all away. Ezra seems happy enough to just change the subject.

"Yeah, let's head back," I say, as we spend the night with my parents, talking about anything but Dallas.

(Oh, and just so you know—my parents knew Ezra was coming over. I did a little thing called telling them in advance. They tried not to act excited, but they have loved Ezra since the day he was born.)

CHAPTER TWENTY-TWO

Because of Dallas

[I see red.]

Today is the twenty-first day that I have lived at Starlight, and I have talked to Zoe zero of these days. Twenty-one days is three weeks, and that is almost a month. I haven't talked to Dr. Martinez, and I haven't talked to any of the weird kids here (except for that time stupid Louis took my stupid fork). Sometimes these kids scream for no reason, and most of the days someone runs away, but they don't get very far. I haven't runned away yet.

I talk to Alicia because she seems nice to me every single day. Sometimes her tells me stupid things I don't want to hear, but mostly she is right. I asked her why she only hangs out with me, and she said that it's her job, just like it was Zoe's job. A job means that people go to work, and then they get money for doing things, so today I found out that the only people who like me are paid to like me.

Nobody paid my mom.

[I see you.]

I walk to my dresser and for the first time in almost a month, I take out the note that Dallas's Mom gave to me. I read it again, this time with tears rolling down my cheeks. I can't believe I have gone this long without speaking to him; I can't believe I have allowed him to feel abandoned by me. I haven't given this child the healing he deserves, I haven't followed through with my promise.

"I like you every day, no matter what," rings in my ears. It was a lie. I didn't like him when he ran out onto traffic. I didn't like him when he stabbed me with a pencil. I didn't like him when he risked both of our lives on the roof at school. I haven't liked him since he got off a ride in the dark, threw rocks at a family, destroyed animatronics, climbed on the roof and was rescued by a helicopter. I haven't felt a single thing for him since the day after the event, when the shock had worn off, and I realized that he knew better than do pull that kind of shit. It's easier to feel nothing than to dwell in anger, so that's what I've done.

Because of Dallas, I'm unemployed.

Because of Dallas, I'm on prescription meds to calm me down.

Because of Dallas, I haven't slept well in a month.

Because of Dallas, I stare at the wall far more than anybody should.

I wonder what kind of responsibility I have towards him now that the dust has settled. I wonder if I'm ready to start looking for new jobs, especially since my emergency financial funds are drying up at a rapid pace. My parents slipped some money into my bank account while I wasn't looking, and I was mortified and grateful at the same time. I wish there was a word for that feeling—Mortiful? Gratefied?

I'm mad as hell at Dallas for what he has done to me, and I'm mad at myself for letting it happen. I've never felt such depths of hatred for another person, especially since I've built my life on a belief that I will never hate another soul as long as I live. I feel like I'm stranded on a desert island with the uncomfortable realization that I don't have the integrity I thought I possessed all these years. There's an elephant on the island, and while I ignore it, he tramples over the very trees that may just save my life.

[I see red.]

Today is the twenty-third day that I have lived at Starlight, and I have talked to Zoe zero of these days. I wake up in my bed, in a room I share with Matthew. He is eight candles, and sometimes he is nice, but sometimes he is mean. That's the thing about the kids at this home—I never really know how they're going to be each day. One time they yell, next time they whisper, and after that they just throw things.

Alicia comes to my room at 8:30am (long hand on the six, short hand between eight and nine) and tells me it's time to go to Dr. Stupid Martinez.

"Did you eat your breakfast?" she asks. I shake my head, and go back under the covers. "Wake up time was an hour ago, Dallas. What have you been doing all this time?"

"Matthew did a meltdown," I admit, through the blankets. "I stayed in bed until he calmed down."

Alicia walks over to the door, where a chart hangs on a clipboard. Matthew's "Alicia," wrote on it this morning about the meltdown. My Alicia (the real Alicia) reads the chart and hangs it back up. She looks surprised.

"OK, Mister. You get a hall pass this time—now get outta bed," she tells me in a pretend bossy voice. "What are you going to wear today?"

I open my drawers, and wear what I always wear—cargo shorts and a black t-shirt. These are the best clothes, because pockets are never not useful. All of my black shirts are a bit different, with all kinds of words and pictures on them. Today I choose a black one with a green dog on it, because he reminds me of Ramsay. Alicia takes me to the dining room, where all the other kids have finished eating.

"What are you going to have?"

"Aren't you going to make it for me?" I ask, confused.

Alicia shakes her head, "I'll help you if you need it, but I won't do it for you."

"You know I used to make all my foods? But they were always six chicken nuggets. Then Zoe helped me make other foods so I could be strong and healthy," I explain. I look at the foods at Starlight, and I know I would have hated all of them before Zoe.

Alicia smiles big and says, "It sounds like Zoe helped you grow into the awesome guy you are today."

"I'm not awesome," I remind her. "If I am even a little bit good, it's because of Zoe."

Because of Zoe, I am eating yogurt and berries for breakfast.

Because of Zoe, I know how to tell the time.

Because of Zoe, I can read books and do counting.

Because of Zoe, I remember what it's like to have someone say, "I like you."

I gulp down some yogurt, as Alicia tells me that it's full of these things called protein and calcium. I tell her how berries have different tastes when they are fresh, frozen, or dried. I put my bowl in the place where dirty bowls go, and the spoon in the place where dirty spoons go. Alicia puts me on her back, and we sing something silly as we go to Dr. Martinez's room.

When she sets me on the floor, I zip my mouth closed. I absolutely will not talk to Dr. Stupid. Whatever he wants to talk about is none of his business, and I have zero space in my heart for a grown up man to know my feelings. My dad never listened to my feelings, him just ran away to make a new family. Jacob told all of my feelings to shut up. Dr. Stupid is not allowed to know my feelings.

They are mine to me.

[I see you.]

Wherever I go, there I am. I'm running away from Dallas as fast as he is catching up with me. Whenever I close my eyes, there he is: on the edge of the building, on the roof of the ride, with a smoking gun in his hands. Truth and fiction are as jumbled as ever, and I know what it is that I need to do in order to have some semblance of peace in my life; yet, I am unsure as to whether or not I have the strength to do it.

I open my computer to search for the contact details of Starlight Children's Residential Home. Suddenly, I see images of kids in their photo gallery—images of the bedrooms and scenery outside. I close the tab, and close my laptop. It's too much to bear—the idea of reconciliation with someone who ruined me like this. He might be six-years-old, but he's responsible for so much of my gradual descent into madness. I spend too much time wondering if I am, in fact, responsible for his state of mind.

Ezra rings the doorbell at 6 pm, and finds me in sweatpants with a messy bun.

"Sorry," I say. Without speaking, he heads over to my wardrobe and chooses me an outfit. He lays it on the bed and smiles.

"I'll wait here while you go take a shower," he orders, kindly.

"Are you saying I stink?" I snap.

"You look like shit, Zoe," he smiles. "You're pretty, but you look like shit."

I grab my robe and storm off to the bathroom. Friggin' Ezra.

[I see red.]

"Dallas, it's almost been a month," Dr. Stupid reminds me. "I want to get to know you, but conversation is a two-way street. In order for us to have a relationship, you need to talk."

"Oh, but Dr. Stupid," I think to myself, "My lips have been zipped closed, and I threw away the key. It's not my fault that I can't speak to you."

The Dr. walks to the door and waves to Alicia who is sitting outside. He talks to her for a second or three, and then she comes into the room as well.

"Dallas," she says, "Is it OK with you if I attend your session?"

I don't say anything, because my lip zipper is stopping me from talking. Everybody knows that. So, I just lay on the couch and close my eyes, because it's about time I climbed on the roof with Zoe to hang out with Grey. Today, Zoe's face looks a bit less like Zoe and a little more like Alicia. In a flash, I open my eyes and start kicking Alicia's body so she'll get the heck out of my personal space, because she is not my Zoe. I know, with all of my heart, that Zoe will come back for me, and when she comes, I can't have an Alicia. There's no Alicia in our new plan, with our new house in San Francisco, in our play dates with ghosts. I kick Alicia a thousand more times because she's the dumbest person ever.

Dr. Martinez grabs my feet and holds them like he wants to kill me, and Alicia quickly goes outside the room. I punch Dr. Stupid in the face, and Alicia gets some other adults to hold me. I shouldn't be here! I shouldn't be in this house with all these crazy kids! I don't belong here, Zoe! I belong with you in a real house, with hot dogs and pancakes!

Matthew's version of Alicia sees my Alicia and hugs her. My Alicia is crying like a stupid baby, and Matthew's Alicia says, "I'm sorry, I know it's been a rough week."

"It's like one step forward, two steps back," the real Alicia says. "He just snaps sometimes, and I have no idea why. It's almost like a seizure—completely out of his control."

Fake Alicia replies, "He was given to you because you can handle him. He's the youngest one here, and probably the most severe case of all sixty of these kids. He's the only kid on your caseload for the foreseeable future because the boss believes you can crack his shell."

"I'm trying," real Alicia sniffs. "I just don't know how long I can take it."

"He's got Reactive Attachment Disorder, right?" the fake one says. "He's trying to push you away, and the minute he thinks he's won, his self-esteem plummets back down to what he thinks he deserves. That is, nothing and no-one. Love on him every single day; that's how you affect change."

Real Alicia blows her nose into a tissue and walks away for a while. She returns to the room where I am sitting with Dr. Stupid. The two other staff members have left the room since I stopped kicking and hitting. Alicia sits beside me, saying nothing. I hold my hand out to her, and she takes it without any angriness. The three of us silently sit in the room together from the time the long hand is on the ten until it goes around to the twelve and the short hand is directly on the nine.

[I see you.]

I am beyond grateful to have Ezra in my life at this time. My lack of motivation is met with an almost drill sergeant approach to spontaneity, and moping is just not permitted on the drill sergeant's watch.

"Get dressed," he says. "We're going out."

"Where?" I whine.

"Does it matter?" he snaps. "You just need to be useful."

I could be offended at his approach, but instead, I reluctantly put on real clothes and twirl my hair into a fresher,

183

albeit messy, bun. We walk Cinnamon to the local coffee house, where I order an almond latte and sit down. Ezra asks for an iced vanilla cold brew, then adds, "Do you guys have any jobs going?"

"I thought you worked for a startup?" the barista responds. Clearly Ezra spends a lot of time here.

"No, I'm asking for my girlfriend," he says, beckoning me to the register to meet the barista.

"Hi," I participate awkwardly, elbowing Ezra in the side. "I'm Zoe."

"Ed," he responds. "Have you got any experience making coffee?"

"Unfortunately no," I shrug. "I've spent the last four years as a Behavior Specialist."

"Oh, like that girl on the news a couple of weeks ago. With that kid who climbed on top of that ride... Log Nation!" Ed laughs. Ezra's eyes grow wide as he meets Ed's gaze, pretending to cut his throat with his hand.

"Yep," I say, looking down. "Just like that girl."

"Oh, shit. Sorry. I—uh- didn't realize," Ed backtracks. "Anyway, we prefer hiring people without experience. So, if you're interested, can you start next week?"

"Don't you need like, a resume or something?" I mutter. Everything is happening so fast, and five minutes ago I never knew I wanted to work in a coffee shop, but apparently that's what I'm about to do. With big fat thanks to Ezra and his big fat mouth.

"You're clearly, somewhat, qualified for the job— so I think a trial would work better than a resume," Ed reasons. "See you Monday?"

"See you in two days," I agree, before punching Ezra in the arm and sitting in a cozy booth. He raises his coffee cup to clink against mine.

"To your new job," he says, with a cheeky grin. I'm extremely uncomfortable.

[I see red.]

Today is the thirtieth day that I have lived at Starlight, and I have talked to Zoe zero of these days.

I think she has forgotten about me. It's like Rachel all over again.

CHAPTER TWENTY-THREE

Zero Day Zoe

[I see you.]

I pick up the phone and dial the number for Starlight Children's Home. It rings twice, and I hang up straight away before anyone knows I tried. I stare at the wall, again. Cinnamon snuggles beside me on the couch. The Christmas tree sparkles as I look at the meticulous decorations Julia made, knowing if it were up to me, there would simply be a banner on the wall that says, "IT IS CHRISTMAS."

I wonder what the holidays look like in a Children's home. I wonder if all the kids go back to their parents, and then there's ones like Dallas who can't go home because they are no longer welcome. The thought that my Buddy doesn't have a home suckerpunches me in the face, and I feel like a coward for exacting retribution by ignoring him. All of the hope I once had for this boy seems to be marred by the supposed human need for revenge. I am a shitty person, and this I know very well.

My phone buzzes, and I'm terrified someone from Starlight somehow called me back. I look at the screen, and it's not the children's home. It's a message from Ezra.

"Dinner at seven. Meet at your house."

I don't deserve Ezra.

[I see red.]

Today is the forty-third day that I have lived at Starlight, and I have talked to Zoe zero of these days. I am in my session

185

with Dr. Martinez, and he has decided to just sit beside me until I'm ready to talk. He hasn't won in forty-three days. Alicia sits beside me and I let her, because I am starting to realize that Zoe has forgotten about me. I don't have a chance at having a new Mom now, so I can forget about the idea of living in a big house with Zoe and ghosty Grey.

A lady who usually works at a desk knocks on the door, and Dr. Martinez jumps at the chance to talk to a person who answers his questions, instead of me, who ignores him. She talks to him, and says that there is someone on the phone who wants to speak to him.

"OK Dallas, we're done for today," he sighs, and walks out the room. He looks back and yells, "Maybe you'll talk tomorrow."

I say nothing, but I pull my head out of my hood and start playing with the blocks again. It's Christmas time next week, so I decide to build a tree and some presents underneath it. After sessions I can build for as long as I like, and nobody ever interrupts me, except for dinner time. Dr. Martinez grabs the phone, and I watch his face get happy when he talks to the person. Maybe it's his wife or Mom?

"I'm so glad you decided to call," he says. "I'm having no luck getting through to him. He's taken to his direct support professional, Alicia, but about once a day he just loses control of himself. We're not sure what triggers the outbursts... he just seems to spend a lot of the day in his head. And he hasn't spoken a word to me yet, and it's almost been six weeks."

[I see you.]

"What..." I stumble, "What do you need from me?"

"I know this is a huge ask, but we were wondering if you'd be able to visit?" Dr. Martinez replies. Damn right, it's a huge ask. I think for a minute about my dwindling financial situation, my brand new job, and the reason I find myself penniless with a dog to feed. I won't give Dallas the power to run through my life like a bull in a china shop—not again. My palms are sweaty, and I contemplate hanging up the phone. I am so angry—jeez—the nerve of this guy. Expecting me to drop everything and arrive on Dallas's whim.

Just then, the puppy snuggles into my lap. He fits just about anywhere, and has a God-given knack of making situations feel better. Then, I look at sweet Cinnamon, and remember the day he came home, and how happy he made Dallas. I wonder if I could go with Cinnamon's help. I think about all that Christmas means to me, and somehow I get caught up in stupid holiday goodwill.

"Zoe—are you still there?" asks the doctor.

"Would it be OK if I brought his dog with me?" I ask, regretting the words as they fall out of my mouth. I don't want to go to East-Jesus-Nowhere Wyoming to see the demon child hellbent on ruining my sanity. I really friggin' don't. I need this trip as much as I need a punch in the face.

"I mean, how big is the dog?" he asks.

I size up the puppy in front of me, "Less than twenty pounds, more than ten."

"As long as he has all his vaccinations, I can't see a problem with that," Dr Martinez agrees. "How soon can you get here?"

Awkward. There's about twenty-five bucks in my bank account until Friday.

"Well, I've got to be honest with you—educating Dallas was my full time job. With him in Wyoming, I'm not making any money at the moment. It's embarrassing to admit," I pause, "But I can't afford to come right away."

"We have grant money for this kind of thing, Zoe," the doctor assures me. "The foundation will cover your costs. I know he's put you through a lot—at least I've read bits and pieces from intake forms his mom filled out pretty hastily. I want to know everything from your perspective. I don't want to put undue pressure on you, but I think he needs you in order to start the healing process."

No pressure at all, thanks Dr. Stupid Ramirez. Martinez? I don't remember. Jeez, I can't handle all this therapist bullshit right now. Maybe he's beyond fixing? Ever thought about that, Doctor Grant Money?

"What about his mom?" I reply, probably a little too snarkily.

"She's…" he pauses, "Not in a good place."

"What about Dallas's little sister?" I ask, with my heart beating out of my chest.

"The baby has gone to live with a relative," he replies.

I ask, against my better judgement, "Not the dad?"

Ramirez/Martinez clears his throat, "No, not the dad."

Thank God.

My heart has hardened like dried clay, and Ramirez/Martinez is trying to plant trees. He can push all he likes, but there's no give in the soil. No matter how hard he pokes, there's nothing but dust. I've always thought of myself as someone who is slow to anger and quick to forgive, someone who could put aside offense for another's benefit—especially the benefit of a child. But here I am looking at a mirror, staring into the eyes of a hypocrite. I know that the worst punishment Dallas can receive is my silence, but I'm too selfish to speak. Am I secretly, sadistically enjoying my win?

"How soon can you come?" he repeats.

"Not before Christmas," I whine, as though it's a knee jerk reaction. This was all set to be my first Christmas with Ezra, my first real kiss under the mistletoe, my first time bringing him home to my family. No, Dallas, you're not taking this away from me. The hairs on the back of my neck begin to stand on end, as I realize just how mad this is making me. If I thought I was quick to forgive people, then I thought wrong. The woman I once thought I was is not the woman who is reacting with such volatility right now. Dallas Jensen has a way of creeping back into my life like an octopus escaping from a jar—spinelessly, silently, and rapidly.

"I'm going to have to think about all this," I reply. "I'll call you back."

I hang up the phone, with my stomach in knots. I catch myself biting the inside of my lip, and grab a piece of gum instead. Scrunching up the wrapper, I realize I've chewed a full pack before eight in the morning. Reaching for a black and white striped shirt and some black jeans, I dress myself for my third shift at the coffee house. Peering at my reflection in the bathroom mirror, I see the face of someone twice my age. I notice, to my horror, that three gray hairs have sprouted in my mane of dark brown hair, and I call each of the wiry old hairs by name—DALLAS JEDIDIAH JENSEN.

For Pete's sake! I'm only twenty-six, I'm not ready for this kind of milestone.

[I see red.]

Today is the forty-fourth day that I have lived at Starlight, and I have talked to Zoe zero of these days. I wake up, I eat, I don't talk in sessions, I play by myself, I eat, I don't talk in another session, I play by myself again, I eat, I shower, I read, I go to bed. That is how forty-four days have gone, and the only people I talk to are Alicia, Grey, and God.

I tell Grey about the weird kids here, and how they get into all kinds of fights together. They yell, and if they punch, they aren't allowed to watch TV for a week. I told Grey if he were on the Earth I wouldn't bring him here, because he doesn't deserve to be at a kid jail. I know it's not a jail with bars and orange outfits, but I have decided that's kind of what this place is. Starlight is a place where parents put kids when they're too naughty to live in normal houses. Grey would never have done anything to end up here.

I tell God about my feelings, and I squeeze his hand, even though it's invisible. God tells me he's here, so I believe Him. Another thing about God is that it is Christmas in five days time, and that means God is getting ready to have a baby. God's baby name was Jesus, and he's the one who died on Easter, but also is still alive. People think it's hard to figure out God and Jesus, but I don't need anyone to explain it all to me. I talked to God and he explained it already, and he told me that I would be OK. Everything is going to be OK.

This Christmas I have a different kind of list. I started to write a normal Christmas list all those times ago when I lived at San Francisco, but I don't want anything like that anymore. I want Zoe to come get me, and be my new mom. When I close my eyes I can see her now, walking into Starlight and walking out these locked gates, holding my hand. Even if the part where Grey is a ghost is fake, at least I can have Zoe back. That's definitely real. I will do anything to get my Zoe back, I really will.

We will have our own kind of Christmas next year, far away from the snowy land of Wyoming.

[I see you.]

"I think you should go," Ezra says, nonchalantly. I can't believe him sometimes—it's like he has no idea what it's like to live with my emotions. Doesn't he know how I am wrestling with this? Doesn't he see how complicated this is? He looks frustrated, and I feel like he's done talking about Dallas. It's almost like he's jealous.

"Zoe," he adds, "You're overthinking. The coffee house will be fine without you, and if they're not, who cares? You're too worried about what other people think."

"It's Dallas I don't want to see," I snap. "The exact person I would be going to see."

"You can't live with him, and you can't live without him. I know you're going through a rough time right now, but it's getting old. It's time to shit or get off the pot," Ezra sighs. "It's not going to be comfortable, but it needs to be done."

I always thought falling in love would feel like rainbows and butterflies, but our story is that of elephants and gray skies. Giant, totally uncoordinated elephants stomping on delicate flowers, and the constant threat of rain on sunny days. Nothing seems graceful or 'on purpose,' instead it feels like a series of chaotic events, one after the other. I wanted someone to sugar-coat difficult conversations, and tiptoe around me in this fragile post-Dallas state. Ezra doesn't mince his words, and I could take the offended road if I wanted to, but the funny thing is, I wouldn't have it any other way. Ezra has taken me at my worst, carried me through depths of despair, and met me on the flipside with a smile. With all the sass and attitude I throw at him, he completely holds his own. I have taken his interest for granted, and with comments like the one he just made, I'm starting to realize I'm not pulling my weight in this relationship.

"Sorry," I mumble.

He shrugs, and takes a bite of his dinner, "Want to see a movie tonight?"

I nod, secretly seething that Dallas has put me in a funk again—this time all the way from friggin' Wyoming. If there's one person I have forgiven less than Dallas, it's myself. But how am I supposed to move forward with forgiveness when I'm knee deep in hatred? I want to change my heart, but my heart is reluctant to change. Ezra's right; if I am to move beyond this season, I need to see Dallas again.

I snap myself out of my mood, keenly aware that I'm on the edge of ruining yet another date. If the tables were turned, I wouldn't like me right now. It's only a matter of time before he's done with me.

#

I arrive at the coffee house at 6 am, with the intent of broaching the subject with my new boss.

"Ed?" I stumble.

"Yeah?" he replies.

"You remember the kid on the roof of Log Nation?" I wonder.

"Yeah," he looks down, clearly embarrassed of his first impression.

"He got placed in a group home in Wyoming, and I'm going to see him the day after Christmas. I know it's short notice, but I'm going to be gone until January third. I understand if that means I don't have a job here anymore."

"It's cool," Ed shrugs.

"What?" I say, taken aback.

"I'll figure it out," Ed says. "Come back when you're ready."

I didn't expect the interaction to go this smoothly. In fact, I stand there with my apron in my hand, ready to hand it in after a measly few weeks of work. I grasp its leather straps and smile, "Thank you."

[I see red.]

Christmas wishes are bullshit.

Zoe is never coming back.

CHAPTER TWENTY-FOUR

Tilling the Soil

[I see you.]

Ezra turns up at seven wearing jeans, a hoodie and T-shirt schwag from the startup where he works. When I open the door, he's there on time, with a steadfast, unconditional smile. Ezra will be my undoing, if in fact I am not already undone. I can't help but shake the feeling that if this relationship were happening at any other time of my life, I'm sure I'd be able to handle it a little more gracefully... I'd be better at being a girlfriend, there'd be more reciprocity, I'd be sunnier somehow. I'm constantly worried that I'm not holding up my side of the bargain. I've spent my life waiting to be in a perfectly ready place for romance, and here I am, caught off-guard in the least available time of my life.

"You look beautiful," Ezra smiles.

"Thanks. So do you," I awkwardly respond on autopilot, desperately trying to fill the empty space with words. He laughs a little; I laugh a bit, and then we both laugh too much. "I mean, you look handsome."

He holds out his hand, and we walk from my front door to his car.

"Old faithful Carlton the car," I laugh, swiftly exhaling from my nose. "I can't believe he's still going."

"Carlton is immortal," Ezra smiles. "And I won't have you saying otherwise."

Carlton is a nineties station wagon with roof racks for a surfboard that Ezra doesn't know how to use. The back windows are plastered with 'coexist' bumper stickers, and 'Keep Santa Cruz Weird,' slogans, which were clearly stolen from Austin, TX. A relic from a different era, Carlton is from a grungy garage-band time, given to Ezra by his uncle. Legend has it that the uncle got rid of Carlton because he grew up, cut his hair, and got married—such is the circle of life. Carlton is functional, for sure, but a grown up man's car he is not. Ezra opens the door for me, and I get in the passenger seat.

Carlton smells like crayons and wet dog.

#

After dinner we walk to a man-made lake in a park that is slightly scary after dark. I tell Ezra about my plans to go see Dallas, and he's just as supportive as I'd expect him to be. In fact, he seems relieved that I might just move past this state of being frozen in a moment—or at least I'm projecting that relief because I know I'm being an ass. Ezra seems to waver between wanting me to talk about Dallas, and wanting me to get past him. I'm apprehensive about all things, to say the least. I've not yet warmed to the idea of travelling to Wyoming, even though I agreed to go. I'm convicted, deeply convicted, by the idea of making amends with this child. The act seems superficial, disingenuous. I'm not ready.

"I don't want to go. A children's residential home is completely out of my comfort zone," I hiss, like he's poked at a bruise on my heart.

"Has anything good ever come out of comfort zones?" he says, as the question fills the air like fog. It hangs there, staring at me with eyebrows raised, unwilling to relent until I respond. I'm uncomfortable, and maybe that's the point. We sit and stare at the lake for a while, watching the water dance in the wind. Ezra puts his arm around me, to elevate my awkwardness level just that tiny bit more as I begin to wonder if I'll ever feel normal again. My comfort zone has become limited to my house, and my adopted dog-in-training. Maybe I need to visit Dallas as much as Dallas needs my visit. Ezra quickly changes the subject, but I remain unresponsive. He exhales.

Once upon a time, my heart was malleable like clay. I could be flexible, I could go with the flow, I could love and be loved freely. Like soil, it was soft and fertile. I grew oaks from acorns; I was part of transitioning kids from demonic to dynamic, shackles to freedom. My heart has sat still these last few months. Caught in arrested development. It's air dried and ready for the fire. With Ezra's help, the firm clay of my hardened heart begins to break a little, as I consider what it would take for seed to grow once more. I'm nowhere near ready to plant trees, but I know it's possible for maybe not a forest, but a garden, to come up from this ground. I grab Ezra's hand, and we sit on that bench for hours.

For the first time in a long time, I feel like someone's got my back.

[I see red.]

Today is the forty-sixth day that I have lived at Starlight, and I have talked to Zoe zero of these days. I have decided not to let her on the roof with me and Grey anymore, because she isn't being kind to us. In real life I am laying on a huge beanbag in Dr. Martinez's office while he waits for me to talk. Of course I'm not actually talking, because I am mostly busy spending the afternoon with Grey. Me and Grey only, nobody else is allowed. Oh, and I don't have any moms anymore, just to let you know. My actual mom fired me, so I fired Zoe from being my new mom. I don't need anyone but Grey.

I climb up onto the roof of our new house in San Francisco, in my mind. Just so you know, there's a waterslide from the roof to the pool, so you get to slide down three stories before splashing your body into the pool and wetting all the bricks around. We have to go from up high, because Grey can't get down from heaven without a ladder. He can only stay on earth ground for like two or five minutes, kind of like how fishes have gills and people don't, so that's why people drown. Grey did a swimming class in heaven, so he's good at it now, but we still go on the slide together so I can save him if he falls under the water. Grey can walk on earth grass for only, like, one minute because it feels like glass to him but it doesn't make blood on his feet. It just feels too pokey for heaven kids.

"Wanna go on the slide now?" I ask.

"OK," him says. "But what if I get drowned in the pool?"

"It's OK, because I know how to save you this time," I say.

"But what about the ouchy grass?" he wonders.

"It's OK, because I will carry you," I say. "I gotted very strong since you've been gone."

I flex my muscles for Grey and he's like, "Wow!"

"But where's Mom?" Grey says. "I never see her anymore."

"She's living at a different place; she never moved to this good house. She has a little baby who is only cool sometimes," I explain. "The baby is half of our sister, and the other half belongs to her dad, Jacob, and him isn't nice. Anyway, we don't have any mom or a sister anymore, but it's OK because I will do all the things you need."

"Let's go on the slide now," Grey says. He doesn't care about having no Mom. Neither do I. Also I don't tell him that Zoe's gone missing, I don't want to worry him. We only have a little while to play, so I will make it a good time by not telling him those kinds of things.

"Dallas?" Dr. Martinez says. I close my eyes tight and pull my hood over my face. He needs to quit interrupting my play date with Grey.

"Dallas—" he says again, with his hand on my shoulder. I put my fingers in my ears and say BLAH BLAH BLAH BLAH super loudly until he stops talking to me.

#

The sun is down, and I say goodbye to Grey, "See you tomorrow, brother. You're my bestest friend."

"You're my bestest, too," Grey says, then he flies to heaven. I look at the sky for a bit, wishing we could just live on the same planet for once. I wish him had a phone, so I could send him texts and photos of the things I do without him. I take off my hood and open my eyes to see Alicia sitting in the beanbag across from me, reading a magazine. Ugh, Grey doesn't need a photo of this boring place.

"You're back!" Alicia says. I make my eyes little at her, so she knows I am not interested in talking.

"I was just reading something I think you'd be into," she lies. "Did you know sharks have the most powerful jaws on the planet?"

I shake my head.

"Each kind of shark has a different shaped tooth depending on their diet—did you know that?" she adds.

I shake my head again.

"You should come take a look at the pictures."

I think for a minute about whether or not I want to listen to Alicia. I put my hands in my pocket and feel the smooth and rough parts of the acorn. I wish it was an oak, but it hasn't been broken yet. I can stop listening to Alicia and stay like the acorn, or I can listen to her and become an oak. I want to be big, I want to be strong, I want to live for hundreds of years… so I sit beside her.

"See this picture?" Alicia says. "It says that sharks never run out of teeth. They'll always grow as many as they need."

I nod my head and sit even closer to Alicia. I wonder if I can rest my head on her arm for a minute, kind of like how I used to hug Zoe before I let her use her arms. I miss hugs; I miss hearing someone else's heart beat. I spent my whole day with Grey, and his heart doesn't have any sound. I want to hear what alive sounds like, in the chest of someone actually alive. I put my hand on my own chest, to see if I still have a heartbeat. It's lazy, but it's still there. Even though I am alive, I sure feel pretty dead.

[I see you.]

Tomorrow is Christmas Eve Eve, or at least that's what my family has always called December 23rd. Ezra, Julia, Cinnamon, and I will leave for Santa Cruz bright and early in the morning—in my car—not Carlton. It's times like these that I am thankful to be dating a guy whose parents live a few blocks from mine, making holiday planning a breeze. With all this easy, breezy holiday planning, I hardly have time to consider the gargantuan knot in my stomach. I sprout a few new gray hairs as my body protests the impending visit to Starlight. I'm grateful for the Christmas distraction between now and then, focused on my time with family, instead of facing the fear of the unknown.

I'm leaving in two days, away until January third. There's so much to organize, so for now, I will make lists. Lists are my happy place, lists are my sanity. I can control how many pairs of undies I pack in my suitcase, but I can not control what will happen on the day I wear my favorite pair. For someone who was a Behavior Specialist for four tumultuous years, I sure like to be in control.

Perhaps I'm making up for lost time.

[I see red.]

Today is the forty-seventh day that I have lived at Starlight, and I have talked to Zoe zero of these days. Today also means there's only three sleeps until Christmas Day. I know a few things about Christmas, and also a few lies about Christmas. Here is the truth: Christmas was invented because Jesus got borned, and He's so important because He's also God. Here's the lie: Santa. A long, long time ago there was a guy who looked like him, but if you go to the North Pole, I bet you any money you won't find a workshop with elves making toys. If you do, them are actors who go home at night to their wives and kids. Elfs aren't true. Also, why do the Santa elfs only make toys made of wood, when really all the kids get video games and bikes under the Christmas tree? Adults shouldn't lie to kids, but them do.

Zoe said I can't tell any kids about Santa being fake, but once I did tell Caroline at my old school. She stomped her foot and told me my pants were on fire. I told her that the only person with their pants on fire was her stupid mom. Then I got sent to time out for being naughty at school on my first day, and that means I'd be on Santa's naughty list too. I don't care a teeny bit. I'll be on a stupid fake list every day, and I'll be happy having a piece of coal for Christmas because presents are stupid. Caroline is always making my life worser.

Alicia and I take a walk out to see the horses at the ranch. There are two in the first stable; one called Arrow, and the other is called Lester. I like being in a stable at Christmas time because it makes me remember how Jesus got born. Arrow walks over to me, and I feed him a fat carrot which I brought in my bag with a few other vegetables like apples, which are actually fruits. He licks my hand, and I laugh so much that snot comes out of my nose. Lester is shy, he barely notices I'm here. He isn't hungry, so Arrow eats all the horse food. I climb up on a gate, and Alicia quickly puts her hand on my shoulders.

"You can't go in there," she says.

"I know," I tell her. "I'm just looking for the manger."

"What do you mean?"

"The thing what animals eat food from, except on Christmas there's a baby Jesus."

Alicia smiles, "I don't think they exist anymore, but we can make one if you like?"

"Not like cardboard and sticky tape. Not like that. Them are made of wood," I correct her, waving my hand in her face.

"I know," she explains. "We have wood, nails, and hammers."

"Awesome!" I yell. "Where? Where are they?"

"We can't start yet. We have to make a plan before we start."

"This is like Project Time. Zoe—um… my old teacher, just this girl I used to know—her and me used to do projects with plans first."

"We don't have any paper or pens out here, so let's head back inside and grab what we need."

I wonder, "Can I start building today if I get the plan done?"

"Sure!" she smiles. I don't know why, because I didn't tell myself to do this, but I just hugged Alicia. She put her arms around me too, and I heard it! I really heard it!

Her heart sounds like boom boom, boom boom, boom boom. I am too embarrassed, so I let go after three beats and pretend it never happened. We go inside to get pens and papers.

CHAPTER TWENTY-FIVE

Tidings of Comfort and Joy

[I see you.]

I wake up to the sound of small rocks being thrown at my childhood bedroom window, and suddenly I feel like I'm a lovestruck teenager in an old Hollywood movie. Ezra rode over to my parents house, from his, on the same bike I remember him owning as a nerdy tween. It's delightfully 90s, like most things at our parents' houses—shrines to the best years of their lives, without them even realizing. I slide open the window to see him grinning from ear to ear, with a present in his hands. Cinnamon barks a couple of times, and I tell Ezra I'll come downstairs. I throw on a bra and furiously chew a stick of gum, to make myself marginally more presentable. Well, as presentable as one can be in an old t-shirt and a pair of satin boxer shorts with cartoon characters all over them. If Ezra wanted to see me all dolled up, he should've given me more than five seconds notice of his arrival.

"Good morning, babe," I say, rubbing my eyes. "It's 6 am."

"MERRY CHRISTMAS!" he comically and quietly yells, so not to wake my parents. Cinnamon has the honor instead, racing downstairs barking at the volume of a screaming toddler. He dances at the sight of Ezra, who swiftly picks him up. I can't help but laugh at the tiny dog and his licky tongue attacking the bearded face of my boyfriend. I can hardly believe I have a boyfriend on Christmas Day—this is already the best Christmas I've ever had. I join the embrace, as Cinnamon decides whose face to lick first.

My parents come downstairs, enthusiastically welcoming Ezra inside before brewing a pot of holiday-flavored coffee. The house smells like cinnamon, cloves, and black peppercorns, mixed with the undeniable scent of pine from the Christmas tree. Mom and Dad are making breakfast together, as they have done every year that I can remember. I am inspired by their teamwork skills, navigating their way around the kitchen like a well-oiled machine (thirty years of marriage looks good on them). They're making grilled leg ham, eggs, tomatoes, and croissants for four this year, for the first time in a long time. My parents always wanted more kids, but it wasn't what life had in store. They used to say they had me and stopped, because I was perfect—but I knew the toll infertility took on their lives. They always dreamed of having three kids, but it wasn't meant to be. Since their extended families live on the East Coast, holidays are often a small affair on the years between family gatherings. Julia became the sister I always wished I had, which makes it harder to admit that we're naturally drifting apart.

Our family might be small, but it's the only one we've got. I hope it's enough for Ezra.

[I see red.]

Merry Stupid Christmas.

For Christmas, I got ignored by Zoe for fifty-one stupid days. And you want to know the stupider part? Alicia isn't even here today, because she's having Christmas with her family. You know who I'm having Christmas with? People I have barely ever seen before. There's only three kids in this whole house who are still here for Christmas, all the other fifty-seven kids went to their parents' houses. Them are the worst kids in the whole wide house; the kind who hit, the kind who poop in their pants, and scream swear words. They're the kind of kids like me, which I know because nobody came to get me. Nobody took me to their home. I think that Santa's naughty list might actually be real and the consequence is worse than coal. I have no family because I'm bad—they gived up on me, even Alicia gived up on me. We haven't even finished making the manger for the baby Jesus. Where will he sleep tonight when he's borned?

"Merry Christmas, Dallas!" says a lady I don't even know. "Come and have breakfast with us!"

I follow her to a room, not because I want to, but because I'm hungry. She serves me a plate of bacon, eggs, and pancakes. I eat the bacon first, because it has the most protein. Alicia telled me about protein. Then I eat the eggs, because eggs also have protein. I think about Alicia telling me that I can either get a food tube in my nose or eat protein, and I gobble up my meal so quickly. My ribs don't look like a guitar anymore, and my muscles are growing bigger every single day. I don't need no stupid food tube anymore. I feel brave eating breakfast with these kids. I feel brave sitting next to grown ups I've never seen before. I wonder what Alicia is eating for breakfast? She usually eats oatmeal. I hate oatmeal, but Alicia always says, "Don't yuck my yum."

That's how she talks. Also, I don't miss her or anything. She can do whatever stupid things she wants to do on Christmas. Doesn't matter to me.

[I see you.]

Ezra latches a necklace around my neck. I move my hair so it won't get stuck.

"It's beautiful," I smile.

"I thought it might help you be brave when you go to Wyoming," he reassures, quite literally, as I look at the pendant. It's an arrow with the word BRAVE emblazoned in rustic silver. My stomach churns as I think about the reason for which I will need to be brave, and I'm simultaneously amazed that Ezra gave such a thoughtful gift (maybe Julia helped him). I kiss him on the cheek and rest my head on his shoulder. What I wouldn't give to feel at home within my own heart again; what I wouldn't do to give the whole thing to Ezra. In my mind's eye, I see Dallas reach into my chest and extract my heart, grinning as he realizes he owns my ass. I'm enraged. That asshole doesn't deserve forgiveness.

I hand Ezra a gift, too.

"Jeans," he says, matter-of-factly, and kisses me on the head. "Thank you."

Ezra doesn't like gifts. He thinks presents are moot; anything he might want, he can buy himself. This puts me in a weird position, come Christmas time, when I realize there's nothing on Earth I could buy that he might like. So I decided to buy him the exact same jeans he's wearing—I have it on good authority that he likes those—considering he wears the same type every day. Sooner or later a pair will wear out, and on that day I will have saved him an errand. In Ezra's mind, this is as romantic as the BRAVE necklace. Also, he's adorable.

We sit at the breakfast table with my parents, who can't keep the smiles off their faces.

"Ezra," Mom beams, "We're just so excited that you're part of the family this year."

"Jeez, Mom, we aren't married!" I snap. Ezra turns beet red.

"Yet," he adds. Everyone laughs, except for me. Now it's my turn to transition to a shade of bright magenta. Whose idea was it to bring my boyfriend to Christmas with my family? Oh, it was mine...

[I see red.]

"Merry Christmas from all of us here at Starlight, Dallas!" a lady who works here says, as she hands me a present. She looks like my old teacher Mrs. Chao. I rip open the paper, and there's a red plastic watch inside. I look at my arm, and I see my dog watch. I put the red one down on the table; I don't need another watch.

"Thank you," I say, because I am learning to be an oak instead of an acorn. She sits next to me.

"My name's Jen. We met last week at Dylan's little birthday party—remember?"

I nod my head, but I'm not really sure if I am telling the truth.

"I work with Dylan, like Alicia works with you," Jen says. I nod my head. "You look kind of upset today."

I nod my head again.

"I wonder if you're missing your family?" Jen asks, and I nod my head. "I bet they're missing you, too."

"Why they didn't bring me home for Christmas?" I grumble.

Jen looks at me, then looks at the table. "To be honest, Dallas, I don't know. It's not really my place to say. But regardless, you are loved."

I roll my eyes, "Yeah. Right! Who loves me?"

"Why don't you tell me?" Jen says, throwing the question back in my face. "Who loves you?"

I think… who does love me? I thought Mommy loved me. I thought Zoe loved me. I think even Alicia loved me a little teeny tiny bit. I don't know what to tell Jen, so I tell her nothing. Big fat nothing.

"Is there anything you'd like to do today?" she asks.

"Yep," I say. "I want to finish building the manger. Me and Alicia started it, but I want to finish it because it's Christmas and baby Jesus needs a place to sleep."

"Do you know where all the materials are?" Jen checks.

"Yeah, but I need you to take me to see Arrow and Lester. That's where the manger project is," I explain. Jen gets up and asks her boss if it's OK to go out to the horse stable, because it's super far away and also it's snowing outside. In San Francisco we never, ever got snow. Jen talks for a bit and I watch her, hoping to see her face look happy, because that's how I will know if we can go to the stables or not. She smiles and walks back over towards the table.

"Let's go!" she says. I smile, too, for the first time all day long. This isn't the Christmas miracle I was hoping for, but it's still a good kind of thing to be happening. I'm still on the naughty list, but maybe I'm one of the better naughty kids. It's for Jesus and Santa to decide.

We put on a hundred pieces of clothes (ski pants, huge furry socks, special boots that used to belong to a different kid, an itchy sweater, gloves, a beanie; those kinds of things) and open the door to outside. The air tastes like a popsicle that's just water flavored, and we walk a long way to the horse stables. My feet are sinking in the snow, all the way up to my knees. I pretend I'm in quicksand, and Jen joins in with my game that I invented. Also, Jen is pretty fun.

At the stable, I say hello to Arrow because him is my favorite horse. He breathes out fast and the air looks like smoke from a dragon. I pretend he's a dragon, and I pretend that I can ride him into the sky and see Grey for Christmas. Grey's feet wouldn't hurt if he walked in the snow, because heaven kids can handle snow because that's how the floor looks in heaven.

"Where's the manger?" Jen asks. I take her to the pile of wood and show her the clipboard that's hanging on the wall from a rusty nail.

"This is my plan," I say. "And this is what I have so far. It's only half made, because we ran out of time."

"Would you like me to help you, or would you like me to just keep you company while you build?" Jen asks. I think for a second, because I am not that good at hammers yet and I would actually like to have help. But also, this was for me and Alicia and not for Jen. If Jen helps me, then I won't have Alicia anymore; just like when Alicia helped me I stopped having Zoe. Just like how I never saw Rachel again in my whole wide life. I wish I could just have one grown up for all the times. I think that's how Moms are supposed to be. But, I wouldn't know, because my mom and dad both stopped wanting me.

I shake my head, "No. I want to just build it by myself."

I grab a nail and start to hammer it, but it falls and I hammer my thumb. I scream and scream, then run into Arrow's stable to hide. I am crying quieter now, because I don't want to be found.

"Dallas, it's not safe to be in the horse stable like that. I know you love Arrow, but he's an animal, and sometimes animals do unexpected things," Jen says. For your big fat information, Jen, I don't care if Arrow kicks me. I am the worst person who needs to be kicked because I can't do good things. I get the acorn from my pocket and throw it on the ground. My thumb feels like it has a heartbeat inside and it's turning blue under the fingernail. Jen climbs into the stable and tries to get me out, so I kick her. She needs to be kicked too, because she's trying to take me away from Alicia. This project isn't hers. She shouldn't be in the stable where I spend time with Alicia. She's NOT ALICIA.

[I see you.]

After Christmas Breakfast we make our way over to Ezra's parents house. Julia throws open the door when she sees us, and yells, "Thank God you're here!"

We are handed Mimosas as soon as we walk in, and I savor it like liquid gold. The champagne calms me almost immediately, and I look around to see that Julia has decorated the entire house, just like she did ours at Halloween. It's a beautiful winter wonderland in sunny California. Their parents swiftly greet us, as we gather around the tree to exchange gifts. I didn't know what to get them for Christmas, so I'm giving them a candle. Candles are my go-to gift in times like these.

They got me one, too, so I know we're on the same page.

[I see red.]

Jen picks me up under my arms and throws me over her shoulder. We walk back to the house as I kick and scream, trying to squirm out of her arms. I see Grey running towards me on the snow, and he's trying to save me. Jen's going to kill me on Christmas Day; I knew I shouldn't trust her! I yell out to Grey, and I tell him he needs to finish making the manger because Jesus is born tonight and the baby needs somewhere to sleep. We have to take care of the baby, or he will be all alone! Grey falls into the snow, and the quicksand eats him up, and soon he's gone. Not even my dead brother will be my friend today.

I deserve this.

#

"He's going to have to earn the privilege to go back to the stables," Jen's boss says. He's a big fat man who I have seen around Starlight but we've never talked. "I'll shoot an email to Alicia and Dr. Martinez to let them know what happened."

I am angry and also embarrassed. Why do they have to tell Alicia? I lay on the beanbag with my hood over my head. I'm so still that I start to feel invisible, and I like it. For a minute I wonder if this is what being dead feels like? Then my thumb starts hurting again, and I know the only other heartbeat I'll hear tonight is the one in my thumb. I want a band-aid, even though I know it won't take the pain away. I want something on my body to show people that I'm hurt, I'm broken, and I'm all done playing. I know that I am a loser. I admit it.

Jen sits beside me, and I roll into a ball. I hear her all muffled through my beanie and huge snow coat.

"Dallas, I trusted you at the stables. I feel kind of sad that our project time didn't work out," she says. I say nothing, nothing, nothing. I stay like a ball, even when my legs hurt, and I start to need to pee. I stay so still until it's time for Jen to leave, because that's how people work. They all leave, and if I can be still like I'm dead, she will go more quicker. Then she says goodbye and goes. I don't mean to, but I pee on myself, on the beanbag too. I cry because I peed in my pants. I cry because I'm not a baby. I cry because I don't want to be here on Earth anymore, I only want to be with Grey.

Then I remember that baby Jesus will be born tonight. I remember what I learned about Christmas at church. I remember that he's the King, and he's a nice king who saves the world at Easter. I cry because I didn't make the manger in time and baby Jesus will have to sleep on the floor tonight. Jesus will feel lonely on the floor.

[I see you.]

As the sun sets, Ezra and I take our traditional holiday amble to the boardwalk—a tradition we started last month at Thanksgiving. Anxiety rises inside of me, or is it the fifth mimosa? I'm uncomfortable. I'm unsettled. I'm exhausted. I'm gearing up for the red-eye in the morning, when Ezra drops me at the San Francisco airport at 6 am. According to my schedule, we're leaving Santa Cruz at 4 am just to be on the safe side. I'll be in Cody by noon, and a couple of hours later at the ranch. Ezra is talking to me, but I'm preoccupied with my own thoughts. I'm going through the steps one by one.

"Hey, space cadet. Are you listening to me?" he teases.

CHAPTER TWENTY-SIX

Seeds

[I see red.]

Today is the fifty-second day that I have lived at Starlight, and I have talked to Zoe zero of these days. Today is the first day since Christmas, and I haven't talked to Alicia in two days if you count today as a day. But it's just the morning—the clock says 10 am, and that means I ate my breakfast and got dressed already. Everybody knows what clothes I put on, since I only ever wear black shirts, gray sweatshirts with hoods, and cargo shorts (I hate jeans the most). Today my t-shirt has a vampire bat on it. Alicia comes out of nowhere and knocks on my door.

"Hey, Buddy! How was your Christmas?" she says. I fold my arms across my body and face the wall. Looks like she didn't read her email.

"Let's go finish our project! You're going to need longer pants on, it's snowing outside" she says, like she can't see how much angry I am with her. The big fat boss of Jen comes to the door and talks to Alicia outside the room. I know what he's saying and I want him to shut his big fat mouth, so I say BLAH, BLAH, BLAH, BLAHHHHHHH so loudly out the door. The stupid fat man tells me to go back in the room, so I fold my arms and stand like a statue just outside the door. He tells Alicia that she can handle me, but if she needs help she just needs to say the word (I wonder what the word is? Probably 'hot dog'). Then the man walks away.

"So, the stable's off limits," she says, looking down. "We're going to have to work our way back to that privilege. Want to talk about it?"

I fold my arms even tighter and sit like a ball in the corner of the room. Alicia sits on my bed, which I am mad about because I had to make it properly and it looks nice, and it will look all messy when her stands up, and I will have to make it all over again. I don't want to talk, so I say nothing. Dr. Martinez comes to the door and tells Alicia something I can't hear, but I think I should know. Alicia sits back on the bed.

"Dallas, I think today's going to be a good day for you."

I frown and make a grunting sound. No days will ever be good for me.

[I see you.]

The drive from Cody Airport to Lovell is around an hour, and I'm beyond grateful to have extra time to warm to this idea. The snow is thick around me, falling from the sky and landing on the windshield. Cinnamon's face is glued to the window, and he exhales foggy snot on the glass. My toes are frozen inside my boots, and I get the sense they'd warm up faster outside of my shoes. This trip is so awkward—Dr. Martinez sent a janitor from Starlight to come pick me up, and he isn't talkative at all. I'd half hoped he'd give me an update on Dallas before I arrived, but I realize he doesn't know one kid from the next—they're all demons to him. His eyes are dead, hair disheveled. This guy's both seen, and cleaned up, some shit.

I fold my hands and pray, looking over the vast plains. I have no idea what I'm about to get myself into. I have no idea why I agreed to stay so long. I want to turn the car around, I want to go back to Ezra.

I want to go back to making coffee.

[I see red.]

I stay in the corner with my arms crossed. I am never ever talking to anyone today. I am not moving, except to eat and use the bathroom. I am going to stay invisible. I hear the Dr. at my door, and I ignore him because that's what I am doing today.

[I see you.]

I see the sign outside the ranch, Starlight Children's Residential Home. I see no evidence of actual children, though, just a big ranch house in the distance and a horse stable even farther away. It looks like the pictures on the website, but with more snow. We drive to the house, and the car stops. I remind myself that nothing good has ever come from comfort zones. Bravery is what I need; I'm grateful for the necklace that Ezra gave me, and I kiss it before getting out of the car.

Cinnamon doesn't know what to make of the snow beneath his paws, as he clumsily dances on the ice like a fancy, furry horse. The janitor takes my suitcase inside for me, as a well-dressed middle-aged man meets me at the door.

"Zoe!" he says. "I'm Luis Martinez—so glad to meet you in person. Come on in—we'll have a chat in my office first."

"This is Dallas's dog, Cinnamon," I add.

"He's sweet," the Dr. says, petting him on the head. Cinnamon's just excited to be running free after five hours of transit today.

"Will Dallas see me if I walk through?" I check.

"No, he's in his room right now which is at the other end of the house. Kids aren't allowed anywhere near the exit points without supervision."

Duh. I should've realized—this is a step before juvie—there's no way anyone's letting kids near the door. I don't know where they'd go if they ran, anyway. There's no civilization as far as the eye can see. Unless they rode a horse to town, which they totally could do if they had a sense of how to do that—I wonder if there are guards here? Ugh, my Behavior Specialist instincts are kicking back in. I'm twenty steps ahead of myself, and I need to scale it back. As we walk through to Dr. Martinez's office, I'm struck by how charming and homely this place is, and I'm relieved to know Dallas has somewhere nice to live. Next minute, a child screams like a banshee and an alarm sounds… suddenly we're not in Kansas anymore.

"By the way," he says, "Dallas doesn't know you're coming. We weren't sure how he would react, so we are going to have him reunite with you in a more controlled environment."

209

The knot in my stomach tightens. He invites me into the small office, one of the few places I've seen in the house that is geared toward adults. Crossing one leg over the other, Luis leans back slightly, which makes his chair bounce a little. I can't work out if he's stretching or using a power pose.

"Thanks for coming," he acknowledges. "I know this must be hard for you."

I try to act natural, "How's Dallas doing?"

The Dr. breaks eye contact, and his mouth becomes an ominous line across his face. Then he admits, "Dallas...Well... he has his ups and downs. We're having a hard time seeing progress."

"He's lost everything," I say, as the hair stands up on the back of my neck.

"I know," he assures. "It's going to take a while for us to see a consistent upward trend with him. We're hoping you'll help him turn a corner."

"Don't you think it's kind of a bad idea for me to come in and out of his life like this? Don't you think a clean break would have been better for both of us?" I snap.

"No," he rebuts. "I don't think that at all. That's why we have you here for so many days, Zoe. It's a significant chunk of time for both of you to heal. Neither you, nor Dallas, have had any closure since the theme park incident."

"It doesn't bother me," I lie. "I've moved on with my life."

"With all due respect," he clears his throat, "I don't believe that for a second."

My heart races and I'm sweating like a pig. I remove my jacket and start fanning myself with a brochure that says, "RAD Kids: Healing Attachment at Starlight." I scoff at the irony.

"Why didn't you bring his mom out?" I hiss, knowing exactly why she isn't here. Dr. Martinez has already told me, and here I am feigning amnesia. Anything to stall the inevitable moment where I will be face to face with my literal demon. I've learned a lot of manipulation strategies from my clients over the years: from the artful young dodgers, the sly foxes, the charming snakes.

"His mom relinquished him to the state, Zoe," the Dr. says sternly.

"Yeah, but that's not immediate. It's a process. Why aren't you getting her here? Why aren't you changing her mind?"

"We are keeping him here for two years, in the hope that she takes him back, but we're not holding our breath. And even if she does take him back—do you honestly believe she's the best caregiver for Dallas?"

I don't. Sarah tried her best, but her best doesn't meet his needs.

"She's better than a revolving door of caregivers at a residential home. How do you think he'll respond to more abandonment?" I acknowledge.

"Dallas has one assigned support professional at Starlight. Her name is Alicia and for the next year she is committed to his rehabilitation," the Dr. explains.

"But she goes home at night, doesn't she? He's six years old, Luis. Who's tucking him in bed every night and reading him stories? Who's cuddling him? Who's telling him they love him? Where does he go when he wakes up after a nightmare?"

"We have house "parents" if you will. They look after a group of six, and are available throughout the night. I assure you, we are providing the most normal experience that we possibly can."

"Is he the youngest kid here?" I ask.

"Yes," he admits. "He's the youngest by a year."

"How many are eight or younger?"

"Just two, and they're in a room together—right beside the house parents' room. Zoe, I know you're coming from a place of protection for Dallas, but I assure you we are giving him the best we can."

I nod, then I kind of regret my outburst. He probably thinks I'm crazy.

"Would you like some coffee or tea before we see him?"

"How about a horse tranquilizer?" I joke. I don't think that helped me look less crazy. He smiles, and pity laughs. "No, I'm ready. No time like the present."

"Great," he says, standing up. I also stand, like my legs are operating without permission from my mind. I'm not ready; I'll never be ready. I grab a hold of my necklace, trying to channel courage from Ezra. We pass through five security gates before Dr. Martinez asks me to wait. Cinnamon is losing his shit, tugging at the leash in anticipation. My heart beats loudly as I wait. The Dr. brings a petite girl towards me, who appears to be in her early twenties—she has velvety brown skin and long hair set in twisted braids. The woman is beautiful, but she looks tired. I can't help but see myself in her face.

"Zoe, Alicia. Alicia, Zoe," he introduces us.

"I've heard a lot about you," Alicia says with a smile.

"Likewise," I lie, mostly because I only found out about her ten minutes ago. "How's Dallas doing today?"

"Well, yesterday being Christmas, I wasn't here… and as you know, he's not great with new people," she starts. I glare at Dr. Martinez, and he doesn't make eye contact on purpose.

"What happened?" I ask.

"Apparently, he was building pretty good rapport with Jen, one of our supports who usually works with a different child. He ate breakfast with her, which has been a struggle since he arrived. He lost a lot of weight for a minute there, but he's getting healthier now. He just refused to eat, and one of our medical doctors told me he would need a nasogastric feed tube unless he started getting adequate nutrition. Anyway, after breakfast, they went out to the stables to finish a project he and I had started. So that you know, going to the stables is a privilege that Dallas had to earn through good behavior -"

I zone out as she speaks, because I'm having an out-of-body experience. I feel like I can finally see who I became with Dallas, from a new and fresh angle. Alicia clearly knows everything about Dallas, because she is with him eight hours a day, five days a week. She's walking in my old shoes, and begging for someone to understand where she's going with this. I understand more than anyone ever could.

"Anyway," she continues, "He apparently freaked out "out of the blue" on Jen, but I don't think any behaviors are "out of the blue." It's more likely that something triggered him, but we're not sure what. He hid in the stables, and she brought him back. Last night he wet his pants, too, which is something he did when he first got here, and he stopped for a while, but it's started again."

"Wow," I nod. "So has there been any progress?"

"Yeah, absolutely," Alicia says. I remember being asked the same thing when I was with Dallas, and I would clutch at straws when it came to progress reports. Anything that wasn't negative became a positive. The smallest of victories is celebrated, and I am glad to see that Alicia does this too.

"We've been talking about acorns and oaks, and Dallas has been keeping an acorn in his pocket to remind him that big things come from things that are small. He's been deciding when he's ready to plant the acorn, knowing that seeds need to break before they're able to grow."

"That's… abstract," I say, doubtful that it's a developmentally appropriate lesson.

"He actually does really well with things like that," she retorts. "I mean, you'd know. He's extremely smart."

I smile. Only someone who knows Dallas, and sees him for who he really is, would call him 'extremely smart.' To the rest of the world, he's 'not the brightest crayon in the box.'

"I'll go in first," Dr. Martinez explains, "Alicia, you stand by the door in case anything unexpected happens."

Dallas running away would not be unexpected, thank you very much.

"I will wave you in, Zoe. Just focus on reuniting—you'll know what to do when the time comes," he finishes.

"Can Cinnamon go in first?" I ask.

The Dr. shrugs, "Sure."

[I see red.]

I have been in the corner for two and a half hours.

Alicia walks in, along with Dr. Poopy and him tells me there's someone here to see me. I say nothing, because that's all I ever say to him. Suddenly I hear something all jangly, and there's this little dog on my lap licking my face. Him sure looks like my old dog, Cinnamon, but him is a lot more grown because this is a different dog. I look at him's collar, and it is the exact same one that Zoe and me bought for the real Cinnamon. Then I notice that there's a name tag that actually says Cinnamon, and I can hardly believe it.

"CINNAMON!" I yell, then I look at Alicia. "Is it really my dog from my old house?"

Alicia nods and smiles. I am so happy to see my puppy, and I hug him so tight that him kicks me when him's trying to get away. I wonder when him is leaving? I wonder if I shouldn't play with my sweet puppy because saying goodbye is harder when you love something.

"Dallas," Dr. Martinez says, "Someone else is here to see you."

Wait. The only persons who could bring Cinnamon here are Mommy or Zoe. My heart is loud in my ears, and I stop moving completely. Fifty-two days without my Zoe and here her is. Her is coming to take me home to our big new house in San Francisco. If we leave now, we can eat hotdogs for dinner with Grey.

Grey will be so happy that our new Mommy is here!

CHAPTER TWENTY-SEVEN

What's Your Name?

[I see you.]
I hold Dallas in my arms and inhale his shaggy hair. His familiar scent transports me back to the endless days we spent at his house, learning life skills on the trampoline with Ramsay. For the first time in a long time I remember Dallas as he was then, instead of the boy rescued by a helicopter.

He rests his head on my chest and cries.

[I see red.]
Boom, boom. Boom, boom. Boom, boom.

I hear she's heart, alive inside of her body. I want to listen to my Zoe living and breathing forever, I want to know what it's like to have someone the same for all my days. I can't believe it's Zoe—the real Zoe. I look up at her face and look away just as quick. There is a thousand and fifty things I want to say to her, but I can only think of one thing.

"I'm sorry," I sniff.

[I see you.]
My tears fall into his wet dog hair, which is longer and shaggier than last time we were together. I hold him closer, deeply ashamed of myself for alienating a child who doesn't know any better. He's so troubled, he's so broken, and I wonder if he'll ever be successfully healed. Attachment trauma is a bitch.

"I'm sorry, too," I whisper. I wonder how long we'll have before he snaps. I wonder if I can handle another outburst, or if I would even need to, since there's two other adults in here. I decide in advance that I will let them handle him if something sets him off. I don't want to induce a meltdown just by being here, and I mentally second guess my visit. Dallas stretches his hand out to mine and holds it to his heart. The cadence is irregular; sluggish then fast.

I was never meant to be the reason for his broken heart and its damaged beat.

[I see red.]

"Where have you been all these days?" I question.

Her doesn't know what to say, and jumbles the words. Her starts to say something and stops, then starts again. "I got a new job."

[I see you.]

It occurs to me that Dallas might not realize that my being with him was employment. I want to eat my words and start over.

[I see red.]

I remember now that Zoe got paid from Mommy. That's how jobs work—people do stuff that other people don't want to do, then they get money in their bank. The plastic card in their wallets connects to the bank who keeps the money. But not credit cards, them are for money that the person doesn't have yet. Mommy always said that her credit card was called Max, and Jacob said she was a stupid bitch.

I remember now.

[I see you.]

I am going back and forth in my mind between elaborating on my new job, and saying nothing at all. The seconds passing by feel like years. I tap the floor so Cinnamon will come sit with us. Dallas stands abruptly and his left arm shoots up, then flails at his side. He jumps twice, as his eyes squint and his face fixes in a strange smile.

I'm scared.

I know this look.

[I see red.]

"YOU A STUPID BITCH, ZOE!" I yell in her face. I kick her, too, and Cinnamon runs away to hide in the corner. Dr. Martinez and Alicia come towards me, but Zoe grabs me first.

[I see you.]

The drive to bring Dallas back to himself is deep within me—dormant but ever present. I grab him involuntarily, and I'm mad at myself for not letting the other two adults take one for the team. I hold him on my lap as he thrashes around, with his arms crossed in front of his body. He's trying to bite me.

"Are you OK?" the Dr. says.

I nod my head, "I've got this."

Alicia's jaw falls to the ground. We spend the next God-knows-how-many minutes bearing through the storm, until Dallas quietens.

"Are you ready to talk?" I ask. He spits, then throws his head back to hit mine. I dodge his skull and wonder if the action hurt his skinny little neck. I turn Dallas around so that I can see his eyes.

[I see red.]

"My name is LOSER!" I yell.

"What's your name?" The *Evil She* says again.

"My name is GREY!"

"What's your name, buddy?"

"I killed my brother, and I can kill you too!" I scream.

[I see you.]

A shiver runs down my spine. He repeats this phrase so often, I'm convinced that he believes he killed Grey—to the point where part of me wonders if he did. We're wading through so much unprocessed grime—he's sinking in quicksand. We're no longer at triage, we're performing open heart surgery. I take my hand and place it on his heart. He swats it away, but I put it back.

"What's your name?"

He looks down, then I see the whites of his eyes as he rolls them back in his head. This is the stuff of horror movies, yet moments like this have become commonplace in my life.

"Dallas," he whispers.

"What's your name?" I repeat, "Say it loud and proud."

"Dallas!" he yells.

"What's your name, buddy?"

"Dallas Jedidiah Jensen!" he yells again. I know he's back, I feel it in the way his weight has shifted. Almost imperceptible to the naked eye, I see his spirit return to his body. I guess I don't 'see' it per se, but rather, I sense that whatever chaotic spiritual grossness just occurred has now passed. He sinks like dead weight, and just as I suspect, he falls asleep on my chest.

I have no idea how much time has passed since this meltdown began, but I get the sense it's been a while. Both Dr. Martinez and Alicia are sitting on the floor staring blankly at what just happened—the air is thick with questions.

"Is... he," Alicia croaks, then clears her throat. "Is he… done?"

"He usually sleeps after these kinds of episodes," I whisper. "When he wakes up he's unlikely to remember what happened. It might come back to him in a few hours or days. What do you guys do when he freaks out like this?"

Alicia looks at Dr. Martinez, and he returns the glance with the same blank expression.

"He doesn't… he hasn't gotten to that level before," the Dr. brags. At least I think he's bragging. Why did he bring me here if I make it all worse?

"He's never mentioned Grey to us," Alicia admits.

And there it is; the huge Grey elephant in the room. The thorn in Dallas's side. The genesis of his problems. The catalyst for his parents' separation, his dad leaving, his self-hatred, his mother's co-dependent relationships with abusive men, and his replacement of a sister.

"We've heard him, I guess, talking to Grey in the times when he's 'gone.' You know that look he gets and he's clearly 'out to lunch,'" Alicia continues. I'm intrigued. We have different names for the same thing, but we both recognize the disassociation

218

going on. We both identify the marked difference between Dallas when he's in his body, and outside his body.

"What does he say to Grey?" I inquire.

"Sometimes he just tells him everyday things—he whispers when he's just making normal conversation. Then other times he screams his name, and he's always looking up when this happens. He tends to climb high when he's screaming, with his arms outstretched," Alicia reveals. The look in her eyes tells me that she's been freaked out by Dallas more than once. She inhales, straightens her spine, shakes her head, and her eyes grow wide. Alicia has clearly seen some shit, but it was just the tip of the iceberg. There's a sobering moment when we all realize the magnitude of damage that has been done to Dallas.

He stirs, and slowly opens his eyes.

[I see red.]

I am like a bear who hibernates all the winter long.

I will eat all the food, then never eat until it's warmer. I will go from fat to skinny. I will become strong in the summer. I will be green like Ramsay, and I will be an oak, not an acorn. I'll do it all this summer. I'll be seven, and seven is big enough to become a good boy. Six-year-olds aren't good. Except Grey... he was good, but then him died.

Only dead six year olds are good.

I wake up from my long, long nap and guess what? It's still stupid winter. I cup my hand and whisper into Zoe's ear, "When are you taking me home?"

[I see you.]

My breath stops. My heart arrests.

What is the best way to tell him that he isn't going home? I want... I need backup on this one, but because Dallas whispered, I'm in a corner. This is just between him and me. I clear my throat, "I'm sorry..."

He holds a defeated expression. "What do you mean?"

This is a familiar manipulation tactic. He knows what I mean, but he's drawing me in with questions and puppy dog eyes. He wants me to feel every burning coal which he is dragging me across. In his eyes, we're still in this together.

He whispers again, "I want you to be my mom."

I'm frozen. The other two adults are staring at me, oblivious to what he's saying. They're watching for my reaction. I stare at the wall, which is an all too familiar feeling.

"I need a break," I hiss towards Dr. Martinez. I try to stand up, but Dallas doesn't budge. He grabs me until his knuckles are white, setting his face like flint and his teeth are closed tight. The Dr. and Alicia both attempt to pry him off, and each time his arms find me again. Finally, Dr. Martinez grabs him from behind and contains his torso. Alicia peels his claws from me, holding each fist in her hands. Dallas is wheezing, absolutely gasping for breath. As they pull him away in the hopes that his legs let up, I fall to the ground—literally crawling to the door.

I need air. I need to be somewhere other than here.

I run for the door.

[I see red.]

"GREY!" I yell. Then I whisper, "She's leaving us. She's leaving us, Grey."

I throw my elbow in stupid Dr. Shit Head's ribs and he makes a sound like it hurts. GOOD! I roll myself into a ball and pull my hood over my face.

If Zoe leaves, then so do I.

[I see you.]

Dr. Martinez catches me as I'm halfway to the stables.

"Zoe!" he yells, rubbing his arms in the cold. I turn around.

"Why did you bring me here? Why do you insist that Dallas and I reopen this giant gaping wound that was closing? Do you know what he said to me in there?"

"No... I was going to ask you. But, can we go inside? It's literally freezing out here."

"Oh? Are you uncomfortable? You're uncomfortable? I just had a seriously emotionally disturbed six-year-old asking me to be his new mother," I yell. "But poor Dr. Know-it-All is uncomfortable in the snow."

He stops in his tracks. "I'm sorry. Out here, if we must—but let's talk about this."

I kick the snow in a seething rage.

"I always thought we could make something out of nothing, you know. I always told Dallas what you're telling him now—that from little things, big things grow. I told him there was hope for his future, and I believed it too. I believed that we could save this fractured child, with these piecemeal interventions. His inevitable diagnoses aren't for kids, so there's over a decade between here and some answers... or medicine to mask the pain. His formative years are closing in on him. He's never going to heal, Luis. He's fucked."

CHAPTER TWENTY-EIGHT

Acknowledging the Elephant

[I see red.]

Zoe walks back into the room after I've already peed on myself. I stay still like a statue.

[I see you.]

Amber liquid is pooling on the floor, before absorbing into the carpet. He never wet his pants with me, not once. He'd use the bathroom as an excuse to skip nonpreferred activities. There's no denying we had our bathroom problems, but the incontinence is new to me. Except I'm not convinced it's accidental—this is textbook reactive attachment manipulation. He knows what he's doing. He might regret it afterward, but he knows what he's doing. I want to scoop him up and change him like a toddler; I want to get him into a warm bath with a rubber duckie, and read him stories while he uses bubbles to make a beard. I want to give him all he missed out on, and nurture the three-year-old trapped in an almost-seven-year-old's body. But in order to break the behavior, our treatment needs to be counterintuitive—we can't show pity for this kid or his demons win. He will go all out to prove he's beyond fixing, and as his adults, we need to show him that there is redemption. Even if it feels impossible, we can't let him drown with his brother. I will choose to see beauty in Dallas, even when everything inside me says he's not worth the effort; he can't be a lost cause, I will go to my grave proving this fact.

Dr. Martinez stays put, and I ask Alicia to show me to Dallas's room. As I walk through the house I see kids drugged out of their minds, staring blankly into space. On the other end of the spectrum I watch as two teenage boys punch each other's lights out while adult men try to separate them. A little girl, maybe around nine or ten, comes and holds my hand. She tells me she likes my necklace. Alicia encourages the girl to go back to her group.

"That's Anastasiya. She was adopted from Bulgaria when she was five. Things didn't work out so well in her new family, and she was sent here after an incident at school," Alicia explains. "She's sweet, but, don't let her draw you in. There are alarms on the doors here for a reason."

We turn a corner and enter room forty-nine, where the dry erase board on the door is marked: Matthew and Dallas. There are twin beds against opposite walls and separate chests of drawers for keeping each child's clothes organized. Two winter coats hang on hooks, two beanies are stored above, and four small snow boots are lined up by the door. On Matthew's side of the room there are family photos, stuffed toys, and love notes. On Dallas's side hangs one lonely drawing of a skinny Victorian house with three people sitting on the roof. Two are boys, and one looks like a lady. They're eating hot dogs.

I open his drawers to get him a new set of clothes. He's got four pairs of camouflaged cargo shorts, nine black t-shirts, and three gray hoodies.

"How did he bring his clothes with him?" I ask Alicia, suspiciously. "I was under the impression he was flown here from the hospital in a medical helicopter."

She shakes her head, "His Mom sent us a bag of stuff after the fact."

"Did she send any photographs… or stuffed toys… or anything?" I clarify.

"Just the clothes," Alicia reiterates. "No return address."

I choose him a t-shirt with a wolf on the front, cargo shorts, white ankle socks, and a pair of undies with dinosaurs on them. He still wears size four clothes, which by Alicia's account, were hanging off him a few weeks ago after he stopped eating. The thought occurs to me that soon enough he will shoot up, even if he doesn't fill out, and these clothes will be way too small for him. Nobody will send him a new bag of his favorite clothes in the next size up. He'll be wearing the hand-me-downs of the big, swearing, fighting boys. I don't want him wrapped in the mantle of societal failure, shoved away in some corner of some town in Wyoming.

I close the drawer and Alicia leads me to a room with all kinds of supplies. We grab latex gloves, cleaning spray, a bunch of paper towel, and some baby wipes, before heading back to Dallas and Dr. Martinez. I look at nothing and no-one, ignoring the group activities being inevitably disrupted by maladaptive behaviors. I ignore Anastasiya as she waves at me with the enthusiasm of a toddler reuniting with a parent at the end of the day.

Dallas is still laying in his own piss; Dr. Martinez sits beside him, yet on dry land. I hand Dallas the supplies.

"Here you go, Buddy. Everything can be fixed," I say, with a positive inflection.

[I see red.]

Zoe doesn't mention the pee, but she gives me a pile of cleaning stuff instead.

"What do you want me to do?" I ask, even if I know what she wants. If I ask her, she'll have to answer me, and if she has to answer me, she'll stay. I've got her all understood.

"I wonder if you can figure it out," she says, then the Dr. and the Zoe leave the room. Alicia turns her back to me, so I try to ask her more questions. I am lonely here.

"What do I do with these?" I ask.

"First, clean yourself. Then, change yourself. Next, clean the floor," Alicia tells me. "I'm turning this way so you'll have privacy as you get changed. I'll set a timer—if you can get it all done faster than five minutes you can have ten minutes playing with blocks."

The timer beeps to start, and I know I can choose to listen to her or not. I take a deep breath, then take off my stinky, wet clothes. I put them in a plastic bag, and use the wipes to get clean. I put the wipes in the trash. I squirt the cleaning spray on the carpet and lay a hundred paper towels on top. I stand on it and watch the pee and spray soak through. It looks like wet footprints on dry paper. I stand on it a hundred times more, then put it in the trash.

"Done," I say in a whiney voice. Alicia turns around."HAHA!" I yell, because I am naked, and I tricked her. Alicia looks away so quickly.

"You're almost done," she says strongly. I put on my undies, then my shorts, then my socks, then my shirt, then my sweater, and then after all of that hard work, I put on my shoes.

"OK, really done!" I yell.

"You have to earn back my trust, Dallas. If I turn around, and you're not ready, you won't be able to play with the blocks."

I look at my whole body, and it's totally dressed. The timer beep beep beeps because five minutes are up. "I'm actually ready, Alicia!"

She turns around a bit nervously, then says, "Thank you, Dallas," in a voice that isn't happy or sad. "Go ahead and play with the blocks—I'll set the timer."

Alicia slides the red part of the special timer clock out to make ten minutes. The red bit disappears as time happens. I wonder if I get to go home with Zoe after I play with blocks?

#

[I see you.]

We're back in the soft room with Dr. Martinez, playing with Cinnamon. Alicia has finished her shift, which is kind of relieving for me. I get the sense that we're competing for something, even though I've taken myself out of the equation.

"Dallas," the Dr. says. "Let's talk about what's going to happen these next few days."

Dallas makes eye contact with Dr. Martinez, nods his head, and says, "OK."

The Dr. smiles and approaches a sticker chart on the wall with Dallas's name on top. There are no gold stars yet, even though the first week was dated in early November.

"Wow! Eye contact, using your body to communicate, responding when spoken to! Dallas, these are your first three stickers on the chart!" he beams. "If you get two more stickers, you get to choose what we do with our next session!"

Dallas looks underwhelmed, but I know it's self-preservation. He is uncomfortable with achievement. But I see that half-smile curling the left side of his mouth.

[I see red.]

Dr. Poopy Diaper gets a piece of paper and starts making a schedule like what Zoe used to do. I remember our home school—it was so good.

"Today is Monday," he says. "Yesterday was Christmas, and today we have Zoe and Cinnamon. Zoe is staying from now until next Tuesday."

As he talks, he writes and draws with the marker that smells good. I follow his writing and drawing with my eyes. I wait for him to tell me that I get to go home with her, but he starts talking about something else.

"We are going to try something very special, but you have to prove that you can handle it," he says with a serious face. I guess this is where he tells me I get to go home with Zoe, and if I'm good, I get to stay.

"Do you know what a service dog is?" he says.

I don't know what service dogs have to do with anything. My eyes get wider, and I'm waiting, waiting, waiting for the part where he says I'm going home.

[I see you.]

He's going to be so excited when he realizes he might be able to keep Cinnamon.

"Dallas," Dr. Martinez repeats, "Do you know what a service dog is?"

Dallas shakes his head, but he's smiling.

"They're specially trained dogs who help people," the Dr. explains. "We'd like to train Cinnamon, so he can stay here with you."

[I see red.]

"...So he can stay here with you."

SO HE CAN STAY HERE WITH ME? No, no, no, no, no.

[I see you.]

226

The half smile morphs. His eyes become narrow slits, then widen as he stands. Oh shit, there go his arms. The volcano is erupting; get ready for the lava.

[I see red.]
"I'M GOING HOME WITH ZOE!" I scream in Dr. Shit Head's face. I spit on him too, but he closes his eyes when it lands on his face. "HOW MANY TIMES DO I HAVE TO TELL YOU? ARE YOU STUPID OR SOMETHING?"

[I see you.]
His words are directly from Jacob's mouth. The phrases spoken over Dallas are spewing from the top of the volcano, from his core, deep underground. They're molten, glowing with anger. They're red: the filter through which he sees life when he's disassociated from his body. His immovable faith that I will be his new mother is haunting, pressing on my shoulders like a heavy ghost. Sarah's face fills my mind, and she's just as haunted as I am, yet by the ghost of Grey. He's the center of all this, an innocent child who ran out of oxygen. Grief never disappears—it can evaporate, but it's ever present, waiting to rain down on a cloudy day.

"Do you need a break, Dallas?" I ask, voice trembling. He starts banging his head against a wall—albeit a soft one. He's certainly not the first kid to meltdown in a soft room at Starlight. There's a stretchy hammock in the corner, and if I can just herd him there, he may calm down without being held. The hammock provides deep pressure sensory input, like a great big hug, with the added benefit of not punching anyone in the face.

I push gently on his back, leading him to the hammock, and of course he resists. So I grab him, and literally throw him in the hammock. He lands softly, bouncing in the stretchy fabric. Inevitably, he thrashes, but he can't get out. Within a minute, he surrenders to the hammock and calms. For the hundredth time today, we sit beside Dallas and wait it out.

There's always tomorrow.

[I see red.]
I'm trapped in this hammock and I'm trapped at this house.

CHAPTER TWENTY-NINE

Rewriting the Story

[I see you.]

At 8 pm I leave Starlight and trudge through the snow to the guest house by the stables. There are three rooms for parents to use when they stay, and the other two are empty—in fact, this whole establishment is pretty empty right now considering the vast majority of kids are home for the holidays. The guest house is dated; decorated with maroon and pine green plaid curtains, oak wood furniture, and a touch lamp by the bed.

It smells musty. Unused.

I fall face down on the bed. What a day.

#

Around 10pm I feel able to dial Ezra.

"Hello," I say.

"Hey babe," he answers. "How did it go?"

"It went."

He takes a deep breath. "Are you OK?"

"I'm exhausted," I admit. "Dallas had several violent meltdowns today, and I had one too."

"I'm sorry," he croaks. "I wish I could be there for you."

I stand by the window, and touch the lamp so it shuts off. I slide it open and feel the freezing breeze on my face, taking in the sight of the stars I haven't seen in years.

"It's beautiful here. A little creepy in the residential part, but I got a guest house out back. It's for parents, but I guess they don't visit much. The whole idea of residential care is tragic, it's like a greenhouse for criminals."

"Are you safe?"

"Yeah," I say, not sure whether it's a truth or lie. "There are tons of staff."

"How's Cinnamon?"

"Cute," I smile, scruffing his furry neck. "He's been a real life-saver. I can't leave him with Dallas yet, but hopefully by the end of the week."

"How's Dallas?"

"Skinny," I choke. "He's peeing his pants, too."

Ezra pushes. "You need to make things right with him."

"I'm trying," I say, holding back tears. "It just didn't happen today."

"There's always tomorrow," he tells me, before changing the subject to something completely unrelated. The conversation doesn't last long, considering I'm emotionally spent, and truth be told—I can't think of anyone but Dallas.

[I see red.]

I wake up alone in my room, because Matthew is still at home with his family. The clock says 7:15 am, and I'm only allowed out of the room after 7:30 am. If I open the door, an alarm goes BEEP, BEEP and I don't want that to happen. I get dressed and wait.

I wonder what time Zoe will be here?

At 7:30 am Alicia comes to the door. Alicia, ugh, wrong girl. I feel like hitting her, but I don't. She takes me to breakfast at the dining hall. I cross my arms and say nothing the whole way.

[I see you.]

I meet Dallas over breakfast and conversationally walk on the very same eggshells that broke to make my meal. All I want is a couple of hours without him flying off the handle, and I wonder if that's realistic. Dallas, Alicia, and I sit around a table for three, and I notice her left foot fixed on his chair. She's pushed the chair in so far that he can't escape quickly, and my respect for the girl skyrockets. Alicia knows what she's doing.

"Zoe, I eated protein all the meals," Dallas brags. "I gotted so skinny that Alicia said her could play guitar on my ribs. She told me that if I didn't start eating, then a doctor would put a food tube in my nose. Not the same doctor that you meeted, him is just a feelings doctor. The food tube doctor is from the hostable."

I mentally note three things:

(1) His speech has regressed—he's lost the ability to use past tense appropriately, the pronouns have slipped, and he sounds basically like a three-year-old again.

(2) He's, in my opinion, deathly skinny—but I'm aware this isn't the worst he's been. He fixed his own meals (chicken nuggets) from the ages of three through six. He didn't know how to accept food from others/this is another power play.

(3) He's himself today. Talkative and free.

After breakfast, Alicia takes Dallas to his first group session of the day. They're doing indoor PE of some sort, since it's snowing like crazy outside. We left Cinnamon in the guest house today.

#

All three primary adults in Dallas's life meet in Dr. Martinez's 'adult' office—a stark departure from the soft room. I, for one, am glad we're out of that God-forsaken padded cell.

"I'm excited to have you both on board for Dallas's treatment plan," Dr. Martinez announces. "Zoe, you come with the most knowledge of Dallas. You can give us context, backstory, and evidence-based opinions on strategies."

Alicia looks a little uncomfortable, redundant even, like I've invaded her area of expertise. I want to tell her I'm not competing — I don't want the responsibility of Dallas. That's why he's here.

"Alicia," he continues, " You are on the front line of this plan. I have only got five hours a week with Dallas, but you have forty. You have seven times more opportunity to make an impact on his life."

She looks less awkward now, and a little more nervous. I would be, too, if I were entrusted with Dallas's life at her age. I wonder if I should suggest that she start working out, doing some weight training or something. With all this protein he's consuming, he's going to get stronger, and Alicia is barely bigger than a twelve-year-old. He'll crush her like an ant.

"Zoe," Luis begins, "Why don't you start explaining your opinions on where we should go with his treatment plan?"

"Grief," I clear my throat. "I believe grief is the driving force behind most of Dallas's behaviors."

Alicia pipes up, "We've heard Reactive Attachment Disorder, Conduct Disorder, Dissociative Identity Disorder, Oppositional Defiance Disorder..."

She bends one finger back at a time as she lists each of the frustrating diagnoses that have been thrown at her. She's drowning in other people's fleeting opinions, and she can't afford to go under.

"It all stems back to the original trauma of Grey's death," I explain.

"Can you elaborate on the details of the trauma?" Luis asks.

"Just so you know," I begin, "I got my original information from Dallas's mom, but I'm not convinced it's entirely accurate. There are major gaps, and most of them involve his mother's alcoholism. She changed the story about three times as she told me."

"Was Dallas in the room when you heard details of the trauma?" Luis asks.

"No," I confirm. "He was in his room making loud noises. I think he knew what was happening, and he didn't want me to know."

"I want you to tell us the most accurate account of the story that you know," Luis requests. "We are unlikely ever to get any more information than you already have. I trust that you'll leave your opinion at the door, and just give the facts."

I think for a moment, about whether or not that is possible. I know, without a shadow of a doubt, I'm going to spin the story in Dallas's favor, but I don't know what else to do. There's a decent part of me that now believes Dallas killed his brother, but in order to save Dallas's life, I'm about to enter into the land of the 'Little White Lie.' My bias gets the better of me as the words leave my lips.

"Four summers ago, when Dallas was three and Grey was six, they were swimming in a neighbor's pool. The dad was inside with friends, and their mom, who has problems with alcohol, left them unattended to refill her drink. When she returned, Grey was face down in the water, and Dallas was still playing, because he didn't understand what happened. Mom immediately blamed Dallas, because she knew she shouldn't have left them alone. Dad only ever heard the version of the story where Dallas held Grey under the water, even though we have it on fairly good authority that's not true."

OK, I made up some of the story. I know for certain that Sarah left to get a drink, and when she returned, Grey had a head injury and was dead. Nobody but Dallas knows what happened in between A and B. The main point of the story is that Sarah shouldn't have left her kids unattended—especially for alcohol.

"Was there an autopsy report?" Luis interjects.

"He drowned," I shrug. What more can I say?

"I feel bad for even asking, but, are we sure that Dallas didn't drown his brother?" Alicia asks. I wince.

It has occurred to me for a while now, that Dallas could really be a killer. There were no eyewitnesses to my knowledge, and right now, I am Dallas's only advocate. I don't know if he held Grey under the water, and he sure as hell doesn't remember the story accurately. He has only ever had a drunken version of the events regurgitated to him. So, in order to save Dallas's life, I lie.

"Yeah, that was concluded in the autopsy," I insist.

"How can they tell the difference between him being held under the water, and him just drowning?" Alicia prods.

"Grey had a head injury," I report, which I know to be true. "Our best guess is that he jumped off the edge of the pool and hit his head on the side."

"Are there any other details to be aware of?" Luis examines. "Some of the story seems kind of fuzzy."

"I told you from the beginning that the story was a jigsaw puzzle, and nobody accurately knows where the pieces should go," I retort defensively. "I've told you all I know."

Dr. Martinez shuffles a bunch of papers, and says, "OK. Now that we know the truth about what happened -"

(I almost throw up, but I don't. The word 'truth' lodges itself in my throat.)

"We can start retelling the story to Dallas. He's assumed responsibility because he's never been told otherwise," Luis continues. "I want you guys to work together to create a social story. He'll probably react to it pretty violently at first, but we'll persevere. Once he knows the true version of the story, we can get to the grief."

"He talks to Zoe about Grey," Alicia comments, "But he doesn't mention Grey to me at all. And let's face it, he flat out ignores you, Luis. How are we going to get to the next step?"

Dr. Martinez and I react in unison, "Time."

"Time's not on our side. We only have Zoe for another week," Alicia worries.

"Let's just take one day at a time," Luis cautions. "We can't project a timeline with kids like Dallas. There'll be progress, then he'll regress, and he'll move forward when he's ready. His brain isn't conditioned for consistency, and we have been given the gift of living with him for the remainder of his formative years."

"What if he has nowhere to go when he's eight?" Alicia worries.

"We'll cross that bridge when we come to it," Luis shrugs. "There's no crystal ball, no magic wand—just brain plasticity and behavior retraining. Truthfully, Alicia, your consistent positive influence in his life is going to make all the difference. You too, Zoe. Your keeping in contact with him will catalyze this process. Don't underestimate your role in Dallas's healing."

We sit in this sobering moment. Two girls in their twenties who can barely be responsible for paying their phone bills on time and keeping up with laundry, staring down the barrel at raising a broken child from his proverbial coffin. I just hope Alicia stays on after a year.

Throwing strategies back and forth across the table for an hour, we finally settle on some ways in which to start a formal treatment plan. We have cumulative reward systems, plans for time-in (instead of time-out), focused attention plans, a set of consistent phrases we'll all use to keep our communication on the same page—a basic playbook. The what-ifs have all been covered. We're stepping into the war with full armor and loud battle cries. This intervention has never been so watertight because Team Dallas is strong and unified. This process is a billion times easier without Sarah on board.

Step one: Fifteen minutes of scheduled attention, following his lead in play, not pushing the conversation. Session three we'll start asking questions.

[I see red.]

After PE and lunch, I see Zoe and Alicia coming to get me. I launch myself at Zoe like a grenade, exploding on her with a hug. I hear the breath go out of she's lungs, like *ugh*! Alicia takes me off Zoe's body, then we all go into the soft room. We set fifteen minutes on the special timer with the red, and Alicia tells me that I can choose any game (as long as it's appropriate) and the three of us will play together for that time. I choose blocks (duh), get the bin off the shelf, and tip it all over the floor. It sounds so loud, and both the girls look at it like they wish I didn't do that. I wonder how long it will be before one of them says, "You know you have to put all of them away when you're done?"

It was five seconds; then Zoe said it. I told her, "I KNOW."

I start building, and they do, too. Sometimes we talk about what we're making, and sometimes we're quiet. For once they're not asking me to talk about my feelings. Before I know it, the red on the timer gets skinny, and it beeps. That's the end of fifteen minutes.

"We are going to play like this every day this week after lunch," Zoe reminds me. We all pack up quickly, and like magic, out come the gold stars. I getted one for packing up on time, another one for packing up with a good attitude, and another one for sticking with one activity the whole time. If I get ten stars, we can add five minutes to the playtime. I wonder how to get twenty stars, so I can add ten minutes?

[I see you.]

We take Dallas to his music class, and Alicia gets permission to leave him unattended as long as she keeps her cell phone on her at all times. Kevin, a floating staff member steps in to provide Dallas with extra support. We make ourselves coffee and grab some cookies from the kitchen—fuel for a full day of intervention.

"Have you ever written a story for Dallas before?" she asks. "One about expectations?"

"Yeah—we had one for our trip to Discovery Country. Obviously, it was super effective," I say. She's trying not to laugh, so I laugh instead. She does too, and I'm glad the ice between us is starting to melt.

"Just so you know," I admit, looking down, "I'm really glad you're on the frontline of this intervention. I know it must feel weird with me here, but I'm being honest when I say I don't want the responsibility of Dallas. I will support you in any way I can; I will be as involved as much as it helps him. Once I leave you'll gain traction, when he comes to terms with our roles in his life. He needs you; a strong, consistent figure in his life. I'll fade to the background."

"Don't disappear too quickly," Alicia desperately chokes, "I need your guidance in this. I'll also probably need to call you when you go home—you're literally the only other person who understands—who sees—Dallas for who he really is."

I hug her, "Of course."

#

Alicia leaves twenty minutes into the session because Dallas called the music teacher a bitch. She's gone for ten more minutes, doing time-in with him (it's like time-out, but the adult stays). He's not angry, just frustrated, and they breathe deeply together. I watch through a two-way mirror, admiring the harmony in which their bodies breathe and move together. I see what was a

235

seed of a relationship blossom to a sapling, with tiny roots going deep. She ushers him back into the music room, and I assume he's repairing the situation by performing an apology of action. He hands her a piece of paper, and I read his lips say, "Sorry."

Alicia returns, and Kevin steps in her place. We pore over pages, motivated to give Dallas the most accurate story about his trauma. These kinds of stories are narratives written by adults to convey, often difficult, messages to kids. They project best case scenarios, they honestly outline events, and explain how life looks, or will look. Like two authors meticulously crafting a best-seller, we begin writing Dallas's history in a way he'll understand. Through the two-way mirror we see Dallas transition to playtime with the group, Kevin herds him like a sheep dog. I'm amazed at his ability to be part of the group today—he looks like the most normal kid in the world. Well, he's a dandelion in a field of thistles at least.

#

Four hours, three calls, one pee-break for Cinnamon, and five cookies later—Dallas's story is written.

CHAPTER THIRTY

Irrevocably Tethered

[I see red.]

Today is the third day that Zoe has been at Starlight. After dinner, I have a special treat—Zoe is going to help me through my night routine and read my bedtime stories. Here's the things what I do:

1. Eat enough dinner to be allowed to leave. Eat the protein.
2. Go to the shower. I need some help getting the hot right—not too icy, not too burny. Alicia normally sits outside the shower saying, "Use soap," and waits with her back turned, so her doesn't see my wiener. Zoe will be the Alicia tonight, and I can only half promise not to run out of the shower all naked. Alicia is so funny when her accidentally sees my weenie. She's so angry, like a toy with red lights flashing. It's so funny. Her's like, "GET BACK IN THERE AND GET DRESSED."

I usually go into my room with Matthew, and we can read books on our own for ten minutes, and at 7 pm the lights go out, out, out. Normally it's dark at 7 pm but Matthew said in summer the sun stays up later than us, but that's why we have fat curtains to make it dark. The House Dad, Pete, says goodnight to us and him says, "If you need me, press the button, and I'll come to you." You know why? An alarm happens if we open the bedroom door in the night. He said it's so kids don't run away, but Matthew told me it's so kids don't kill anyone with knifes. Also, Matthew wears a diaper to bed, and him is a whole year older than me.

#

[I see you.]

Dallas runs out of the shower stark naked, and my hands go over my eyes as fast as lightning. Alicia warned me about his new found love of flashing, and I'm sure she'll find it hilarious that he gave me the same surprise.

"Shower. Now!" I command emotionlessly. He dances around for a while, realizes I'm not going to laugh at him, then gets back in the shower. When he's out of sight I giggle to myself and send Alicia a text message:

Thanks for the heads up about the nudie run. Dallas: 1, Zoe: 0.

She replies straight away with several laughing emojis, and I realize that all the hours we've spent without Dallas have turned us into comrades rather than competitors. Dallas turns the shower off, and I get ready to prompt his next move.

"Are you decent?" I ask.

"What means decent?" he yells, and I hear him splashing around in the puddle of water on the tiles.

"Do you have clothes on?"

"Yeah."

"If I turn around, and you're naked, we can only read two stories instead of three tonight. I'll ask again—do you have clothes on?"

He rustles around and delays his answer.

"Wait—um," he says in an elongated tone, then quickens his speech. "Dressed!"

He is technically dressed, but I think he skipped the part where he's supposed to dry his body. I try not to laugh, as he stands there in his adorable pajamas with his damp skin sticking to the fabric. His hair is wet and stuck to his face.

"When's the last time you had a haircut, Buddy?" I giggle.

He looks up to the left and puts his finger on his chin, "Hmmm. When you took me in San Francisco."

238

That was the day before Discovery Country. I don't know how things like haircuts work here, so I make a mental note to ask Alicia when we can get his mane trimmed. Dallas hangs his towel and grabs my hand to lead me to his bedroom. When we get inside, he gives me the grand tour.

"This is my bed; that's Matthew's bed. That's our books. Them's our clothes. Matthew is at him's parents house, but that's where him normally sleeps. You can sleep in him's bed tonight if you like?" he suggests, with big, puppy dog eyes.

Speaking of puppy dogs, I say, "I'd love to—but I need to go back to the guest house and look after Cinnamon tonight."

"Can you bring him over here tomorrow?" he pleads.

"Let me check with Dr. Martinez first, but if he agrees, I think it would be super fun. Now, which books do you want to read tonight? Three small-ish books is our limit."

He stumbles out of bed to the room's shared book collection. I wonder if they belong to Starlight or Matthew, because none of them are Dallas's. He selects three fiction stories, none of which are about vicious animals. Hope rises, as I realize not everything has been a regression. His academic skills are more advanced, and he has an age appropriate appreciation for literature. He gets in bed and pats the space next to him—I lay beside, just as we used to snuggle on the trampoline. I hear his heart racing, and I kiss him on the forehead. He half-smiles, then his breath deepens and slows. His heartbeat catches itself, now steadily drumming inside his chest. I'm reminded of how little affection he's received since Grey's death—Dallas is nobody's son. His love tank is dry, and with Alicia's help, we will start to fill him up, step by step, bucket by bucket.

#

By the end of the third story, I notice he's asleep. I stroke his wild hair, and lay beside him for a while, enjoying the closeness without fear of vacillation between sweetness and rage. My heartbeat steadies too, the symbiosis between Dallas and I strengthening with every beat—he heals me as I heal him.

For better or worse, my life is irrevocably tethered to this child.

#

Pete places his hand on my shoulder and wakes me. It's midnight, and I've fallen asleep beside Dallas, holding his hand.

"Zoe," he says, "Sorry to wake you, but you need to go back to the guest house now."
I sit up and rub my eyes, swiping my hair out of my face.

"Thanks," I mumble to Pete. I pull the blanket over Dallas to make sure he's warm enough, and place a spare pillow in the gap I've left. He stirs but doesn't wake. I kiss him on the forehead.

#

Cinnamon bolts out the door when I return, desperate to go pee. Poor thing, I've left him too long today, and he's left me a turd on the carpet in return.

#

[I see red.]
Zoe has been here for five whole days now, and her brought Cinnamon to see me. A visitor comes from the place who trains service dogs, and she does a test to see if he can be my service dog.

"Thanks to all the training that Zoe put in early on," the lady says, "Cinnamon is a good candidate for becoming a service dog. We'd like to involve Dallas in the training—is that OK Luis?"

I wonder who Louise is, then I see her looking at Dr. Poopy.

"Dallas, if you want to keep Cinnamon here at Starlight, you'll need to train him five days a week with Lynda," Dr. Poop Head says. "Do you agree to commit to the training? That means you stick to it, and don't give up."

I nod my head. I really want to keep Cinnamon. Dr. Poop talks a grown up conversation to the dog lady. He tells her about money because her said usually parents pay it, but mine can't because nobody told them about it.

"...Starlight has grant money that will pick up the costs associated with the training. You'll come here Monday through Friday, 4-5pm? That's free time in Dallas's schedule," he tells.

"Perfect," Dog Lady says, then she goes.

[I see you.]

After lunch, Alicia and I usher Dallas to the soft room for our focused attention session. He's earned ten extra minutes, which is mutually beneficial since today we add a little more agenda. He hasn't flipped out with us since the first day, so we tread lightly, deciding not to ask questions. We'll introduce the social story at the end of the session.

"Set the red to twenty-five," Dallas instructs, and I'm amazed at his ability to mentally add his regular time plus his reward. Mere months ago, his report card stated he couldn't count to ten. I move the hand on the timer, as Alicia sits on the floor with Dallas. She and I share a glance of nerves and excitement, and I'm glad we're in this together. He chooses blocks, again, and we do our best to stay present while following his lead. Honestly, I've never met an adult who enjoys playing with kids. Being on a rug, surrounded by blocks is my own specific kind of torture, especially when anticipating the moment where we begin reshaping Dallas's life story. If a watched pot never boils, a watched timer never moves. My stomach churns.

[I see red.]

"I maked a river, Zoe! Hey, Zoe! ZOE!" I yell, waving my hand in her face. "Earth to Zoe!"

She shakes her head and tells me sorry, then says, "Wow! Yeah. I see a river."

I have made a thousand things with blocks, and always I put them away at the end, and it's like they never existed. Every day I make new things, and I never get bored.

"BEEP BEEP, BEEP BEEP, BEEP BEEP!" goes the timer. I kick the blocks with my foot to break them down, but I'm not angry. That's just how I pack up now, it's my new way.

"Let's see who can put most blocks back in the bin," Alicia says, then all three of us start putting blocks away. I notice at a toy car I've never seen before, and it looks awesome. I zoom it on the ground, and its wheels keep spinning like crazy.

"It looks like Alicia and I are winning!" Zoe yells, and I remember what I am supposed to be doing.

"No! I win!" I say, and put a hundred thousand blocks away. When we are done, I walk to the door, but Alicia takes me to the beanbags. Zoe and Alicia sit both sides of me, and bring out a game tablet. I think we are going to play that Zombie game with guns.

[I see you.]

I scoot my beanbag across the threshold to the door, the room's only exit point. Apart from a few toys, everything in this room is safe and soft. Even the blocks are made of foam, so if he throws them at us, they won't hurt. I tell myself not to be afraid of his meltdowns, knowing that I've been through the worst of them already. It's quite possible that I've just locked us in a room with a tiny murderer, but today's the day we erase his past.

Did he kill his brother? I'd sooner think his alcoholic mother made it up than believe the shaggy haired kid I fell asleep beside last night was capable of cold-blooded murder. Maybe he was just curious about what would happen, and wasn't developmentally ready to understand cause and effect. Maybe Grey just hit his head, and nobody is to blame. But, I'll blame the lady who gave him up, and take my doubts about Dallas to the grave. Regardless of the truth, a three-year-old can't be held accountable for something like that. Dallas loved his brother, of this I am sure.

"Hey Buddy," I say. "We're going to read you a story."

[I see red.]

I never get to play the zombie game anymore! UGH.

CHAPTER THIRTY-ONE

This is Your Life

[I see you.]

I open the story app and start reading the first page, "My name is Dallas, I am six-and-three-quarters years old, and I live at Starlight House."

"Hey! That's me!" he comments, pointing to a picture of himself with Arrow the horse.

"A long time ago, I lived in San Francisco with my mom, dad, and brother Grey," I swipe to turn the page, seeing Dallas tense his body in my periphery.

"That was a thousand years ago. BORING!" he snaps. "Can we do the zombie game now?"

"I tell you what," Alicia bargains. "If we can get through this story together, you can play zombies afterward. But that deal only works if you're paying attention to the story. Deal?"

He rolls his eyes, and says in the whiniest voice, "Fine."

It's not a deal I would've made myself, because I'm pretty sure it's not going to end well—but Alicia is his person now, so I need to let the rope out a bit. The next page is a photo of Grey and Dallas, one I stole from the house while Sarah was at work. I may or may not have found it in her closet while Dallas was pooping. He pooped, I snooped. Hey, the end justified the means, didn't it?

"Grey and I were best friends. We had bunk beds, we played on the trampoline, we swam together. One day Grey and I were swimming," I pause, because Dallas has his fingers in his ears.

"Think of how fun the Zombie game will be," Alicia encourages, and to my surprise, he puts his hands by his side and pays attention. He taps his foot, because he knows what's coming.

"... And Mommy left us alone in the pool. When kids swim, adults are supposed to watch to make sure they're safe. Everybody makes mistakes, and Mommy thought we would be OK for just a minute. Grey jumped from the side of the pool and hit his head on the bricks which made him fall asleep. I thought he was being silly, and it was part of the trick he was doing, so I laughed," I continue, cautiously. Dallas is shaking his head furiously, but saying nothing.

"Hey Buddy, looks like you've stopped listening. Do you need a break?" Alicia prompts. Dallas stops shaking his head.

"No," he says. "Keep reading."

"People need to breathe air, and when Grey was underwater for so long, he had no air. He breathed water, which went in his lungs. He died because he spent too long without air in his lungs, and this is called drowning," I read.

"I KNOW! Why do you think I wouldn't know what drowning meaned? I was there. I know what means drowning!" Dallas yells. "Also, this story is fake because that's not what happened. I killed him."

I put my arm on Dallas and he shrugs it off. Sitting beside him, without eye contact, I calmly stray from the written story, explaining succinctly, "You didn't kill Grey. Nobody killed Grey. Grey died from a head injury, which caused him to drown. It wasn't your fault."

"Them are lies," he whispers. "Why did Mommy say I killed Grey? Why did Daddy tell me that too? And Jacob?"

I don't want to blame Sarah, but then again, if she was there, none of this would have ever happened. "Buddy," I say, "Mommy was supposed to be watching you in the pool. She made a mistake, and she felt really guilty. Do you know what guilty means?"

Dallas shakes his head.

"You know how sorry you feel when you think about not saving Grey? That feeling you get when you've done something wrong? That's called guilty," I explain. "Mommy felt guilty about leaving you and Grey in the pool, so she blamed you and your daddy believed her. She didn't kill Grey, but she didn't take responsibility for leaving you alone. Mommy made a mistake, Dallas. But the bigger mistake was when she said it was your fault."

"But I remember it," he says.

"You remember this version of the story, because that's what Mom and Dad told you. Your parents should have been watching you and Grey in the pool, and they weren't. Grey died by accident, Dallas," I inform, somewhat desperately. "It was an accident."

"You're a liar!" he yells, standing up, waving his finger in my face. Blood rushes to my head, and I brace myself for the impending meltdown. Alicia pats her lap, then gestures for Dallas to sit with her. To my surprise, he perches himself calmly, and allows Alicia to wrap her arms around his waist. I know he's triangulating—trying to make Alicia the good guy, and me the bad guy—but he's contained, and far more calm than I had anticipated. He spent most of the last few days giving Alicia the cold shoulder, so I'm glad he's made me the bad guy in this situation. For Dallas's life to change, he needs a secure attachment to Alicia.

"I know it's really hard to change your thoughts, Dallas. I can't even imagine having someone tell me that my memories weren't real. The problem is, little kids' memories are made stronger by adults. Imagine you saw a blue square, but your Mom told you it's a green circle. Before you're big enough to know what you saw, you'll remember the green circle because that's the story you've been told," I ramble, knowing this is all going over his head. I'm speaking for my own benefit now. I want him to understand, but I'm not sure it's developmentally possible.

"Finish the story," he grumbles, with his foot rapidly tapping the floor. Alicia is holding his arms across his body, which makes all the difference to his ability to regulate his behavior. I bring the tablet back, and now there's a picture of Grey's grave. I'm not sure Dallas ever saw it, but it's a photo of a photo I saw in Sarah's closet. Subsequently, it's blurry, because I felt dirty for stealing a picture of a grave.

"Grey isn't with us on Earth anymore. He lives in our memories. It's OK to miss him, it's OK to cry, it's OK to talk about Grey. I need to talk about Grey, so I can grow into a healthy kid, a healthy teenager, and a healthy man," I pause, taking in the expression on Dallas's face. He's staring at nothing in particular, sucking on his left middle and ring fingers. His right-hand twirls his long, curly mane, and I watch him tug at individual hairs. He's this odd mix of infant and disturbed adult; a child caught in a moment far above his maturity level, with the coping skills of a baby. Alicia gently removes his hand from his hair, and I remember that I need to ask her about getting him a long overdue haircut. Now, he's just sucking his fingers and staring.

He takes his hand out of his mouth and says, "OK."

Alicia and I look at each other in disbelief.

"OK… meaning…?" I check.

"OK, I'll talk about Grey," he shrugs. "Is the story over? I want to play the zombie game."

Alicia reaches for his star chart and swiftly adheres a sticker in today's space. "Dallas, thank you for using your words!"

I take another sticker, "You get a second sticker for controlling your body."

We're careful to reward without praise, crafting each sentence by fact, instead of judgment. We know that too much celebration brings him crashing down in a wave of self-sabotage, so we keep our tone relatively neutral. He half-smiles, unwilling to acknowledge his successes in this area, yet something deep inside of him basks in the recognition. Alicia hands him the tablet, and he flips through the story again, pausing on the picture of himself with Grey. His eyes are different in this photo—different than they have been since I've known him, but certainly a stark departure from what they are today. His face holds a sunken quality that no six-year-old should know, a worn-out expression, like a fugitive running with no rest. He takes a deep breath, then changes the screen to the zombie game.

Dallas looks up and says, "I forgot how Grey looked."

[I see red.]

Today I learned some things:

1. How to make a peanut butter sandwich. I am not good at knifes yet, but of course, we don't use sharp ones. You know why? Them alarms I already explained.
2. In PE I learned more of soccer, and one day maybe I can play on a team. I learned about service dogs and how them need to behave. I am happy to keep Cinnamon here, even if we need to do a lot of work for him to stay.
3. I didn't kill my brother. Nobody killed my brother. Him just died because it was a mix between a mistake and an accident.
4. The zombie game is more fun than I remember.

#

[I see you.]

"I miss you," Ezra echoes from the other end of the phone. "How many more days?"

"Six," I croak.

"Who am I going to kiss on New Year's Eve?" he whines.

"You better not kiss anyone," I laugh. "Kiss your hand."

He laughs, and I realize I truly miss him, too.

"I… love you," I blurt nervously. There's a pause on the other end.

"I love you, too, Zoe," Ezra admits.

#

I breathe easier tonight, staring out the guest house window to the snowy plains stretching as far as the eye can see. I brought some dinner back with me from the residential house, and while it's warming in the microwave, I open the bottle of red wine Dr. Martinez left in the guest house for me. It came with a handwritten note that says, "You are brave. Thank you for coming to Starlight." The small gesture looms large on a day like today, even though I know one glass will be enough for me. I shove the cork back in, hoping it will keep for tomorrow night.

Cinnamon chows down on kibble, before curling up on the couch. I sit with him, knowing this furbaby won't be mine for much longer. He never really was mine, just a borrowed soul who got me through a rough time. Something tells me we've turned a corner today, locating Team Dallas on a map, working together to get to the next destination. I lift Cinnamon's floppy ears and let them drop. He looks like a cartoon character sometimes, especially when he's fast asleep and I'm making him do funny faces.

I whisper, "You are brave, Cinnamon. Thank you for coming to Starlight."

It's not like he had a choice, but I have a feeling he was born for this.

#

[I see red.]

Today is the last day of the year, which is called New Year's Eve. Zoe has been here for six whole days, and here are some things what are happening for New Year's Eve:

(1) We put up streamers and balloons at the living room in the house. Ten kids are back now, but fifty are still at them's parents houses. Seth is ten, but him is scared of balloons, so he won't come into the living room. I told Alicia I would help him, but since Seth was kicking his legs, her said to stay away.

(2) We got new calendars. Alicia buyed me a yoga dog calendar, which is so funny. Every page has a dog doing a funny pose that them can't do in real life. Alicia sat with me and we wrote all special dates on the calendar, like; my birthday (February 28), Zoe's birthday, Alicia's birthday, Dr. Poop Face's birthday, Christmas, Easter, Grey's birthday, Grey's death day, and we also invented International Armpit Day. That's June 5th if you wanted to know.

Tomorrow is a new year, and Alicia told me that it would be a good chance for me to start my life fresh. I want to go back to the stables to find my acorn. The seed is ready to break, so the big fat oak can grow.

[I see you.]

I laid low most of the morning. Dr. Martinez thinks it's wise for me to step back a little as the visit comes to a close, so I stayed near the guest house until lunch. Alicia worked with Dallas on his calendars, as our next step towards honoring Grey's life with some kind of memorial. The team agreed that Dallas would benefit from creating a monument of some sort at Starlight, and we're working on commemorating Grey's birth and death days. We suggested a garden, a statue of something Grey loved, or planting a special tree—none of which seem to appeal to Dallas. We have so few reliable memories of Grey available, so inevitably, some of what we're teaching him to remember is fictional.

All of the memories that Dallas expressed about Grey, I've stored them in my heart. I've done my best to sort them into reality and fantasy, but nobody will ever really know the difference. Sarah won't answer the phone, so I have no choice but to answer the proverbial call to assist Dallas's healing. We've created as much of the story as he's going to get, and this is the foundation on which the new house of Dallas will be built. He won't have the big house in San Francisco, but he will have a renovated house in his heart. Somewhere inside, he knows this is more important, and whether we like it or not, Starlight is where he needs to be right now.

Dallas is more resilient than we realize.

#

[I see red.]

We aren't allowed to stay awake until midnight, which is when the new year actually happens. But we stay up until nine o'clock and make a pretend Happy New Year. I have never done this before, and I didn't even know it was a thing. Alicia throwed a streamer at me, and she said it's OK to do that on a special occasion like Happy New Year, but in regular life, you shouldn't throw stuff. Zoe kissed me on my head, and I wiped it off straight away because I was so super embarrassed that her kissed me in front of the cool kids. Her said that new year's kisses are a thing.

Just after the long hand is on the twelve and the short hand is on the nine, the guy in charge of the party tells us it's bed time. I already had my shower, so I go back to me and Matthew's room with Zoe. She stays outside until I'm changed into my PJs and tells

249

me, "No stories if you pretend to be dressed but you're actually naked."

(Matthew is still away.)

"Are you decent?" says Zoe.

"Yep," I answer, and it's the truth because I want stories. Also, now I know that decent means 'clothes.' She climbs into bed while I choose three small-ish books from the shelf, then I jump over her and into my space beside the wall. She starts to read, but I stop her.

"Zoe," I say, "Where does my Mom live now?"

"I don't know," she answers. "I tried calling her but she won't pick up the phone."

"Who takes care of Aurora?" I wonder.

"I'm not sure about that. I know she was living with a relative for a while, but I think your mom planned on keeping her," Zoe tells. "I know she doesn't live with Jacob, though."

"I want the baby to be safe," I explain. "I hope Mommy do's a better job growing her up than her did with me and Grey. She only kept us both until we were six, so she better not give 'Rora away when her is six. Kids are supposed to need their moms."

Zoe kisses me on the head, and I don't wipe it off. She doesn't say anything for a while, then says, "You are brave, Dallas. Even though you don't have your mom, you have me, Alicia, and Dr. Martinez. You have people who love you."

"But you're going home soon," I say. "You'll forget me again."

"I'll never forget you, Dallas. Your name is written on my heart forever," she tells, and I wonder what that means. "I won't be here for you, in person, every day. But I will leave you Cinnamon, and I'll write you letters. You can call me any time Alicia agrees— and I will visit you again in a couple of months."

She didn't do any of those things when I got here, and I wonder if she's telling the truth. "Do you promise?" I ask.

"Of course," she says, squeezing my hand.

"Why do you need to go home, anyway?" I whine.

"Well, I have a job so I can make money to live. And...I have someone very special in San Francisco. He's a grown up man, one I love very much," she explains. Yuckkkkk, Zoe is in love! I get a bit scared that him will steal all her kisses and she won't have any left for my head.

"Who is him?" I say, sitting up with my hands on my hips.

"Ezra."

"How many candles does he have?"

"Twenty-three."

"You're more numbers than him," I tell.

"I really am," she smiles all big.

"Bring him next time, OK?" I say.

Zoe agrees, then I get her to start reading the stories. But it's so late, and I'm so tired, I hardly hear anything other than Zoe's heartbeat as I fall asleep.

CHAPTER THIRTY-TWO

Grey's Good Garden

[I see you.]

I'm heading home on the red-eye tonight; stoked to see Ezra, but nervous to leave Dallas. The new year is three days young and blissfully meltdown-free. He hasn't peed his pants for four days now, either (here's hoping he stays dry for the new year). Knee deep snow piles outside the guest house, and I have to call Luis to shovel the snow so I can get out the door. Part of me is hoping the flight is delayed by the weather, but most of me was ready to leave the minute I arrived. I've made peace with the idea of Starlight House, and I'm truly glad to see Dallas here. This is the best place for him to grow.

Yesterday the house hairdresser came by, and Dallas had his wild mop shorn. We had him pick the style from a magazine, because giving choices is imperative for a child like Dallas, who's had everything chosen for him. This morning he greets me with a short back and sides, fading to a longer top with a side part and long bangs. He's had tracks cut on the sides of his hair like lightning bolts, and I laugh, because that's what you get when you ask a six-year-old what kind of haircut he wants. Dallas is a step closer to being more of himself, and that's all that matters.

The ban on stable visits has been lifted, and today we finally get to hang out with Arrow and Lester. On the plus side, we have a ratio of two adults to one child, which seems appropriate for Dallas. We play a game on the way to the stables, which is fun for him, and imperative for us.

"Go!" Alicia yells, and Dallas runs.

"Stop!" I scream, and he stops. Just like obedience training for dogs, we're testing his ability to comply with directions, even though we know he's a wild cannon during a meltdown. I tell him to go this time, because Alicia should be the one getting him to stop. Goodness knows she'll be saying it a whole lot over the next year.

Dallas's face lights up at the sight of Arrow, and I swear he looks brighter today. He stands a little straighter; he smiles a little wider, he breathes a little deeper.

Truthfully, so do I.

[I see red.]

I run to the acorn, and put it in my pocket before anyone sees. I have a plan for this little guy—something real special.

"Arrow is the brown one with the arrow shape white bit on him's nose," I explain, because Zoe has never ever seen these horses before. "Lester is black and white, and I have no clue why him's called that name."

I climb on the fence to pet Arrow. He's gentle and kind, and he lets me kiss his nose.

"Yuck, Dallas," Zoe says with her face all screwed up. "You probably shouldn't kiss horses."

"But I love him," I say. "You kiss my head because you love me, and I kiss Arrow's head because I love him. That's what kisses are for."

Anyway, I wipe off my mouth because her meaned that horses have germs. I show Zoe around and we feed the horses some carrots. We stay for a hundred years, then it's time for lunch.

[I see you.]

I sit across the lunch table from Dallas, as he scarfs his chicken, rice, and vegetables. I can barely believe he's eating such healthy food, and Alicia can hardly believe he's eating so much. We roll with it, crossing our fingers that this progress continues.

"Did you like them horses?" he sputters, with a piece of rice flying out of his mouth.

"I loved them, thanks for taking me to the stables," I say.

"Will you miss them when you go home?" he tests.

253

"Not as much as I'll miss you," I smile. He smiles too. With only a few precious hours left together, I wonder how we can keep things as meltdown-free as possible. I'll put him to bed tonight, and in the morning, Alicia's on her own.

"What should we do this afternoon?" I ask.

"I have a plan," he replies with an eyebrow raised. History tells me I should be wary of Dallas's plans.

[I see red.]

I eated the proteins, also the rice. Now I grab Zoe and Alicia's hands and take them outside. Them are freaking out because them don't know what's about to happen.

"Dallas, where are we going?" Alicia says. Next, we're at a garden which is dirt and nothing else is in it. I take the acorn out of my pocket and open up my hand.

"I want to plant it," I say, digging a hole and poking it in.

[I see you.]

I want to tell him that's not how oaks work. I want to tell him that if you plant a hard, closed acorn in a garden bed and barely cover it with dirt, it absolutely won't grow. But I fight the urge to correct him, and so does Alicia — in his own way, Dallas is telling us he's ready to move on. He's accepting Grey's death, and finding healthy ways to remember.

"I want to make a garden," he announces. "I want to call it Grey's Good Garden, because them all start with the letter G."

Alicia and I smile at one another; our glance narrowly escaping Dallas's periphery. Then, expertly, she comments without judgement, "What else would you like to put in Grey's Good Garden?"

Dallas thinks, with his finger on his chin. "Hmm… Flowers. And fish. Them start with F, and that's one before G. Them are for remembering stuff that happened before Grey died."

"By the time Zoe comes back to see us again, Grey's Good Garden will look amazing," Alicia says. "I can't wait to work on it with you."

"Come for my birthday!" Dallas demands. That's two months away.

"I'd love to," I reply, before doing the rational things, like making sure that date works with everything else happening in my life. Then I see Dallas's crazy hair and sweet face, and realize that his milestones trump anything else in my calendar. He hugs me spontaneously, with his skinny belly hanging out of his now, too-short, shirt. I swear he was wearing that exact t-shirt the day I arrived, and it fit perfectly.

It's true what they say, "From little things, big things grow."

#

At 4 pm Dallas starts training Cinnamon with Lynda, and I borrow Dr. Martinez's car to drive to the nearest department store. Making a beeline to the little boys' clothing, I stock up on camo cargo pants (the kind that zip off into shorts), gray hoodies, and black t-shirts emblazoned with dinosaurs, skulls, horses, and dogs. They're sizes 5, 6, and 7—because who knows how big he'll be at the end of February?

[I see red.]

When the long hand is on the twelve, and the short hand is on the five, Zoe comes to pick me up from dog training with Lynda. Cinnamon barks some happy barks when him sees Zoe, so I join in, too. Zoe tells me that barking is only for dogs, then tells me she's taking me to Dr. Poopy's for a session. I have decided that I am talking to him now. Sometimes I even call him Louise, even though that's a girl's name.

Zoe gets down and cuddles Cinnamon before Lynda takes him away to her house. Him will live there for most of the day until he's trained enough to be my service dog. Zoe got tears in her eyes, and I wonder if her is sad about saying goodbye to the fluffy little dog.

"I'll miss Cinnamon," she says, which I suspected.

"It's OK. You can see him on my birthday," I tell, holding her hand. "What's in all the bags?"

"I'll show you in the soft room," she tells. Then she wipes her face and has no more tears.

We get to the soft room and Dr. Louise isn't there yet, so I grab the bags from Zoe and we spread the stuff all over the floor. There are so many cool clothes here, and Zoe said them are for me! Dr. Poop opens the door.

"Wow! What's all this?" he says.

[I see you.]

"I noticed Dallas was getting too big for the clothes he brought from home," I explain, "So I got him some things to grow into."

Dallas looks at each item with wide eyes, examining the different designs on the shirts. He hugs me spontaneously and whispers in my ear, "Thank you Zozo."

"Dallas has grown quite a bit lately," Dr. Martinez announces. "We've been able to talk about Grey almost every day this week. His sticker chart is getting full, too."

I gesture to Dallas, "Can you tell Dr. Martinez about Grey's Good Garden?"

Dallas shakes his head and looks down. It's all a bit too much for him—growth is uncomfortable for someone accustomed to being stunted.

"Maybe you'll tell me next time," Dr. Martinez smiles.

#

[I see red.]

The long hand is on the eleven and the short hand is very close to the seven. Zoe has read two and a half books, and Matthew comes back tomorrow. My eyes are closing, and I am trying with all my muscles just to stay awake. Tomorrow, Zoe will be gone.

"I love you, Dallas," she whispers. "I love you exactly as you are, no matter what."

She kisses me on the head, and I fall fast asleep.

[I see you.]

At seven thirty I pull the blankets over Dallas and pat his hair for the last time. I tell myself he'll never be like this ever again, for better or worse, but mostly better. I punch the code in the

256

door, avoiding the supposed knife alarm. Pete sees me out, and thanks me for my help.

Dr. Martinez catches me in the hallway, with a professional handshake, and kind smile.

"Thank you, Zoe. Honestly, without your visit, we could never have achieved this much with Dallas. We're really looking forward to having you back at the end of February."

I think about the thousand things I could say back to him, and settle with a smile. We part ways, and Alicia helps me to the car before driving me to the airport. The hour from Lovell to Cody is slow, with minutes passing in silence.

"When," I croak, and clear my throat, "When Dallas loses his next tooth, can you be the tooth fairy?"

"I don't work nights," Alicia replies, "But I'll work something out with Pete."

We sit in awkward, tense, silence.

"Can you tell me when his shoes wear out?" I add. "I'll get him some new ones. I just don't want him wearing the clothes the big boys pass down to him. I don't like the idea of Dallas walking in their shoes."

"Sure," Alicia smiles from the driver's seat. I see the airport on the horizon, and suddenly my anxieties about leaving Dallas rise to the surface.

"Can you start modeling correct pronouns and past tense? I'm worried about his speech regressing. He's capable—" I ramble, and Alicia stops me.

"Zoe, I can see it's hard for you to leave him behind. It's hard for you to trust me with him—and I can't promise I'll raise him perfectly for the next year—but I'll do my best. Luis will be there to advise. We have the treatment plan, and we have you as our best resource."

I feel kind of embarrassed about not trusting Alicia, but she's hit the nail on the head. I need to cut the cord; Dallas is now in her capable hands. It really does take a village to raise a child. The car slows, then stops by my ticketed airline.

"Thank you for everything," I sniff, as tears fall down my cheek.

"You're brave, Zoe. Thank you for coming to Starlight," she says, while I wonder if that's a marketing phrase used by Starlight House, or just an honest sentiment. I watch the taillights disappear in the darkness as she drives away, then wheel my suitcase to the kiosk.

In just a few hours I'll be in Ezra's arms, and I seriously can't wait to see him.

CHAPTER THIRTY-THREE

Home is Where You Make It

[I see you.]
 I stumble deliriously through the San Francisco airport arrivals just after 5 am, to find Ezra waiting with coffee and a smile. I've gotta believe it's love if he would wake up this early for me. His face is sunlight on this pitch black winter morning, and he's even more handsome than I remembered. He takes me home like a gentleman and comes back to see me after work.
 I sleep the day away, feeling the empty space left by Cinnamon.

[I see red.]
 When I wake up, there's no Zoe in my bed. I knew her would be gone, but I (a little bit) hoped she'd fall asleep and miss her plane. I want to be brave, but I cry instead. Alicia opens the door, so I pretend I'm sleeping—she says nothing, her just sits with me. When I'm ready, I open my eyes.
 "Want to wear one of your new outfits today?" she asks.
 I run to the drawers and look at all the cool new things that Zoe left me. Them look exactly like my old clothes, except newer and bigger. I choose the shirt which has a dog on it, because him looks like a wolf, and wolfs are cool. Wearing Zoe clothes makes me feel like her is still here. I look at the yoga dog calendar and count some numbers.
 Fifty-six days until I'm seven and Zoe comes back.

#

[I see you.]
    I've been home a week now, and can't begin to explain how light I feel without the Dallas-monkey on my back. The medication, the night terrors, the giant rock of unforgiveness lodged in my heart—they all seem like a distant memory. I can finally think about Dallas without feeling sick, remembering the acorn in the ground, instead of the boy in the sky.

#

[I see red.]
    Alicia helps me press buttons on the computer so we'll connect with Zoe. I see her face first, then hear her voice.
    "Hey, Buddy!" she says through the screen.
    "Twenty days until my birthday," I remind her.
    "Yeah! You know what else is coming up?" Zoe asks. I shake my head, then she says, "Valentine's Day!"
    "Eww. You're just going to kiss your boyfriend all day long!" I say, then pretend to vomit.
    "Actually, I was going to tell you to look out for a special Valentine's package in the mail. I sent it yesterday, and I know you're not crazy about surprises," she smiles, and now I'm so excited wondering what it is. "Anyway, how's the garden coming along?"
    "It's good," I say. "Alicia is helping me, and we ordered some flowers from the internet. They will get here tomorrow, so that's when we start planting. I was going to make the flowers gray, but then I thought that might be an ugly garden."
    She laughs, "Yeah, maybe Grey would have wanted something brighter."
    "We got blue and orange ones, because blue was his favorite color and orange was the color of his fish stuffy that he cuddled at night," I explain.
    "I remember you telling me about the fish when we went on the underwater ride. Do you remember that?" she asks. My face feels hot. I don't like remembering that day because I wasn't the boss of my own body. I do remember the underwater ride, and I

also remember the log ride. I feel a knot in my tummy about the Discovery Country day, so I don't answer with words, I just nod my head.

[I see you.]

"Is Alicia there?" I ask, adjusting the camera on top of my computer.

"She's right here," Dallas says, as Alicia slides into view.

"Hey Buddy, are you all done talking?" I check. He nods his head. Alicia prompts him to say goodbye, then directs him two doors down to Dr. Martinez's room for a session. I see her stand at the door and wait for him to go safely inside. She makes a thumbs up sign, to Luis I assume, then she sits in front of the computer to continue our video call.

"Hey," Alicia says. "Thanks for calling. Even though he didn't say much, he's been looking forward to this all week."

"How's Cinnamon's training?" I inquire.

"Dallas has been really committed, and Cinnamon is a really fast learner because he's so young. Lynda said he should be able to come live with Dallas in June. Usually, it takes longer, but since Dallas's needs are different than, say, a child with diabetes, there are less specific things for Cinnamon to learn," she explains. I'm glad to hear it.

"Dallas looks bigger," I observe.

"He's growing like a mushroom," she agrees. "He's put on five pounds, grown an inch, and we've had to donate all his size four clothes. We're so grateful you got him the bigger sizes, he's in fives and sixes right now, depending on the day."

"What about his shoes?" I ask.

"They're getting snug," she admits, clearly too embarrassed to ask for more items. I thought as much.

"How many teeth has he lost? Looked like a few," I note.

"Four! You saw him with the bottom ones out—the adult teeth are coming in now. The top two became loose the week you left," Alicia reports. "Pete has been on tooth fairy duty—the part where he takes the teeth and replaces them with money. I've been writing notes for him to leave under the pillow."

I smile, "Thank you. I've gotta be honest, you're doing an amazing job with him. His speech has developed leaps and bounds

261

in just a few weeks. Things seem to be really happening for him right now."

"It takes a village, Zoe," Alicia deflects the praise. "You're a vital part of that village."

I don't know what to say, so we make small talk before creating excuses to part ways.

#

[I see red.]

Today is Valentine's Day. I used to think it was called Valentime's Day, but that's actually not how the word is said. When Alicia comes to the door, she's holding a package from Zoe which is covered in love hearts. I rip it open, and first, there's a card. I don't need Alicia to read it, because I know how to read now.

"Der..." I try.

"Dear..." Alicia helps.

"Dear Dallas, Happy V-Valentime...Oops! ValentiNe's Day. Love Zoe. XXX," I read. "What do the X's mean?"

"They're kisses!" she says, and I poke my tongue out, pretending to vomit. I see the present, and it's a box, too. I rip open the paper, then open the box to see the best pair of shoes I have ever seen! Green boots with a white circle and blue star. I take off my tiny, old, stinky shoes and undo the zip at the back of the new boots. I don't even need to do the laces on these ones! I slide my foot in, and there's extra room for my toes to wiggle around. I zip them up, up, up and they are the perfect shoes for me.

#

[I see you.]

On Valentine's Day, I start work at 6 am, like any given Tuesday. I think about Dallas opening his gift, and I'm thankful that I can still love him practically, albeit from afar. Ezra and I have plans to go out for dinner, so I am surprised when I see him knocking on the door of the coffee house at 6:58 am—two minutes before it opens.

"Hey babe," I say, "What are you doing here so early?"

"I didn't want to wait until after work to see you," he smiles, and kisses me. "OK, I got what I came for. You can go back to work now."

Ezra disappears as fast as he arrived, and in my early morning daze, I wonder if he was really ever there at all. Happy Valentine's Day, indeed.

[I see red.]

Today is the last Tuesday that I will ever be six. This day in one week (that's the next line on the calendar) will be my seventh birthday. Zoe is bringing her stupid boyfriend, but I told her to do that, so it's actually fine with me, I just don't know if I will like him or not. If he brings me a present, I might like him if the present is cool enough. If it's a bad present, like toilet paper or something, I will tell Zoe to break up with him. Alicia and I are calling her now.

"Did you ever meet her boyfriend?" I ask Alicia.

"No, I have been here with you the whole time! Do you think I flew out to California to meet him while you were in bed?" she says, tickling me.

"Stop!" I yell, but I like it. I'm laughing, then she stops, and I say, "I don't know what you do while I'm in bed!"

"I go home and sleep," she laughs. "I don't have a life outside of here. You're my life."

The computer makes dialing noises; then we see Zoe and a guy with a beard on the screen.

"Hey!" she says. "Dallas, meet Ezra."

[I see you.]

Dallas disappears under the table, and I see Alicia become flustered trying to usher him back to the computer.

"Sorry," she whispers. "He was just telling me he was nervous about meeting Ezra. Is it OK if we call you back in a few minutes?"

"Sure," I say, and we disconnect.

Ezra looks awkward. I knew he was excited to meet Dallas, so he's probably a little disappointed. It's hard to understand why kids act the way they do, unless you've been around them enough.

"It's not you," I tell him. "Dallas doesn't do well with men in general. He's only ever had really shitty male role models, so it's a process."

"Isn't his therapist a man?" Ezra wonders.

"Yeah," I agree. "It took him seven weeks to actually speak to him. The house parent for his room is a guy, too. At first, Dallas decided not to need anything, so he wouldn't have to talk to Pete. Almost four months later they're pals. They have to prove they're safe, and not leaving; it just takes a while."

We sit in silence, as Ezra taps on the table. I can see he's a bit offended. After a couple of long, awkward minutes, Alicia and Dallas return our call. Dallas is sitting on Alicia's lap, and she's holding his arms. She whispers something in his ear to prompt conversation.

"Hi," he says. "Hi, Ezra."

"Hey, Dallas! Great to meet you," Ezra replies with a beaming smile. Alicia whispers something in Dallas's ear.

"Do you have a dog?" he says.

Ezra giggles, "No, I don't have a dog, but I know you do. Me and Cinnamon are great friends."

Dallas puts his hands on his hips and squints his eyes, "How do you know my dog?"

"Zoe and I took very good care of him for a while," he responds. Alicia whispers in Dallas's ear, then he shakes his head, appearing to reject the words she's feeding him.

"Thank you," he mumbles, before whispering to Alicia. We can hear him say, "I didn't want him to know my dog before he knows me."

Alicia whispers in his ear, then Dallas says in a robotic tone, "Thank you for calling, OK BYE."

He disappears from the frame, and we watch Alicia send him to Dr. Martinez. She comes back to the computer.

"He's in a bit of a mood today," she admits. "Some days are harder than others."

"Meltdowns?" I ask.

"No, nothing like he did with you," she assures. "I shouldn't complain. You bore the worst of it."

"He's never going to be "normal," Alicia," I say, using my fingers for quotations. I hate the word, but it holds the most weight.

"I know," she admits, defeated. "Sometimes I just hope."

Ezra looks uncomfortable. This is a world of which he's been locked out; this is my domain, my comfort zone, not his. Alicia and I understand each other in a way that Ezra will never even scratch the surface. We're trench buddies, connected by the war zone. He exhales, uncomfortably realizing that he's disconnected, and there's nothing he can do about it. We end the video call, not knowing whether it's a good idea for Ezra to come to Wyoming, or if his presence will send Dallas's progress packing. I wish I could understand this kid—one minute he's asking for Ezra, the next he's pushing him away. It's hardly a surprise, since his early attachments were ambivalent at best. I feel Alicia's pain; that hopeful wish he will grow out of all of this and find himself a nice 'forever' home.

I tell Ezra not to worry, though I can see he still cares. He's never had to deal with deeply wounded kids before, and I explain that following through with the visit is the best thing for Dallas. He's not so sure, and heads back to his house early.

We don't talk for the rest of the day.

#

I stay up late, wondering if Dallas will ever be adopted by another family. I wonder if he could live a valuable life in the foster system. I wonder what happens if he gets to 18 without a family to call his own. I know he expects me to be his mom if nobody else steps up to the plate, but I can't be manipulated like that. I'll love this child to my dying day, but I won't raise him as my own. I'm not old enough, established enough, brave enough, or patient enough. I want him to have one of those strict, no-bullshit, badass Moms—someone who can give him all the time in the world. Someone who isn't me.

Sometimes love is a bitter pill to swallow.

CHAPTER THIRTY-FOUR

Seven

[I see red.]

I open my eyes and see Matthew still sleeping. Jumping on his bed, I rip the covers off and yell, "It's my birthday! It's my birthday!" I wish I had a streamer to throw at him: because that's for special occasions, and this is definitely a special occasion.

I'm seven!

[I see you.]

Ezra didn't say much on the flight to Cody, and now that we're waiting in line for a rental car, things are starting to get awkward. Once we jump through all the hoops, pile into the car, and set the GPS, I decide I need to ask what's wrong.

"I'm worried..." he chokes. "I'm afraid in some way, some time in the future, you'll choose Dallas over me."

I'm flabbergasted—this couldn't be further from the truth.

"I don't think you need to worry about that," I say, quickly deflecting the statement.

"You say that now," he warns, "But I know how much you love that kid. You won't admit it, but you'd do anything for him. What happens when he's eight and needs to leave Starlight? Who's going to take him in?"

"Not me," I maintain.

"So, you'll let him go into the foster system? You'll be totally fine with him living with a random family who may or may not be a good fit?" he snaps.

"I just don't think we can plan that far ahead," I shrug. I can see that he's been struggling with this since we made the video call to Dallas. The air between us has been thick with tension since that day, waiting for this conversation to happen. Mere minutes away from Starlight, the emotional volcano erupts.

"One day when they ask you to adopt Dallas, and you know they will, you're going to have a really hard time saying no. If you take him on, I don't know where that leaves us," Ezra blurts, gripping the steering wheel with white knuckles. I extend my arm, placing it on his shoulder, not sure what to say.

"Are you saying that he's a deal breaker?" I ask.

"Yeah… kind of. I mean, I'm not an expert like you, but I know that I don't have the bandwidth to raise a kid like Dallas," he says.

"I never said I wanted to adopt him," I reiterate. "I've actually said the opposite, repeatedly."

"Zoe, it's not that I would leave you if you adopted him. It's just that I think he has the potential to drive us apart. He's not interested in a relationship with me, he's just scoping out his competition," he admits.

I sit with his words for a moment, then say, "I think he genuinely wants to meet you. And, you know I love you, Ezra."

"I love you, too. You have no idea how long I have loved you—and now that I have you, I don't want to lose you."

"Nobody ever really knows how long they will have someone in their life," I reply. "Let's not see the end before we've even begun. I can't promise you I'll never adopt Dallas, but I can promise you that right now, that's not my plan."

We sit in silence for the remainder of the drive to Lovell, deep in thought, as I wonder whether it was wise to bring Ezra here. I wonder if he's mad at me for trying. I'm under no impression that we're playing happy families.

Besides, I never said I wanted Dallas long-term.

[I see red.]

I see a silver car driving down the long, long, long driveway, and I hope like crazy that it's Zoe. Then an old lady gets out, and I know I'm wrong because it's Lynda bringing Cinnamon for a visit, which is still a really good thing. Waiting for Zoe takes forever! Alicia comes to the room with Cinnamon, and also presents and streamers, and we have a little dance party with Matthew.

"Would you two like to have a picnic breakfast at the stables?" she asks, and we jump up and down on the bed saying, "Yes! YES! YESSSSSS!"

[I see you.]

We stop at a bakery in Lovell, to pick up a birthday cake I ordered for Dallas. The baker opens the box to reveal the most incredible dog cake, looking exactly like our sweet little Cinnamon. I smile big, and so does Ezra, breaking the ice that's formed between us in snowy Wyoming. He carries the cake to the car, placing it on my lap in the passenger seat. I balance it precariously for the next fifteen minutes as we roll up to Starlight.

Ezra reacts to the ranch like I did two months prior. The look on his face appreciates the beauty, while simultaneously takes stock of the sadness. On my second visit, I can recognize the full worth of rehabilitation, instead of being struck by the weight of why these kids need the ranch. It's even more beautiful at the end of winter; still, ice capped, but with hints of the green to come.

In the distance we see two little boys running and stopping, over and over again, trailed by a lady with a leashed dog calling out commands. As we get closer, I see that it's Dallas and Alicia, with who I assume to be Matthew. The top of Dallas's head is now the height of Alicia's shoulders, and Matthew almost looks her in the eye. Like watching a handler interact with growing tiger cubs, I wonder what will become of their relationship when the babies tower over their master, knowing it won't be long before they grow into their gargantuan paws.

"There he is," I tell Ezra. "He's the smaller one."

Ezra looks overwhelmed, yet glad to finally lay eyes on the child who has indelibly changed me. He smiles, "He's going to be so happy to see you."

[I see red.]

A green car drives in the driveway, and as soon as I see it, I stop dead in my tracks. It's her this time! And him! I start running, but Alicia says to stop, and I listen. It's hard to stop when you really want to keep running.

"It's Zoe!" I yell. Alicia asks me to wait until the car stops moving, and when we hear the car turn itself off, I run with all my speed, and nobody tells me to stop.

[I see you.]

Hurdling towards us, Dallas throws himself on the parked car. I roll the window down, and he practically crawls inside. He stops halfway, realizing there's something on my lap. Cinnamon recognizes Ezra and subsequently goes into full barking mode.

"What's in the box?" he yells. Alicia pries him from the open window as Ezra opens the car door, allowing me to reveal the cake. Dallas's eyes grow wide.

[I see red.]

Alicia—I mean, Zoe—has a big cake that looks like our dog, Cinnamon!

"Happy seventh birthday, Buddy!" she says, as her beardy boyfriend gets the cake off her lap so she can get out of the car. Cinnamon seems to like him, so I guess he's OK. I jump up, hugging Zoe with my legs around her waist, and arms around her neck. She's the best human, and she's here with me now. I feel her heart beating on my heart, like twins.

"Matthew!" I yell. "Look it! A dog cake!"

"WOW," he says. "Can we eat it?"

"We were just heading to the stables for a special birthday picnic," Alicia explains to Zoe and the beard guy. "Would you like to come?"

[I see you.]

"Sure!" I agree. "By the way, Dallas, this is Ezra."

He looks down and says, "Hi," with his foot tracing lines in the snow.

Alicia prompts, "Eye contact, strong voice."

Dallas looks up and extends a hand to Ezra, "Hi, I'm Dallas. Nice to meet you." Ezra shakes his little hand, as I just about die from how cute their meeting has turned out to be, and replies, "Nice to meet you, too. I've heard a lot about you."

Alicia doesn't skip a beat, introducing Matthew to all of us, since he was away with family when I visited last. Matthew's face holds a familiar depth: eyes that have seen too much, a mouth reluctant to smile, and the fast, jerky movements of a kid living from the fight-or-flight mode of his reptilian brain. I don't know how he got this way; I want to pity him, but I know he has a family who wants him rehabilitated. In that respect, he's lightyears ahead of Dallas. While the window of Matthew's formative years has recently closed, Dallas's is wide open, with the curtain dancing in the wind.

Hope lives in the breeze of change.

[I see red.]

"Let's play the stop/go game," I tell Zoe. We run, she yells stop, and we stop.

"You're getting really good at this," she says. "Let's add Ezra to the game."

We run, and Beardy says stop. For a millisecond I think I'll keep running, but I don't, because Zoe would be mad, and I don't want her to stop liking me. Also, seven is my year to be green. I stop, and he says, "Go."

Arrow and Lester are neighing in the stables, so I climb a little on the fence to pet them. Alicia doesn't stop me because she knows I can be trusted now that I am seven. Ezra stands next to me, while Zoe sets the cake on the wooden outside table.

"Who's this?" he asks.

"Arrow," I say, softly. "He's my favorite."

"How should I get to know Arrow?" Ezra says. "He's never met me before, and I don't want to scare him."

I think, with my finger on my chin. I whisper, "Just be his friend slowly. He won't bite you, but if he does something mean, it's probably because he's just a little bit scared."

Ezra talks to Arrow for a bit, then I let him know it's OK to try to pet him. He touches Arrow's nose, and the horse breathes out quickly, which scares Ezra, so he pulls his hand away. I whisper to Arrow, "Easy, boy. Ezra is nice. Ezra is safe."

I grab Ezra's hand, and let him touch Arrow again. This time they both stay calm.

[I see you.]

While I'm setting seven candles on the cake, I look up to see Dallas and Ezra petting the horse. They're both smiling—genuinely smiling—which makes me think they'll get on just fine. I leave the table, with matches and a knife, and walk over towards them. Matthew makes a beeline for the table, and Alicia tackles him before he gets there. I've been out of the game for so long I've forgotten about the small details of keeping young, vulnerable humans safe. I apologize profusely, keeping the contraband safe by my side. Alicia is tuned in beyond belief, intuitive and ready.

[I see red.]

We get around the table, all of us, like a family. There's Ezra on one side of me, and Zoe on the other—then there's Matthew and Alicia facing us. The candles are warm when Zoe puts the flames on the top, and Alicia hugs Matthew's arms tight, tight, tight so he doesn't get burned. As the fire goes on the candles, I think about how I was nervous to meet Ezra and I was sure I wouldn't like him. I remember how I used to not like Zoe, and then she showed me she was on my team. I haven't known Ezra long, but I think he's on our team, too.

"One, two, three, four, five, six, seven," I check, giving Zoe a thumbs up for good work. "Seven candles."

I know I'll be here for eight candles (maybe nine), and I don't even mind anymore. For some weird reason, Starlight is now just as much my home as the place where my mom was. Matthew is like my new brother, so I don't need to talk to Grey so much anymore. I didn't forget him, I can just let him be gone now. Grey's Good Garden helps me remember.

[I see you.]

"Happy birthday to you, Happy birthday to you! Happy birthday, dear Dallas, happy birthday to you!" we sing, before Dallas extinguishes the candles with one enormous breath. I hug him, and kiss his head. We cut the cake into generous chunks, laughing at the ridiculous sugar rush before 10 am. The boys run the excess energy off by the stables before Dallas takes my hand and leads us to Grey's Garden.

It's a raised patch, teeming with vibrant orange and blue flowers which are uncharacteristically healthy for this time of year. Hand painted clay fish are perched atop sticks, and there's a plaque that says, in Dallas's precious handwriting, "Grey's Good Garden." A small sprout has emerged from the garden bed, and Dallas shows me, treating it like a precious gem.

"It's my acorn, Zoe," he beams. "From little things, big things grow."

"Something from nothing," I smile, holding him tight. "That's what we do."

[I see green.]

    I am Dallas.
    I am seven.
    I see green.

ACKNOWLEDGEMENTS

This book has been written with deep gratitude to the following people:

- Amelia Bennett: Your generosity and pursuit of this project has blessed me more than you know. If anyone reading this is also an author, I highly recommend Amelia's editing services. She will work with you throughout your entire project, not just the tail end - find her at bookwife.com
- VK: You gave me a second chance in the USA, and a job that taught me more about forgiveness than anything else I've ever experienced.
- My beta readers: Nichy Nott, Kelly Six, Megan Warren, Courtney Quinn-McCabe, Neil Abellanosa, Ella Henry, Abby Stanford, and Jordan Dodson. Thank you for catching continuity errors and weak plot points, thank you for encouraging my efforts, and most of all, thank you for taking the time to read and respond to my work.
- Baby Piers: You better get ready for a thousand kisses – your dad and I can't wait to smooch your face.
- Jesus: the way, the truth, the life. I live to worship you.

ABOUT THE AUTHOR

Amy Piers grew up in the placid hills of rural Lockyer Valley, and the calm shoreline of bayside Victoria Point in Queensland, Australia. A prolific writer from the time she could hold a pencil, some of her favorite childhood memories involve sitting at a desk for hours, scribbling stories into notebooks. Her earliest ambition was to become Jennie Garth, or a waitress, but later relented to the idea that she was born to write. Her first published piece was a story about her family's cow, featured in the *Toowoomba Chronicle* in 1992, which won her a Happy Meal at McDonalds. She later moved onto blogging, ghost-writing for a Silicon Valley catering company, and screenwriting feature-length films.

Amy lives in San Francisco with her husband Daniel, as they eagerly await the arrival of their first baby in early 2017. Amy enjoys 90s music, dogs in costumes, cringeworthy reality TV, storytelling podcasts, and almond lattes. For more of Amy's writing, visit her blog at **amypiers.com**

Made in the USA
Lexington, KY
05 June 2017